OUTLAW MOUNTAIN

OUTLAW
MOUNTAIN

A REESE GOLDEN MYSTERY

CINDY KEEN REYNDERS

**CAVEL
PRESS**

Kenmore, WA

CAMEL
PRESS

A Camel Press book published by Epicenter Press

Epicenter Press
6524 NE 181st St.
Suite 2
Kenmore, WA 98028

For more information go to:
www.Camelpress.com
www.Coffeetownpress.com
www.Epicenterpress.com
www.cindykeenreynders.com

Cover design by Scott Book
Design Melissa Vail Coffman

Outlaw Mountain

Library of Congress Control Number: 2023945717

ISBN: 978-1-68492-157-7 (Trade Paper)
ISBN: 978-1-68492-158-4 (eBook)

As always, thank you to my husband and my family
for their patience and understanding when
I go into my office and disappear for hours.
They appreciate my writing addiction
and for that I will be eternally grateful.

ACKNOWLEDGMENTS

THANK YOU TO THE GREATER POWER that has blessed me to have my way with words. Also, I appreciate that Camel Press has allowed me to join the ranks of their authors.

ONE

MILLIONS OF YEARS AGO, IN WHAT IS NOW KNOWN as southern Wyoming, the Earth's crust folded into a ridge, thrusting upward to create mountains of layered rusty red stone. In order to provide water for modern day residents, engineers created dams in the lower valleys of the geologic feature, offering not only a flowing supply, but a recreational paradise.

Fire Peak Reservoir now gave Wyomingites and state visitors a place for boating, fishing, and swimming throughout the summer, and into the fall's lingering warmth. It also happened to be one of Reese Golden's favorite places to escape.

Relaxed in a folding chair along the sandy shoreline, Reese dangled her fishing pole, waiting for one of the silver-finned creatures to grab her hook. A cool September breeze generated rippling blue-green waves beneath her outcast line.

Stone monoliths shaped like giant chunks of layer cake, some of it bearing the color of blood, surrounded the reservoir. The early morning sun cast pale pink and lavender light on the surfaces, giving the rocky angles an ethereal glow.

A tree beside Reese arched into the blue sky; its branches bent with the weight of several crows. The black birds hopped back and forth, their scolding caws raking the air. Perhaps they complained to each other, angry about the noisy humans who had invaded their space.

Reese's grandmother used to say, "Where crows are, there is prophecy and magic."

Gran had never explained what it meant, she'd only given Reese a sly smile and told her that one day, she'd understand.

I'm probably too thick-headed to ever get it, she thought.

Overhead, geese flew south in a perfect V, which Reese had heard helped them conserve energy by using the air pressure of the bird in front to support their lift. Poor unlucky duck, it sure had a crappy job.

Beside her, Jeremy Savage perched on a boulder, his fishing pole arched over the lake. An eager expression etched his face as he watched his thin plastic line trailing in the water. With perfect concentration, he waited for that first sacred nibble.

It occurred to her that they both wore flannel shirts, old jeans, and scuffed hiking boots. A black Stetson shadowed his face, and she wore her grandfather's comfortable old cowboy hat. Obviously, both of them were accustomed to outdoor activities. Covering up one's body with sturdy clothing helped to avoid ticks and other creepy crawlies, along with preventing major sunburn.

A police detective in her hometown of Meadowlark Valley, Jeremy often hired Reese to consult on cases. Like so many government agencies these days, his unit was understaffed and overworked. He'd told her plenty of times how much he appreciated being able to rely on her private detective skills.

Although she had plenty of other work to keep her busy in her new business venture, Reese valued being able to contribute to the local law enforcement scene. Since she'd left the Denver Police Department to strike out on her own, she still had blue blood running in her veins. No doubt, she probably always would.

And, she had to admit, she liked working with Jeremy.

Lulled by the lapping waves, Reese almost nodded off. A second later, she snapped back to attention, propping her eyes open with invisible toothpicks.

"Are you okay?" Jeremy asked.

"I feel like the walking dead," she admitted.

"Fish bite the best at sunrise," he reminded her.

"Suckers."

They both laughed.

"Aren't you glad I invited you to join me this morning?" The corners of Jeremy's eyes crinkled with amusement.

"You bet your sweet bippy I am," she said. "There's nothing I love more than getting up at the butt-crack-of-dawn."

Even though copious amounts of coffee hadn't brought her fully awake yet, Reese's mouth watered at the idea of frying up tender, flaky fish—preferably Rainbow Trout. Add some hash browns and *voilà*, breakfast fit for the gods.

"It's good to get out from behind your desk and breathe some fresh air," Jeremy commented. "Clears the mind."

"Yeah, I know," Reese said. "But I was up late doing paperwork, which is why I'm not so chipper."

"Workaholic."

"That's like the pot calling the kettle black," she said.

"True," he said. "I worked late last night myself, but I got to bed at a decent hour."

"It was one o'clock in the morning for me," Reese admitted. "That's typically my drop-dead hour."

"I'm going to start calling you the punisher," Jeremy said.

They both fell silent again. The pleasant morning serenity, broken only by the sound of buzzing insects and bird calls, wrapped around Reese like a warm blanket. Nature's sweet lullaby threatened to put her to sleep again.

Only the hungry fish, swimming in the blue lake's murky depths, mattered, even though they managed to avoid her fat, juicy worm.

From down the shore, a shrill, blood-curdling shriek echoed. A flock of frightened birds burst from the bushes and scattered to the east. A dog's wild barking added to the chaos.

"Shit," Jeremy said as he set aside his pole, slid down from the boulder, and took off running.

"Double shit," Reese said, following him.

Boots crunching along the gravely lake shore, the two pushed aside tall grass, and tangled weeds as they rushed toward the distraught cries.

TWO

"HELP, SOMEBODY!"

A young Asian woman stood in a gravelly cove beside a muddy pool, looking around with a wild glint in her eyes. A white headband held back her dark shiny hair. Dressed in black leggings and a red sweat shirt, she stared at the bald man with a gray beard and mustache stretched out along the shoreline.

Gripping her dog's leash—a reddish-brown Boxer with a white chest and paws—her gaze remained transfixed on the body. The pooch continued woof, woofing until she slipped a treat from her pocket, which it immediately gobbled.

Spotting Reese and Jeremy, the woman began to stammer.

"I . . . I just found him like this," she said. "My husband and I are staying over in the campground and I was out walking my dog. What do we do?"

The dog began barking and the woman said, "Hush, Morgan."

The pooch complied, but continued pulling at the leash, seemingly desperate to be free. No doubt it wanted to sniff the newcomers to determine whether they were friend or foe.

Reese hurried over and knelt next to the guy on the ground, noting he wore a T-shirt and brown bib overalls. She gripped his shoulder and spoke loudly. "Sir, are you okay?"

He didn't respond

Jeremy hunkered down next to Reese as she placed two fingers on the man's neck, feeling a faint throbbing in the carotid artery beneath his jaw. He laid in a sideways position, and his chest moved up and down with shallow breaths. A slight blue tinge colored his face, no doubt from lack of oxygen. His skin felt cold and clammy.

"He's got a pulse," Reese said. "It's weak, though."

"Looks like the guy was out fishing," Jeremy said as he nodded toward the gear strewn across a metal folding table. An old gray pickup truck sat nearby.

"He must have been in that camping chair before he fell," Reese said as she spotted the overturned object positioned nearby.

"Heart attack," Jeremy suggested. "Or maybe a stroke."

"Some sort of health episode," Reese said as she looked for any visible wounds like bleeding cuts or bruises. All she noticed were his scuffed palms where he'd probably reached out to try and break his fall.

"I just tried 911, but there's no service up here," the woman said as she held up her cell phone.

"I'll call for help on my two-way," Jeremy said. With long strides, he hustled back toward his Trailblazer.

The woman lifted her brows.

"Jeremy is a detective with the Meadowlark Valley Police Department," Reese explained. "He's got a police radio."

"Thank heavens," she said. "I really didn't know what to do. I'm so glad you two were nearby."

"I'm Reese Golden, and you are?" Reese asked.

"Cricket, Cricket O'Donnell. My first name's actually Catherine, but folks typically use my nickname."

"Are you from Meadowlark Valley?"

"Yes, that's where my husband and I live," Cricket said. "I'm sorry I didn't know how to help this poor guy. I feel so useless."

"It's fortunate you were walking this way, Cricket. Otherwise, it might have been a long time before anyone else found him."

Cricket nodded. "Is he going to live?"

"We won't know until the EMTs do an evaluation," Reese said. "It's a good sign that he's got a pulse."

"Thank heaven for that," Cricket said. "Is there anything else we should be doing? Like move him so he's more comfortable? I can get a pillow from my camper—"

"No, we don't want to do anything in case he's got a spine injury," Reese said. "Right now, the best thing to do is to stay with him and wait for the ambulance."

THREE

R EESE CHECKED THE CHEST POCKET of the man's overalls, removed his leather wallet and slipped out his driver's license.

"Who is he?" Cricket asked.

"Wade Gentry," Reese read aloud, then replaced the license and wallet.

"I wonder if he's one of the Gentry's who belong to the Gentry Ranch," Cricket said. "They've got a huge spread right outside of town."

Jeremy pushed through the bushes. "An ambulance is on the way," he told them, nearly out of breath after his hasty trek.

"They need to get here fast," Cricket said. Morgan growled again, and Cricket patted her head, calming her in a quiet voice.

"I checked the guy's ID," Reese told Jeremy. "His name is Wade Gentry."

"I've heard of him," Jeremy said as he hunkered down next to the elderly man again. "He's one of our local ranchers. The Gentry Ranch is a short distance away from Meadowlark Valley."

"I knew it," Cricket said.

"Hope we found him in time," Jeremy added.

Fortunately, the reservoir wasn't far from Meadowlark Valley and emergency services dispatched an ambulance right away. After it arrived, Reese stood nearby as the paramedics assessed Gentry, administered oxygen, loaded him onto a stretcher, and lifted him into their vehicle.

Relief steadied Reese's nerves when the paramedics announced that they'd stabilized Mr. Gentry's condition.

A MVPD police cruiser had also shown up, and the paramedics talked briefly with the officer—a thirty-something man with cropped brown hair who looked trim and fit in his uniform.

After everyone exchanged basic information, the ambulance rushed from the scene, emergency lights flashing. Jeremy introduced Reese and Cricket to the officer, and they all shook hands. She noted his name tag identified him as Officer Rhett Ketcham.

For a brief second, she wondered if Ethel Ketcham, the president of the local flower club, was his mother. Probably in her late sixties, Ethel would be about the right age.

Morgan took a defensive, four-legged stance, and the short brown hair on her back stook up straight. Obviously unhappy about meeting yet another stranger, she resumed growling, her graying muzzle showing teeth. Cricket handed her another doggie treat.

Jeremy seemed to know the officer pretty well, and Reese listened as the two of them evaluated the scene.

"Cricket found Gentry while she was walking her dog," Reese added for context.

"I'm sorry you've had such had a rough morning, Ms. O'Donnell," Officer Ketcham said.

"Thanks," Cricket said. "I sure never expected something like this."

"What did you notice when you found Mr. Gentry?" Officer Ketcham reached into his cruiser and pulled out a notebook, and a pencil.

Cricket frowned, then cleared her throat. "Unfortunately, I froze. Then I screamed like a ninny. I'm so sorry."

"I'm sure it was a shock," Jeremy said.

"Fortunately, you and Reese showed up," Cricket said.

Officer Ketcham scribbled something on his lined paper, then asked, "Can you recall if you witnessed anything unusual or something that might have seemed out of place?"

"No," Cricket said. "All I saw was poor Mr. Gentry collapsed on the ground. I panicked. Everything after that is a blur. Frankly, I didn't know what to do."

"Everything's under control now," Reese said as she reassuringly patted Cricket's arm.

"I sure do hope he'll be okay," Cricket said as she gave a trembling smile.

"From what I can tell, I'd rule this an accident," Officer Ketcham said. He made more notes, then tapped the small notebook against his leg. "Doesn't look like any foul play is involved."

"It appears that Gentry was out fishing," Jeremy said. "Nothing suspicious there."

"I'll notify his kin that he's in the hospital," Officer Ketcham said.

"I can take care of that," Jeremy said.

"I believe Gentry has son and a daughter," Ketcham said. "His wife disappeared a while ago, so she's not in the picture."

"I heard she left her husband," Cricket said. "The word around town was that she'd met someone else."

"Rumors aside, Reese and I will go talk the family." Jeremy folded his arms across his chest and nodded at Ketcham. "I'm sure you've got plenty of other things to follow up on."

Officer Ketcham nodded. "Sure do."

"Gentry Ranch is about 10 miles east of Meadowlark Valley, isn't it?" Jeremy asked.

"Give or take," Officer Ketcham said. "It's off of Jackrabbit Road."

"Reese and I will head over," Jeremy assured him.

"Ladies," Ketcham said, nodding at the two before he got into his cruiser and drove away.

"I'd better get back to the campsite or my husband's going to think Morgan and I fell in the lake," Cricket said.

"You've been a big help," Reese told her.

"I didn't do anything," Cricket protested.

"Yes, you did," Reese reminded her. "You found Gentry. You probably saved his life."

Cricket blushed. "It's you guys who saved the day."

Cricket walked a panting Morgan down the road toward the campground.

"We've got a house call to make," Jeremy said.

"That, we do."

"You don't mind that I volunteered you for the trip to the ranch, do you?"

"Nope," Reese said. "I'd rather visit with the Gentry's than face the paperwork piled on my desk."

"It's Saturday," Jeremy pointed out. "Don't you ever take a day off?"

"On the rare occasion," she admitted. "And maybe if I'm sick. Otherwise, I like to stay busy."

"All work and no play," he quipped.

"Whatever," she interrupted.

The two hiked back to their fishing spot. Now and then, Jeremy helped her climb across some of the rougher spots.

"After we stop by the Gentry's, I'll take you to breakfast," he said. "How does that sound?"

"Peachy."

They gathered up their fishing gear, then loaded everything into Jeremy's Trailblazer. As he drove down the highway headed toward the Gentry Ranch, Reese studied the passing prairie with its dips and swells covered in tall, buff-colored grass and endless sagebrush.

Even though Meadowlark Valley wasn't a huge metropolis, which boasted maybe around 40,000 inhabitants, including people in the county, there seemed to be plenty of trouble.

FOUR

A N ENTRY GATE TO THE GENTRY Ranch consisted of large beams erected over a dirt road. At the top of the structure, metal letters spelled out the name, and two metal horse cutouts stood in perpetual reared back positions on either side.

Split rail fencing lined the property, which stretched into the distance. Dotted with grazing cattle and a random dog or two, the acreage rolled toward the horizon. A number of outbuildings nestled in low sections. A bubbling blue creek meandered past them, surrounded by thick shrubs and Russian olive trees.

Reese loved the feathery, pale silver-green leaves on the woody plant, however, she realized that it was listed as a noxious weed in Wyoming, due to its tendency to displace native vegetations such as buffaloberry, golden current, chokecherries, and cottonwood. She considered that unfortunate since it grew so hardily around here and in other parts of the west.

Low hills covered in blue-green sagebrush and grass covered the landscape, with the late September sunlight casting everything with burnished haze.

Both her mother and little brother, who had passed years ago, had loved autumn. Jesse especially treasured Halloween with its trick-or-treating. For her mother, it had meant an end to tending the family garden and preserving the fall harvest that consisted of canning tomatoes, corn, beans, squash, and other culinary delights.

The car accident that had taken their lives lived forever at the back of Reese's mind. Her heart squeezed with bittersweet remembrance, and she pushed away the unpleasant memory. No use dwelling in the past, it only dragged a person down.

"What are you thinking about?" Jeremy asked as he rounded a corner and steered toward the Gentry's large log home.

"Not much really," Reese told him, not wanting to admit to thinking about her mother and brother. "It's amazing how fast time goes by."

"You look worried," he said.

"Do I?" Reese sighed. "I hate seeing anyone get hurt."

"We can check on Gentry later."

"Hopefully he will have improved."

Jeremy wheeled his truck up a long gravel driveway, past rusted plows, and several large wagon wheels. Surrounded by groves of pine and spruce trees, no doubt planted as wind breaks, the residence consisted of one log level, and supported a good-sized porch running along the front.

Clumps of orange and yellow blanket flowers, interspersed with tall pink cosmos, brightened the stone foundation. A breeze rippled the American flag attached to the top of a tall post.

Reese and Jeremy got out, then walked toward the wooden paneled front door which held a grapevine wreath decorated with small pumpkins, autumn leaves, and a black-and-white checkered bow.

Hitching her purse on her shoulder, Reese rang the doorbell.

"I hate being the bearer of bad news," she said.

"Same here," he returned.

The front door opened, and a man, probably in his mid-twenties, wearing jeans and a plaid, western shirt appeared. He held a cell phone to his ear, talking to someone.

"Yes, yes, I understand," he told the person. "I'll be there as soon as I can."

He disconnected and stared questioningly at Jeremy and Reese, his blue eyes piercing, his expression questioning.

"I'm Detective Jeremy Savage of the Meadowlark Valley Police Department," Jeremy said. "We're here about Wade Gentry."

"That's my dad," the man said, ushering them inside. "I'm Taggart Gentry. I was on the phone with the hospital talking about him."

Reese and Jeremy exchanged glances, then stepped through the doorway.

"How's he doing?" Jeremy asked.

"He's in stable condition," Taggart said, lines of concern etching his countenance.

A blue striped western-style rug covered polished floorboards. A large wooden chest displayed several pottery bowls, a thick white candle resting on a rusty base, and a fall floral arrangement. Thick beams hugged the ceiling and an antler chandelier sprinkled light across the room. The ambience was warm and inviting, although a sense of urgency radiated from Taggart Gentry, and no wonder.

"Your father collapsed at Fire Peak Reservoir this morning and we found him unconscious," Reese explained.

"I've begged him not to go out fishing on his own," Taggart grumbled. "He's got a heart condition, but he's stubborn. It's hard for him to admit he's slowing down, and he keeps going at life like he's 20."

"I get it," Reese said. "My grandpa was the same way."

Reese's grandfather had continued his rigorous schedule nearly up until the day he'd died. He had been a tough, sturdy man, and he, along with her wise grandmother, had raised her after her mother and brother died. She'd only been 12, but somehow, they'd managed to help heal her broken heart.

She knew it would be difficult for her to admit her own limitations, someday when the time came for her to slow down. No wonder others had such difficulty when facing the same reality.

"I appreciate all you did," Taggart said, running a hand through his dark, curly hair. "I've got to get to the hospital to be with him now."

"Of course," Reese said, ready to leave and allow the man to go to his father.

"Tag, what's going on?" A very pregnant woman entered the hallway, a curious look on her face. She wore a long, loose dress in amber and yellow hues, and she looked tired.

"It's dad, hon." Tag walked over and took her hand, kissing the back of it. "He collapsed at the reservoir while he was out fishing."

"Oh, God," she said, brushing coffee-brown hair away from her face. "How is he?"

"Don't upset yourself, Sylvia," he warned. "We don't need anything to happen to you, too. Think of the baby."

"I'm not feeble, Taggart." She slid her blue, Cat-Eye frame glasses on top of her head. "Your father needs us."

"He does, and we've got to get to the hospital." Taggart removed a leather jacket from a wooden hall tree, and pulled down a brown and red fringed poncho, which he handed to her.

"I'm having contractions, too." Sylvia placed a hand on her rounded stomach. "I'll go to the OB/GYN department to get checked out while you talk to the doctors about your dad. Let me get my purse."

"I hope the baby's not coming yet," Taggart said as his wife ambled away. Lips pursed, he opened a closet door and rolled out a small suitcase. "He's not due for two weeks."

"We'll be on our way," Jeremy said as he removed a business card from his back pocket and placed it on the chest. "Here's my number if you have any questions."

Reese also removed a business card from her purse and laid it next to Jeremy's. "Don't hesitate to call me either."

"Sure, sure, and thanks again," Taggart said.

As Reese and Jeremy walked back to his truck, Jeremy shook his head. "That poor guy has got a lot on his plate."

"No kidding," Reese agreed as they climbed inside the vehicle.

"Where to?" Jeremy asked.

"The Western Moon Café," Reese said. "Best food in town."

"I'll second that," he said.

FIVE

After breakfast, Jeremy dropped Reese off at her small bungalow. Surrounded by trimmed bushes and autumn flowers that included day lilies and rust-colored mums, the house always filled Reese with familiar warmth. Her family may be gone, and she lived alone, but her loved ones lived on in her heart.

As Jeremy walked her to the front door, he leaned closer and said in her ear, "Earth to Reese."

She turned and met his gaze. "Huh?"

"Where'd you just go?"

"Sorry," she said. "I was thinking about my grandparents and how much they appreciated having this house."

"It's a nice place," Jeremy said.

"I miss them."

Reese glanced toward the flower beds and other places in the yard where the two had left their mark. Over there sat the tree stump grandpa had hollowed out and made into a planter. Nearby perched the plaster garden gnome grandma had lovingly placed beneath a lilac bush.

"My grandmother was always planting blooming things, and my grandfather tended the trees like they were his babies," Reese said. "They traveled some when they were younger, but as they aged, they said their favorite place was home."

"They sound like great folks."

"And my mom, and my brother," Reese added. "You'd have liked them, too."

He tilted his head to the side and grinned, his handsome face lighting up. "Are you sure you don't want to spend the afternoon with me? We could take in a movie or just hang out?"

"I've got a snowstorm of paperwork on my desk to sort through, along with several reports to write. Otherwise, I'd do it."

He sighed. "More federal background investigations?"

"Yep. And some local cases I need to start working on before my clients get antsy."

"That reminds me, I need to swing by the department and see how things are going. But I'd rather play hooky with you."

Reese shook her head. "Not today. Sorry."

"It's just as well," Jeremy said.

"Need help with anything?" Reese asked.

"Maybe. I'll review our cases and let you know," Jeremy said.

"Okay," Reese said.

He headed to his Trailblazer, turning briefly to tip his hat at her before he got in and drove away.

Inside the house, Reese walked past her old, but comfortable furnishings and headed toward her office. Mr. Bojangles, her black cat, wrapped himself around her legs, greeting her with a loud meow.

"I missed you too, buddy," she said. "Unfortunately, the fish weren't biting this morning, so there's no treat for you."

Tail held high, he padded along behind her as she entered her office, which she'd converted from the old garage. Her Bronco, an older model she'd restored with her grandfather, now lived outside under a metal carport.

Plopping her oversize purse on the floor, she sat down at her desk. Bo jumped up and made himself comfortable on a stack of bills she needed to mail. Reese shook her head at his antics as she turned on her computer, then began working on one of her projects.

A couple of hours later, she'd bulldozed her way through most of the items that had been staring her in the face. Pleased that she'd done a good job of catching up, she sat back and closed her eyes as she massaged her stiff neck.

When her cell phone rang, she reached over and pulled it out of her purse, noting the individual's identity. She'd been working for Olivia Clarkson for a week, investigating her fiancé. Reese's efforts so far had uncovered information indicating he'd been cheating on his bride-to-be.

Preparing herself for the woman's unrelenting questions, Reese put the call on speaker.

"Golden Private Investigations. May I help you?"

"It's about time you picked up," Olivia said sharply. "What have you found out about Luther? I'm sure absolutely nothing because I completely trust him. Big Daddy insisted I have him checked out, though."

Abrupt and to the point. Reese couldn't fault the woman on that—Olivia surely didn't waste time beating around the bush. Nevertheless, she just wasn't the most pleasant chick on the planet. Reese found it difficult to get a word in edgewise with her.

Olivia's father, Gunnar Clarkson, who everyone called Big Daddy, was the mistrustful sort. He figured people would try every way they could to scam his family out of their millions. As far as his future son-in-law went, it appeared he'd been correct.

"I was just about to call you," Reese replied, feeling a tad guilty. *Liar.*

Sorting through a stack of folders, Reese located the Clarkson file, which was full of notes about Luther Hale's nefarious activities.

Reese cleared her throat. "Would you like me to tell you what I found out over the phone or in person?"

"Tell me now," Olivia said impatiently. "This wedding nonsense is about to drive me insane. I swear, Luther and I should have just gone to Vegas. But I know if we did, Big Daddy would kill me."

Reese winced. The idea of telling the anxious bride-to-be that

she'd uncovered a mountain of dirt on her beloved wasn't a pleasant prospect. She could tell Olivia was hot to marry Luther, but her
wealthy family wasn't about to give their blessing unless she had
him thoroughly checked out.

"Hopefully this clear weather will hold out," Olivia rambled. "I'd
hate it if we had a freak blizzard during our wedding next month.
It's going to be held in the hot house garden of the Worthington
Hotel in Denver, and it would be awful if people had to travel
snowy roads to get there."

Reese leaned back and propped her feet on her desk, waiting
for the right moment to speak.

"What do you have to tell me?" Olivia finally asked.

"You might want to sit down."

"It . . . it's that bad?" Olivia sucked in a deep breath.

"He's seeing other women."

Silence echoed on the other end of the line and Reese envisioned what Olivia may look like right now. She pictured the woman's livid expression and tightly clenched fists.

Finally, Olivia shrieked, "Seriously? I mean, Big Daddy suspected Luther might only be after my inheritance. You know
we own the Rhineland Beer distributorships located throughout Wyoming. My father is leaving all of his children with huge
trust funds."

"That's what I understand," Reese said, trying not to be irritated that Olivia continued pointing that out each time they talked.
At every opportunity, the woman dangled her family's prestigious
background and gobs of money.

"Do you have photographs and videos? I want to see the proof.
And Big Daddy will absolutely insist on it."

"That's the final work I need to do," Reese said. "I've got a lead as
to where Luther takes his flings and I need to conduct surveillance."

"You're going to catch him in the act," Olivia translated.

"Right," Reese said. "Should I email you the photos and the
report or should I send it to your father?"

"I want to see everything," Olivia said in a cold, determined voice. "Shoot them over to me, and I'll show them to my father. I'm going to have to eat crow since he warned me about Luther. But I d-didn't want to believe him."

Olivia began sobbing and sniffling.

"I dislike giving you unpleasant news," Reese said.

"The wedding is definitely off, if what you've told me is true," Olivia said in a trembling voice. "My friends said you were good. And now I know you're worth every penny. Damn it, anyway."

"For what it's worth, I'm sorry."

"Big Daddy is right. Luther probably just wanted my money. You know, sometimes it sucks to be filthy rich. I feel so . . . so betrayed."

Even with all the pitfalls, Reese wouldn't have minded giving it a try. Nevertheless, she kept that tidbit to herself.

Reese promised Olivia she'd get busy with her stakeout in order to supply photos of Luther's romantic escapades. When she hung up, she began planning a trip to the no-tell-motel where one of his former lovers, Wilda Peacock, had told Reese he took his floozies on weekends.

Wilda hadn't been easy to convince it was in her best interest to confide in Reese her secrets about Luther. However, a crisp $100 bill had helped her spill the beans.

This being a Saturday night, Reese hoped she would be lucky enough to catch Luther in the act of treating one of his floozies to a romantic interlude.

SIX

THE SUN WAS SETTING IN A METEOR OF ORANGE, the dramatic color no doubt fueled by the smoldering, nearly extinguished mountain wildfires that persisted on filling the sky with a smoky haze. Reese didn't like the idea of shoveling snow from her driveway and sidewalks, but a wet blanket of moisture would surely quench the sizzling fires.

It didn't surprise her that Luther Hale had managed to locate the ultimate in sleazy motels for his clandestine rendezvous. Gravel crunched beneath her truck tires as she drove into the parking lot and stopped.

She wrinkled her nose as she studied the run down, dirty pink brick and green-shingled structure. A low-slung building, it featured a row of connected, cottage-style rooms. Reese imagined one of their features included beds with genuine magic finger vibrators to provide 15 minutes of bliss for a quarter. Or maybe these days it cost a dollar for the thrill. Inflation would not be denied.

The appropriately titled Lover's Hideaway Motel rented rooms by the hour. Reese knew she'd never have been able to find it except for the solid directions Luther's jilted former girlfriend, Wilda, had given her.

Wilda had warned Reese to be careful not to miss the motel since it was tucked away amongst thick, concealing foliage. She hadn't been joking. The place was nearly buried in tall, tangled weeds, giant old birch, maple, and pine trees, along with an over-grown lilac bush hedge that looked nearly dead with its dry, skel-etal branches.

Luther drove a sporty red Camaro—an older model more befit-ting the budget of a Bigmart warehouse manager. Slowly perusing the vehicles parked in front of the motel, it was easy to spot his ride, nearly hidden by a large black Silverado.

"Now I just need to figure out which room he's in," Reese mur-mured aloud. The prospect of peering in windows to determine Luther's whereabouts didn't appeal to her. Being arrested as a Peeping Tom definitely was not on her bucket list.

Mulling over her dilemma, she pulled her Bronco into one of the shady, empty spots. As if the stake-out gods had heard her con-cerns, Luther walked out from one of the rooms and sauntered up to an ancient, red-and-white soda machine.

He dropped in coins, then pulled out a can and took a swig. With a lazy grin, he watched as a rusty, dented car pulled in next to his. A pretty young redhead in a short, tight dress got out and hurried toward him.

In an instant, Reese had her cell phone ready to grab photos when the two hugged and kissed. Fortunately, the couple remained oblivious to her as they linked arms and strolled toward Luther's motel room. In the doorway, he unzipped her dress, and she began unbuttoning his shirt.

They left nothing to the imagination as they went at each other, and it seemed fairly obvious to Reese what was about to go down. After they closed the door, she slipped out of her truck and headed over to their room.

It was located at the end of the building, so she walked around to the side, feeling lucky to find a window, albeit cracked and streaked with grime. She peered through the pane, snapped a few more shots of the lovers rolling across the bed, making out. When more clothes came off, Reese backed away.

She'd seen enough.

A branch cracked as she stepped on it, so she froze in her tracks, hoping and praying it hadn't alerted the paramours. No such luck.

A second later, Luther burst from the motel room. When he spotted Reese, he shook his fist and began shouting at her. "What are you, some sort of pervert? I'm gonna call the cops if you don't get lost!"

His face turned a purplish-red color and he started chasing her, despite his unzipped fly and bare feet.

Reese's heart hammered as she beelined toward her Blazer. Glancing at Luther over her shoulder, she decided he looked like an angry bull being taunted by a Spanish matador.

Relieved when she finally reached her vehicle, she opened the door and jumped inside. She dropped her cell into her purse and started Betty's engine, revving it into life.

Glancing at her rearview mirror, she noted that Luther had finally stopped following her. Nevertheless, his caustic glare could have melted the paint on Betty if he'd possessed super powers.

"Another cheating, two-timin' scum bag bites the dust," she joked as she backed out and drove away. "Wait until Olivia sees what her beloved fiancé has been doing. Actually, who he's been doing."

SUNDAY PASSED BY IN A BLUR of attending church services, some house cleaning, and then catching up on reading. Not fiction reading, which would have been pleasant. No, Reese needed to catch up on some of her law enforcement magazines. Amazon had also recently delivered a book about private investigators that she wanted to dive into.

The next morning, she met her friend Kiki Morningstar at Meadowlark Valley Park. Dressed in track suits, she and Kiki did their warm-up routine, then jogged along a familiar trail. It might be Monday, the first day of the work week grind, but Reese felt invigorated by the blood pumping through her veins, boosting that good old endorphin high.

Trees arched overhead, the branches covered in a mixture of yellow-tipped and rusty -brown leaves set against a clear blue sky. The adjacent lake's surface mirrored the rising sun's brilliant rays.

Reese's long brown hair bounced across her shoulders, while Kiki had knotted her frizzy black hair into a bun atop her head. In the chill morning air, their heavy breaths puffed in front of their mouths.

When winter wreathed the city in drifts of deep, white snow, Reese and Kiki went to the gym to do their running. However, as long as the weather held out, the two of them preferred staying outdoors where they could enjoy nature.

Reaching the stone water fountain donated by a local family, Reese slowed down and jogged in place, waiting for Kiki to catch up. She studied the circulating water bubbling from the surface. The feature, surrounded by tall, ornamental grass and shrubs, created a lovely focal point and the silvery liquid offered soothing sounds.

A crow winged toward the grass and landed. It hopped past a bush and began pecking at a French fry someone had dropped. Reese wondered what it would be like to rely on discarded food scraps to satisfy random cravings. The bird looked at her, gulped down the rest of the food, then flew away.

A few seconds later, Kiki eased up beside her and they began walking toward their homes.

"Another three miles under our belts," Reese said.

"Does it bother you that we run all those miles every day, but we never go anywhere?" Kiki sent her a curious glance.

Reese chuckled. "I never really thought about it like that. But you're right. Maybe we ought to change it up and find somewhere else to jog. Get some new inspiration."

"What's your day looking like?" Kiki asked.

"Not too brutal," Reese said. I've caught up with most of my background checks, but I have some client calls to return."

"I'm going to try and get some inventory done between customers," Kiki said. "Then I've got a meditation class later this afternoon."

In Kiki's downtown shop, The Celestial Eye, she offered exclusive crystals, spicy incense, and other mystical wares. She also lived on the top floor the green and white Gothic-style home, which reminded Reese very much of a storybook cottage.

"Are you staying busy these days?" Reese asked.

"Amazingly so," Kiki said. "It seems I chose just the right niche of business to offer our fair city's citizens."

"That's good," Reese said. "Otherwise, they'd probably have to drive to Cheyenne or Laramie to find their tarot cards and wind chimes."

"Which reminds me, are you coming to class today?" Kiki asked.

Reese, who had been enjoying the sound of dry, crunching leaves beneath her feet, suddenly realized Kiki had asked her a question.

"Yes, sure, I'll be there," she responded. "Unless something comes up and I can't make it."

"Perfect," Kiki said. "I believe the meditation is helping you. You're not so uptight these days, my friend."

"It does clear my mind," Reese agreed.

Being shot on the job had done a number on Reese's ego, but time really did have a way of easing her qualms. At first, she'd felt vulnerable; so vulnerable she'd decided to resign. Her confidence had begun to flag and she didn't feel she was offering her best services to the police department.

All these months later, she'd come to terms with what had happened. She believed returning home had allowed her to rebuild trust in herself and her abilities. Returning to a familiar routine acted as a balm on her soul, along with living alongside the people in town she'd known all her life.

When Reese's cell phone rang, she fished it from a pocket, noting the caller ID. "Hi Jeremy."

"I need you down at the station," he announced.

It seemed to be more of a demand than a request. She knew when Jeremy got wrapped up in work, he didn't mince words.

Reese couldn't think of any pressing matters that would prevent her from complying.

"What's up?" she asked.

"I've got Taggart Gentry in my office."

"How is his dad?"

"They put a stent in a clogged artery, and he's resting now," Jeremy said.

"I'm wishing for the best," Reese said.

"Tag's got another issue he needs our help with," Jeremy pressed.

"Give me half an hour," Reese said. "I just finished with my run, so I need a shower."

"Hurry," Jeremy said.

Frowning, Reese put away her cell.

"What's going on?" Kiki asked.

"I'm not sure," Reese said. "When Jeremy and I were up fishing at the reservoir Saturday, we found a local rancher, Wade Gentry, unconscious along the shore. After the ambulance came to get him, Jeremy and I drove to the Gentry Ranch to let the family know."

"You met Tag and Violet Gentry?" Kiki asked. "They are very prominent in the community. They do a lot of volunteer work and serve on many different boards."

"I see," Reese said.

"Tag's wife comes into the shop a lot—she really loves my pillar candles and essential oils," Kiki said. "I combined a selection of several different varieties that specifically help expectant mothers support a healthy pregnancy. The tin they come in contains lemon, lavender, geranium, cypress, and sandalwood."

"Umm," Reese said as she picked up her pace. "Anyway, Tag Gentry is in Jeremy's office right now."

"Jeremy didn't give details?"

Reese shook her head. "Nope."

"Maybe Tag's got more questions about how you found his father."

"Could be," Reese said, her mind churning with different theories. Spotting her house down the street, surrounded by a brown, leaf-strewn lawn and ancient cottonwood trees, Reese said, "Well, this is where we part."

"Call me later," Kiki said. "Now you've got me all curious."

"I promise," Reese said.

Reese jogged toward her house, her mind teeming with possibilities about why Taggart Gentry had shown up in Jeremy's office.

SEVEN

A<small>T HOME, REESE SHOWERED, APPLIED A DASH</small> of makeup, then knotted her hair atop her head. She dressed in a leopard print blouse, a black leather vest, black jeans, and well-worn boots that used to belong to her grandfather. He hadn't been a large man and had stood maybe an inch taller than Reese, so his boots fit her perfectly.

Over time, the sage advice Reese's grandfather had imparted became embedded in her mind. Wearing his boots gave her self-assurance and made her feel as though he walked alongside her, encouraging her to maintain his ethical standards.

Bo hopped onto her bed and curled his black furry body atop the multicolored granny square Afghan her grandmother had crocheted.

"Sleep tight, little buddy," Reese told the cat as she reached over to scratch between his ears.

Hooking purse handles over her right shoulder, she headed outside to her vintage, restored Bronco, which she'd nicknamed Betty years ago. A rush of wind swept past her, setting aflutter orange and yellow leaves. Reese watched them for a few seconds, deciding they danced on the air like tiny ballerinas.

After climbing into the truck, she backed out of her driveway and headed downtown to the Meadowlark Valley Police Department. As usual, blue and white squad cars lined the parking lot in front of the white cinderblock, two-story building.

Reese recalled that when she was a kid, the lower floor had held Red's Butcher Shop, and the upper floor held an apartment where Red lived with his wife and two children. About 10 years ago, the building had been refurbished to hold the offices of Meadowlark Valley's finest.

She parked Betty, then got out and walked toward the station, avoiding the gnarled roots of a cottonwood tree that had broken apart the sidewalk. Her boots crunched on tiny chunks of crumbling cement and dried leaves as she strolled past two poles bearing a United States flag and a Wyoming flag. Opening the glass entrance door, she walked inside.

The waiting area featured a black leather couch, a couple of mauve chairs, and an artificial Ficus tree. Beyond a half wall, several office workers sat at desks, concentrating on computer screens. TV monitors hung on walls. Filing cabinets, printers, and book shelves jam-packed the area. Fluorescent fixtures on the ceiling gave off harsh light.

Steve Daniels, the administrative coordinator, sat at a desk in the front reception area. With his short spiky hair and bulging biceps showing beneath the sleeves of his dark blue polo shirt emblazoned with the Meadowlark Valley Police Department logo, he always reminded Reese of a Marine recruit.

"Hey there, Reese," Steve said in a friendly tone. "What's up?"

"Detective Savage asked me to come down here," Reese said.

"Ah, yes, he mentioned that you'd be coming," Daniels said. He grabbed the phone receiver, then punched in a number on a black handset. After touching base with Jeremy, Daniels met her gaze again.

"You're cleared."

Reese breezed down the hallway. She walked through a door and entered a room that held a sea of desks. A few uniformed officers leaned over stacks of papers, studied their computer screens, or talked on the phone. Some of them looked up, and recognizing her, waved.

"Hi, Reese," one of them said. "How's life treating you these days?" he asked.

"Good, Officer Sherman," she replied.

"Call me Ray," he said. "You're one of us, after all. You just don't wear the uniform or have a badge."

"Sure," Reese said. "Take care."

"You too," he shot back.

She stepped around a wall of room dividers and spotted Jeremy seated at his desk, wearing crisp, dark blue jeans, a white button-down shirt, and a classic tweed sport jacket.

Tag Gentry sat across from him in a molded orange chair. He wore the same clothing he'd had on yesterday. Wrinkles covered his western shirt and he looked agitated. His shoulders sagged, and dark circles ringed his bloodshot eyes.

Assessing people was a habit Reese had picked up after so many years of working with the public. You could tell a lot about someone by the way they dressed and behaved.

Such as, were they sincere? Were they lying? Or had life handed them a crap fest?

It was all about body language.

"Reese," Jeremy said, "have a seat."

He pointed to another orange molded chair wedged nearby, where she made herself comfortable.

Jeremy rocked back in his chair and nodded at Tag. "There's a problem at the ranch."

"It's about my sister, Violet," Tag said.

Reese gripped her knees. "What's going on?"

"I can't get a hold of her," he said, his brows knitted. "Sylvia and I have called and texted, but she's not responding. And she hasn't come home for the last three nights. I know in my gut there's something wrong."

"She lives there at the ranch?" Reese asked.

"Yes," Tag said. "After graduating from college, she came home and has lived there for the last five years managing our ranching operation."

"I see," Reese said.

"Can you two help me?" Tag said in a near pleading tone. He perched on the edge of his seat, tapping one of his boots as he glanced back and forth between the two of them. "I'd go out looking for her myself, but I don't want to leave Sylvia in her condition. And I sure can't leave Dad."

"I explained to Tag that the police department often works with you on cases," Jeremy said. "Since you have a knack for finding people, I wanted you in on this."

Reese tucked strands of stray hair behind her ears as she considered her work commitments. Since she'd slaved over the weekend to catch up, she was at a good point to help.

"I have some basic questions that I ask in all missing person's cases," Reese said. "So please don't take offense if they sound too personal or if you've already answered them for Jeremy."

"I get it," Taggart said in an anxious tone. "I'll do anything to find Violet."

"Has Violet ever done anything like this in the past?"

"You mean has she taken off without telling any of the family where she's going?"

Reese nodded.

"No," Tag said.

"Does she have any concerning medical conditions or emotional issues?"

"She's definitely not a head case," Taggart said. "She's as steady as a rock, believe me. It isn't like her at all to drop out of sight."

"Does she have a boyfriend? Maybe she's with him."

"She's never mentioned it." Tag shook his head. "I'm pretty sure she'd have told me if she was seeing someone."

"You're close with her then?"

"Yes. Being older, I've always felt the need to protect her and we have this . . . this connection. Now I can't shake this feeling that she's in trouble."

"Did you look through her room to see if she maybe left a note?"

Tag nodded. "We couldn't find a thing that seemed out of place and there were definitely no notes."

"When was the last time you talked to your sister?"

"Late Friday afternoon. She planned to meet a friend for dinner."

"Where did she go to eat?" Reese crossed her legs.

"To the Prairie Shopping Center," Tag said.

"Did she mention a specific place where they planned to eat?"

"She didn't say exactly, but I know Violet likes a restaurant there called Sweet Clementine's. She raves about their steak salad, so they could have gone there."

"Maybe after they had dinner, they decided to go out of town and forgot to tell you," Reese suggested.

"I thought of that. Saturday morning, I tried to call her friend, Sabrina, to see if she could tell me anything. But she didn't answer, either."

"Hmm," Reese said, frowning.

"Then I got preoccupied with dad's accident. At the hospital, they rushed him into surgery. We were also worried that Sylvia was going into labor." Tag ran a hand through his hair. "Sunday came and went, and I realized Violet hadn't checked in. I want to respect her privacy, but she's been gone too long without any contact."

Reese pulled a small legal note pad and a pen from her purse, which was big enough to hold a kitchen sink. She preferred her handbags that way so she could carry plenty of gadgets. At a moment's notice she could come up with whatever oddball item she might need.

She jotted some notes, then said, "Violet's friend's name is Sabrina?"

"Right, Sabrina Byrd. She works at a local advertising and web development agency." Tag seemed to catch his breath. "Violet mentioned she's graphic artist."

"I need Violet's birth date, her height, weight, eye, and hair color," Reese said. "Also, her phone number and yours. And a recent photo."

"I'll burn you one of these," Jeremy said, holding up a work-sheet. "Tag filled out this form with pertinent information."

He walked over to a Xerox machine and put it under the lid. A few seconds later, he handed Reese a copy.

"I'll text you a pic of Violet from the other day." Tag pulled a cell phone from his pocket and began punching on it. "She was taking a class of school kids on a field trip to our pumpkin patch."

A ding sounded on Reese's cell. She fished it from her purse, examined the photo of Violet, a tall, thin woman with her short, feathered hair featuring burgundy streaks, then tucked away her phone. She scribbled more about Violet on her note pad, allowing herself think of any and all the reasons Tag's sister may have failed to get in touch with her family.

Maybe she'd spent a wild weekend with her friend. Could be she hadn't felt like calling home yet. From the way Tag had described his sister, it seemed she would have been more responsible, though.

"Does Violet have any ex-boyfriends?"

Taggart snapped his fingers. "That never occurred to me, but there is one. His name is Austin Buell. The two dated for a while in high school, but they broke up before graduation."

Reese wrote down the ex-boyfriend's name and added a couple of ideas about what might be going on with Violet. Possibly she was sick or there might be a specific reason she didn't want to talk to her brother. Something might have happened that made her want to remain silent for a while.

Reese pursed her lips and let her mind wander. Did Violet Gentry have a secret life her family didn't know about?

Through the years, she'd investigated a multitude of miss-ing persons cases—the husband with a second family no one was aware of; the daughter who funded her college classes by stripping, the father who had gotten in too deep with gambling debts. There were a surprising number of reasons why people disappeared.

"Did you and Violet have a falling out of any sort? Perhaps an argument?" she asked Tag. "Or maybe she had a disagreement with another family member."

Tag shook his head. "No. We all get along fine."

So, he says, Reese thought. Sometimes people didn't want to air their family's dirty laundry. Even when it became a dangerous bet to keep things quiet, they didn't want the family name tarnished.

"Is Austin's family living in town?" she asked Tag.

"I don't know," he said.

Perusing the form Jeremy had handed her, she noted Tag had listed Sabrina Byrd as the last person he knew had been with Violet. He'd also listed her phone number.

"I'll start by trying to track down Violet," Reese said. "I'll check social media, too. Have you done that, Tag?"

He shook his head. "Nope. I don't like that shit, but Violet's really into it."

"That might give us some leads," Reese said.

"Money's no object," Tag said.

He pulled a tooled leather checkbook from his front shirt pocket. "How much do you need to get started?"

Reese held up her hand. "That's not necessary."

"The department will take Reese's expenses since she's working with us on this case," Jeremy said.

"I see," Tag said. He closed his eyes and rubbed his forehead, as if his temples were pounding. "Man, I'm so crazy worried that I can't think straight."

"You're under a lot of pressure," Reese said. "Rest assured, I'll start looking for your sister right away."

"I appreciate it," he said, sounding more convinced.

"By the way, how does Violet get around?" Reese asked.

"She owns a 2000 Ford Ranger," Taggart said. "It's light blue. The license plate number is on the form I filled out."

Reese checked the sheet and made note of it. "Does Violet have any typical haunts? Like bars or clubs?"

"Geez, I didn't even think of calling them," Tag said. "She likes the Roadhouse Bar down on Cross Street."

Reese jotted that down.

"If I think of any other places she goes or things she does, I'll text you," Tag said.

"Thanks," Reese said.

"I can't help but feel like a dirtbag." Tag glared out the window at the rushing traffic, the strain evident in his voice. "I'm choosing to focus on Dad and Sylvia, rather than trying to find my sister."

"Don't think of it that way," Reese told him. "You're doing the right thing by asking the police department to investigate."

"We have databases and other things at our disposal," Jeremy pointed out. "Things average citizens don't."

"I know you don't want to hear this right now, Tag, but Violet may not be missing exactly," Reese said. "She's maybe just not communicating with you right now. There may be good reasons why she hasn't checked in."

His gaze pierced Reese as he stood. "I don't believe that for one minute."

Jeremy stood and gripped Tag's shoulder. "Hang in there, buddy. We know this isn't easy."

"We'll be in touch as soon as we hear something," Reese assured him.

"I'm headed back to the hospital to see my dad," Tag said in a tired voice. Lines of defeat etched his face as he left the office.

Reese chewed on her lower lip for a few seconds. As always, the concerns people had for their missing loved ones weighed heavily on her conscience. The responsibility of being entrusted with finding them was not a simple undertaking.

And time was of the essence.

Reese met Jeremy's gaze. "It isn't good that Violet's already been gone this long."

"I know," Jeremy said. "I mentioned that to him, which frustrated him even more."

Reese nodded. "You know, Violet may have a simple explanation as to why she hasn't returned anyone's calls."

"It is possible," Jeremy agreed.

Reese walked with Jeremy to the door. "I'll keep you updated."

"I'll call local hospitals to see if she's been admitted anywhere." Jeremy rubbed his chin with his thumb and forefinger. "I'll also check law enforcement databases to see if she got arrested in any of the towns nearby."

"Thanks for covering those," Reese said.

Jeremy grasped her hand and squeezed it. "Talk to you later."

"I'm looking forward to it." Reese was tall, yet she still had to stretch up to kiss Jeremy. At first, as her lips met his, he seemed caught off guard. Before long, he pulled her close and wrapped her in his strong embrace.

For a few, all too brief magical seconds, Reese felt delighted, and thoroughly content. Sizzling warmth spread from the top of her head, down to her toes.

Finally, with seeming reluctance, they both pulled apart. He gave her a lopsided grin. She smiled back, then spun on her boot heel and left. A part of her wanted to continue the kiss somewhere private, but unfortunately, duty called.

EIGHT

O UT IN HER TRUCK, REESE CALLED Violet's cell. Just as Tag had said, his sister didn't answer. In fact, the call went directly to voice mail, indicating the battery was dead. Same thing with Sabrina's cell when Reese dialed the number.

It wasn't a good sign that Violet and Sabrina hadn't recharged their phones. It wasn't completely ominous, either. It concerned Reese, though. These days, most people made certain their cells were active, and in fact, relied on them too much, in her opinion.

Reese drove out of the police department's parking lot and headed directly over to the Prairie Shopping Center—the last place where Violet Gentry had gone. Located a short distance from the older part of Meadowlark Valley, the old strip mall had originally been built in the 1960s.

The construction consisted of dull boxes built in a row. Some of the bygone stores, such as Radio Shack and K-B Toys, had been replaced by a Great Clips beauty salon, an antiques store, a small bank, and a few other locally owned shops. The old Kodak Film drive-through kiosk in the parking lot had been torn down and replaced by a large stone planter that currently held bushes and flowers.

Sweet Clementine's resided at the end of the mall, with its hand-painted sign featuring green ferns and pink roses above the door. Several customers walked out of the restaurant, and a couple of more walked inside.

Reese drove through the parking lot, checking out the vehicles, but didn't see a powder blue Ranger like the one Tag said his sister drove. Since it was morning, most people were at work, so there were plenty of parking spots.

She was about ready to stop and go into the restaurant to show Violet's picture to the staff and ask if they remembered seeing her Friday when a patch of blue flashed from the side of the building.

Reese wheeled her truck around and drove toward the parking area tucked around the corner. A Ford Ranger truck, just like the one Tag had described, sat there. After parking, she got out and inspected the vehicle, which had a black cover buttoned down and stretched over the bed.

The license plate number matched the one Tag had given. Red fabric stuck out of the tailgate, and Reese's heart skipped a beat. Did it belong to Violet?

Sliding her cell phone from her back pocket, she dialed Jeremy's number. When he picked up, she said, "I found Violet's truck in the Prairie Shopping Center parking lot beside Sweet Clementine's restaurant."

"That was fast," he said. "Any sign of her?"

"No, but there's bunched up material sticking out of the tail gate."

"Are you thinking what I'm thinking?"

"I bet so," Reese said. "I'm afraid when we open up the tailgate, we'll find Violet's body stuffed in the bed of the truck."

"I'm on my way," he said, a note of urgency in his voice. "I'll radio for a patrol car and get some investigators over there."

"I think you'd better send for the coroner," Reese added. "Just in case."

SIREN WAILING, A MEADOWLARK VALLEY POLICE cruiser, along with a black Crime Scene Investigations van, and the black coroner's van, rolled up and parked near Reese. That garnered the interest of onlookers, who gathered around to stare. Their voices punctuated the air as they talked amongst themselves, and some began to snap cell phone photos.

"Man, what's going on?" A young man wearing jeans and a white T-shirt covered by a tan trench coat called out. He had jet-black hair and dark sunglasses, which he whipped off and shook at Reese when she didn't answer. "Hey, lady, I asked you a question!"

"Move along, sir," she finally said. "This is a law enforcement matter."

When he scowled and gave her the finger, she turned around, ignoring him.

A cop got out of the patrol car, and Reese recognized Officer Rhett Ketcham with his cropped brown hair as he strode toward her. "Hello, Ms. Golden. Detective Savage said you've got a lead on a missing person's case?"

"I've located Violet Gentry's vehicle." She pointed toward the blue Ranger.

"Let me call it in." Ketcham spoke into the radio on his shoulder, then read the license plate. A few minutes later, he got a response. "Yep. It's registered in her name."

Ketcham waved over several crime scene technicians, who wore black pants, black polo shirts and black vests bearing the MVPD logo.

"Let's secure this truck," Ketcham instructed as he pointed to the Ranger.

Her ID badge flapping on a black lanyard, one of the investigators got busy tacking up yellow crime scene tape and another investigator produced a supply of yellow A-Frame evidence markers. Another team member got busy taking photographs, outside and inside the truck.

In a clump of gnarled trees, crows sat silently observing the activity. Reese took note of them, wondering what the birds thought about all the fuss.

Jeremy arrived in his Trailblazer, just as Dr. Pepper Beckwith, the coroner, exited her van. They spoke briefly, then they walked toward Reese and Officer Ketcham.

Dr. Beckwith's long, reddish-brown hair fell over her shoulders, and she wore a black windbreaker with a Granite County logo and the word, CORONER stamped on it.

"We've met before, haven't we?" the doctor asked as she approached Reese. "You look familiar."

"Briefly, at a prior incident."

Dr. Beckwith nodded. "I remember now. You're a private investigator, right?"

"Guilty as charged," Reese affirmed. "And I'm working on this case."

"What do we have here, Officer Ketcham?" the doctor asked.

"I was about inspect the bed of this truck," he said.

"I'm afraid we'll find a body under the tarp," Jeremy said, hooking his thumbs in his utility belt.

"Let's have a look," Dr. Beckwith said in a grim tone as slid examination gloves from her pocket and put them on.

Also wearing gloves, Ketcham unsnapped the black plastic and rolled it aside, releasing a foul stench. Everyone stood back, frowning at the unwholesome odor, that could only mean one thing.

Although familiar with the reeking smell of death, Reese quelled her gag reflex. It was something a cop never became accustomed to. She scowled down into the truck bed at a young woman with wheat-colored hair, probably in her late twenties, wearing brown pants and a brown tweed jacket. Her body rested atop a mound of sweaters, and jeans—which looked very much like a rolling closet. Fast-food wrappers, makeup, drink cups, and soda cans littered the space.

The victim's head rested at a strange angle on a striped horse blanket, revealing her bruised and mottled face and neck. Her glassy eyes bulged and she stared lifelessly at the blue sky above, her twisted body quiet as a marble statue.

"Jesus," Officer Ketcham exclaimed, a frown on his lips.

Jeremy shook his head.

Investigators began snapping photos of the body, the flashes like lightning during the brightness of day.

Reese's insides withered. The cruelty heaped on homicide victims always disgusted her. A breeze brushed past her cheeks, but shock prevented her from brushing away strands of hair that dropped across her forehead.

Brow furrowed, Dr. Beckwith touched the victim's neck. "Those ligature marks over her larynx indicate she was most likely strangled. By the rigor mortis condition of the bluish body tissue, lividity, I'd say she's been dead more than 24 hours."

"Yep," Jeremy said.

"If I find her hyoid bone is fractured, it'll be a sure sign of strangulation," the doctor added.

"She doesn't match the description of our missing person, Violet Gentry," Reese said.

Officer Ketcham slid out a purse that had been smashed beneath the victim's hip. After opening it, he withdrew a wallet and slid out a drivers' license.

"Her name is Sabrina Byrd," Ketcham said.

"Violet's friend, the one she met for dinner," Jeremy said.

Reese crossed her arms over her chest. "Now the question is, where is Violet?"

"You've got your work cut out," Jeremy told her.

"For sure," Reese said, her heart sinking to discover that her missing person's case now involved a murder. "Tag's going to be crazy worried to discover Violet's friend is most likely a victim of homicide."

NINE

Dr. Beckwith donned a face mask and examined the body at different angles. She'd brought a clip board from her van which she used to jot down observations.

Technicians lifted fingerprints and gathered hair, fiber, blood, and other DNA samples. The coroner took her time, which Reese knew from experience was very important because the tendency at a crime scene was often to remove a decedent too quickly.

Once a body is removed, it cannot be replaced.

It's always best to wait until the evaluation is complete and all evidence is collected to determine the manner and cause of death. Otherwise, there might be a potential to cause emotional trauma at a later date to concerned family members.

"I'm ready to take the body to the morgue," Dr. Beckwith told Jeremy. "I'll need to perform an autopsy."

Jeremy nodded. "Whatever you need Dr. Pep—"

"No Dr. Pepper jokes," Dr. Beckwith said, a sparkle in her eye. "That's way inappropriate right now."

"You're right," Jeremy said. "This routine always gets to me. There's really no way to lighten the mood."

"Exactly," Dr. Beckwith said.

Dr. Beckwith nodded toward her two assistants waiting nearby. They rolled over a sheet-covered gurney and transferred the body onto it. After securing it with a black plastic covering, they strapped it down and rolled it toward coroner's van.

"I'm off now," Dr. Beckwith said. "I'll have more findings in a bit, Detective, in case you'd like to contact me with any further questions."

"Appreciate it," Jeremy said.

"Can you tell the victim's family?" she asked.

Jeremy nodded. "Will do."

Dr. Beckwith followed her assistants, climbed into the van, and drove off.

"Dr. Pepper?" Reese met Jeremy's gaze. "Seriously? Is that a bad department joke or what?"

Jeremy scratched his brow. "Yeah, it is. Really bad. We deal with a lot of depressing shit, so sometimes we screw up."

"Did you find out if Violet has been admitted to any local hospitals or if she's been arrested? Reese asked.

"I checked, but those are both a big negative," Jeremy said.

"It honestly looks like she's been abducted," Reese said, watching as one of the investigators removed a purse from the blue truck, along with a cell phone. "Otherwise, she wouldn't have left those behind."

Jeremy snapped on a pair of plastic gloves, strode over and collected the purse from the investigator. He withdrew a flowered wallet and returned to Reese's side holding up a drivers' license. "It's Violet's."

Reese nodded.

Jeremy dug through the purse's contents again and produced a phone.

"Looks like somebody nabbed Violet in a hurry," Reese said. "I don't believe she'd leave that behind."

"Chances are that Sabrina simply got in the way," Jeremy said. "That's why somebody took her out."

"Collateral damage." Reese frowned. "I'm going to check inside with the restaurant to see if anyone saw or heard anything unusual Friday night. Hopefully they have surveillance footage covering this area."

"I'll check with Violet's cell phone carrier to see if we can get a copy of her call records," Jeremy said. "Her abductor might be someone she knew."

"Do you think you'll have any trouble?" Reese asked.

"Some carriers are cooperative with law enforcement, some aren't," Jeremy said. "If they refuse to hand over the records, I'll get a court order."

"Let's hope that's not the case," Reese said.

"Yep, it'll delay our investigation," Jeremy said.

"Which sucks," Reese said.

One of the technicians walked up to Jeremy. "We're about done here, sir."

"When everything's finished, tow the Ranger to the lab for further, in-depth processing," Jeremy said. "I want every inch of it covered."

"Got it," the technician said, then headed back to the truck.

"Let's go see about that restaurant surveillance footage," Jeremy said.

"Right behind you." Reese followed Jeremy inside Sweet Clementine's, walking past the crowd of people who had gathered to observe the police and the CSI team.

"Hey, what's going on?" a lady called to them.

"This is our neighborhood," a man added in an indignant tone. "We have a right to know."

Both Reese and Jeremy ignored the taunts.

"Please stand back," one of the uniformed officers advised the individuals.

A bell on the door tinkled as Jeremy opened the restaurant's entrance door for Reese. He stood aside as she went in first, then followed. The small restaurant boasted a mixture of exposed brick, corrugated steel, and creamy white walls.

A jungle of Boston ferns, dangling philodendrons and spider plants suspended from the ceiling and draped from wooden shelves. Mosaic green and white tiles graced the floor and rustic pendant lighting flooded the area with illumination.

Some of the customers sat eating and chatting with each other at light wood tables with matching chairs. Several others had lined up along the window front of the restaurant, where they had obviously been watching the show outside. Quizzical expressions lined their faces. Upon spotting Reese and Jeremy, they whispered amongst themselves.

Reese and Jeremy walked toward the wooden counter where a woman in a long, colorful skirt and a white top stood. She tossed long, glossy black tresses over her shoulders. Large, gold hoop earrings danced alongside her smooth, light brown cheeks.

Beautiful and exotic, were the descriptive words that came into Reese's mind. Smiling, she said, "We're looking for the owner."

"I am Neeta Poole," the woman said, her gaze questioning beneath dark, arched brows. "My husband Troy and I own this restaurant. He isn't here at the moment, though."

"Reese Golden." She handed Neeta a business card.

Neeta examined it, then looked up when Jeremy spoke.

"I'm Detective Savage of the Meadowlark Valley Police Department," he told her, then pulled aside his jacket so she could see his badge.

"What's going on?" Neeta asked. "Why are the police outside?"

"We're investigating an incident." Reese withdrew her cell phone from her purse and showed Neeta the photograph of Tag Gentry's sister. "Do you know this lady, and do you recall her coming here Friday night?"

"That's Violet Gentry," Neeta confirmed. "She comes here a lot with friends. She always praises our food, which is a mixture of American cuisine and authentic Indian dishes from my home country."

Jeremy pulled a small journal and a pencil from his jacket pocket and made a note.

"I hope Violet is all right," Neeta said, her dark eyes flashing. "She is a nice lady."

"When did Violet and her friend leave Friday night?" Jeremy asked.

"Not until we were getting ready to close," Neeta said.

"What time was that?" Reese asked.

"Midnight," Neeta said. "We stay open late on Friday and Saturday. Weeknights, we close in the evenings at 10 o'clock."

"Did you hear or see anything unusual?" Jeremy asked.

Neeta shook her head. "Everything was fine. Violet and her friend, I think her first name was Sabrina, were the only two customers remaining at closing time. They'd already paid for their meals, so they were just talking. Troy and I had everything done for the evening, so as soon as they left, we locked up and left through the back door."

"Do you have surveillance footage of the corner out here?" Reese pointed outside to where the police were finishing up.

"Yes, we do." Neeta gestured toward them. "Please follow me and you can review it in the office."

TEN

NEETA'S OFFICE APPEARED TO BE MORE of a converted closet, but Reese decided it seemed functional enough. She and Jeremy perched on well-worn chairs at Neeta's small, battleship gray desk. It appeared to have come from an army surplus sale, which gave it retro appeal.

They studied the computer screen, watching over and over the security footage dated from last Friday. Unfortunately, it had a grainy quality, which made it difficult to determine details.

"I am so sorry," Neeta said. "I keep telling Troy that we need to upgrade our security system with better software and cameras. And put better lighting out there. It's just so expensive, you know?"

"The overgrown bushes also obscure a lot of the view, too," Reese added.

Neeta made a frustrated sound.

"Hang on," Jeremy said, adjusting the camera footage backward and forward, trying to capture some still shots. He stopped the video and leaned forward, peering closer at the images.

"There," Reese said, pointing out two women entering the restaurant. "That looks like Violet, and that must be Sabrina."

"Yep," Jeremy said.

"Go forward to when the two left," Reese suggested.

Jeremy moved the footage closer to midnight. Sabrina walked out of Sweet Clementine's. When she got close to the blue Ranger, someone in dark clothing, a dark coat with a hood, and a face mask jumped up. The figure grabbed her and covered her mouth with a cloth that had most likely been soaked in something noxious.

"Look at the size of that guy," Reese commented. "I'd say with those broad shoulders and muscular form, it's probably a very large man."

"I'd have to agree," Jeremy said.

"Looks like he used chloroform to nab her," Reese said. "That's not easy to obtain."

"He could have concocted a home version," Jeremy said.

"True, you only have to mix acetone and bleach," Reese noted.

When Sabrina slumped down on the ground, the attacker rolled her over, no doubt in order to see her face. After a second, he leaned over and wrapped meaty fists around Sabrina's throat. At a certain point, he dragged her body toward the truck bed, pulled off the cover and dumped her inside.

Reese bit her lower lip as she watched how the man treated Sabrina's body like so much garbage. It disgusted her.

Returning the cover to its former position, the large man hunkered down beside the driver's side of Violet's truck again. The screen flashed, and the footage filled with fuzzy lines. Then the monitor blacked out.

Jeremy swore, and Reese placed a hand on his upper arm.

"My apologies," Neeta said, her hands clasped.

"Not your fault," Jeremy said, fiddling with keyboard. "It's the damn technology."

"We've already seen some good stuff," Reese said, tossing Neeta a glance over her shoulder.

A few seconds later, the video cleared. Jeremy stopped fiddling and removed his hands from the keyboard.

Reese leaned in to watch the screen closer.

Violet appeared, sauntering toward her truck. Once again, the attacker jumped up and clamped the cloth against her mouth. She struggled briefly, then sank back against him.

The man looked around, no doubt to ascertain that he hadn't been seen. Then he picked up Violet and carried her into the bushes.

"Chloroform again," Reese growled.

"Looks that way."

Neeta pressed her hands against her cheeks, her eyes wide. "This is terrible! Those poor women. Can our restaurant be blamed for any liability?"

Jeremy stood. "Parking lots are the most vulnerable crime area for a business. Do you have an attorney?"

"No," Neeta said.

"You'll want to retain one," Reese said. "To be on the safe side."

"Wh . . . what could we be sued for?" Neeta's voice trembled.

"Negligent security," Reese said. "Just be prepared."

Neeta nodded, but remained silent—her face pale and drawn.

"We need a copy of this security video," Reese said.

"Of course." Neeta removed a jump drive from a desk drawer. Sitting in a chair, she slid it into a port and copied the video. Finished, she handed Jeremy the drive.

"Contact us if you have any more questions," Jeremy said.

"Also, think back to Friday night when Violet and Sabrina came in for dinner," Reese suggested. "Try to remember what they were talking about that night. It could be important."

"Of course," Neeta said.

"If you recall the details, give me a call."

Reese and Jeremy left the office and walked back outside in time to see Violet's blue Ranger being towed away.

"Nothing to see here, folks," Officer Ketcham told the people who continued to mill around. "Go on about your business, please."

Murmuring, most of them walked away. A few die-hards continued to hang around, probably chewing the fat with one another about what they'd witnessed. And videotaping as much as the excitement as they could.

A gust of wind whipped a dirt devil through the south end of the parking lot. Dark tresses flew around Reese's face, obscuring her vision. She reached into her pocket, located a scrunchie, and used it to tie back her hair.

Then it hit her.

An unusual, tingling sensation started at the base of her neck and raced down her spine. Her pulse beat in a staccato rhythm. As if being controlled by someone or something, her gaze was drawn to the parking area where Violet's truck had been.

In her mind's eye, she witnessed the same scene she'd watched in the surveillance video. A tall, dark man dragged an unconscious Violet across the asphalt. Rather than being limited by the camera's view, Reese saw beyond. The perp pulled the woman through the bushes next to the lot.

Amazingly, on the other side of the shrubs, a worn, weed-filled dirt road appeared, along with an old, beat-up station wagon. The vehicle color seemed indistinguishable, but Reese judged it to be white, although plastered with rusty spots. The bumpers and the body displayed stickers covered in wording she couldn't read from this far away.

"Reese?" Jeremy asked.

Ignoring him, she continued watching as the large man opened the station wagon hatch, lifted up Violet, and dropped her unconscious body inside.

A sinister laugh sounded. Had it come from Violet's abductor? Reese couldn't tell. She watched as he reached into his pocket, pulled out a lighter and a cigar, and smoked briefly. Then he tossed the stub on the ground, climbed in the driver's side of the station wagon, and drove off.

"Reese!" Jeremy said in a more urgent tone. "Ride with me to Sabrina's house to let her family know what's happened."

Shaken by what she'd just seen, or imagined, or whatever, Reese turned to him. "Huh?"

"Come on," Jeremy urged as he headed toward his unmarked police vehicle, a dark blue Chevrolet Trailblazer. "It's not far from here."

"Just a minute." Reese hustled toward the bushes and pushed her way through the leaves. Just as she'd envisioned, there was indeed a worn dirt road running along the back side of the strip mall.

Next to the toe of her boot, she spotted a half-smoked cigar. Grabbing a couple of short sticks to use as tongs, she picked it up and read the label.

"Especial Romeo Cigarro."

Stepping back through the bushes, Reese walked it over to Jeremy. "DNA test this. I think our suspect dropped it."

"I bet there are plenty of mall workers who go out there for smoke breaks," Jeremy said. "What makes you think our guy dropped it?"

"Gut instinct," Reese said, not confident enough to talk about what she'd seen transpire in her mind.

They held each other's gazes for a second, hers insistent, his mistrusting. Finally, Jeremy called for Officer Ketcham to fetch him an evidence bag, which he did. Jeremy dropped in the cigar, wrote on it, and handed it back to Ketcham.

"Potential evidence," he explained, then turned back to Reese.

"Did you hear someone laughing a second ago?" she asked.

"No, Reese," Jeremy confirmed. "No one's laughing."

"I didn't really think so," she said. "Maybe I'm losing it."

"You're not," Jeremy said. "The things we see in this line of business are bound to get to us on occasion."

"Yeah, you're probably right," Reese agreed.

"Let's stop by the hospital first and let Tag know about what we found here."

"Good idea," Reese said, still reeling from her unusual episode.

ELEVEN

AT THE HOSPITAL, TAG AND SYLVIA met Reese and Jeremy in the waiting room. The pale gray walls, bright fluorescent lighting, and bare table surfaces gave off sterile, cold vibes. The practical, hard-wearing carpet—the color of stone, added to it.

"What's happening?" Tag asked, impatience threading his voice.

"We watched the security footage at the restaurant where Violet went with her friend Sabrina on Friday night," Jeremy said. "It's not good."

Sylvia grabbed Tag's arm and clung to it, tears brimming in her eyes. "And?"

"Violet's friend Sabrina was killed and she was taken," Reese said, hating to share the terrible development with them. "The video was grainy, but the suspect appears to be a big, tall guy. Does that sound like anyone she might know? Or that you know?"

Both Tag and Sylvia shook their heads.

"Oh my God," Tag said in a trembling voice. He led Sylvia toward a gray- and cream-colored couch, where they both sat down. Studying the floor, he rubbed his temples, apparently coming to grips with the disturbing news.

Sylvia placed a protective hand on her swollen abdomen. "Who would have done such a monstrous thing?"

"We're trying to find out," Jeremy said.

"I knew something bad had happened," Tag said. "I just knew it."

"I feel like my heart's being ripped from my chest," Sylvia said, then hiccupped, which was followed by sobs.

"We're doing all we can to track down Violet." Reese walked over and patted Sylvia's shoulder. "Believe me, I'm determined to find her."

"God, I can't believe this is happening," Sylvia said.

"How are you feeling?" Reese asked.

"I keep having Braxton-Hick's contractions, but they're not the real thing yet," she said.

"How's your dad doing?" Jeremy asked Tag.

"His surgery went well," Tag said. "Thank goodness he's resting and the docs say he ought to make a full recovery. We haven't told him about Violet, though."

"It wouldn't be good to upset him, especially with this latest update," Sylvia said.

"We're on our way to talk to Sabrina's family after we leave here," Jeremy said. "Maybe they know something that can help us."

Sylvia leaned against Tag. Tears rolled from her eyes.

As for Tag, his eyes were rimmed with red, and he looked exhausted. "I want to go break that guy's neck," he said, sniffing.

"We want to see justice served, too," Reese said, remembering that's exactly how she'd felt all those years ago when she discovered her mother and brother had been hit and killed by a drunk driver.

"Keep us posted," Tag said. "Meanwhile, I'm going to start putting out missing posters. I plan to do everything I can to help find my sister."

Jeremy met Reese's gaze. "Let's get going."

The two of them walked down the hall and stepped inside the elevator. Outside, they climbed into Jeremy's vehicle and he drove them downtown to a modest-sized, Tudor-style home. It was an older housing area, probably built in the 1920s, but most of the structures had been updated. The Byrd's place boasted a nice green yard and lush bushes. The tall cottonwood and elm trees had been neatly trimmed. Freshly painted white trim complemented the home's red brick.

Jeremy parked along the curb in front of the house. After exiting his vehicle, they walked up the sidewalk toward the entrance. Reese stepped onto a small concrete porch and rang the doorbell, her mouth pursed. She very much disliked being the bearer of bad news, and she knew Jeremy wasn't a fan, either.

"I hate the color," Jeremy muttered, frowning at the door.

"The burnt orange?" Reese studied it close. "I think it's cute—it makes the décor pop."

"Pop?" Jeremy shook his head. "What does that even mean?"

"It means if you ever get married, let your wife do all the decorating."

"Ha, ha, aren't you the comedian?" he said jokingly.

Reese shrugged. Several seconds ticked past, then she stepped down from the porch and eased up beside Jeremy.

"I don't think anyone's home."

"They're probably at work," Jeremy suggested.

A motor's humming interrupted Reese's thoughts. She turned, along with Jeremy, to see an electric-green sedan pull into the driveway. A woman in a black sweater dress and matching boots got out on the driver's side of the car, then walked around the vehicle toward them. Her curly, cinnamon-colored hair bounced across her shoulders as she studied them with an enquiring expression.

Jeremy pulled aside his jacket to flash his MVPD detective's badge, then he handed the woman one of his business cards. "Is this where Sabrina Byrd resides?"

"Yes, and I'm her mother, Belinda." She glanced at the card. "Hopefully this won't take long. I'm only on a short lunch break from Morgan Falls Bank. What's this about, Detective Savage?"

"We've got some news about your daughter," Jeremy said.

Belinda's brows knitted. "She never came home Friday night, but I thought she'd gone somewhere with friends and had forgotten to tell me. I tried calling, but she never answered her cell."

"Can we go inside and sit down?" Reese hated to tell her about Sabrina while they stood out here. It was never easy for a parent to hear of their child's death.

"Tell me here," she said, sounding frustrated as she glanced at her watch. "It's usually my daughter Mandy who gets herself in trouble. How bad could it be?"

Jeremy pressed his lips into a grim line. "It appears Sabrina's been the victim of homicide."

Belinda blinked several times. "Who-what? I don't believe it! There must be some mistake—"

"We found her this morning," Jeremy explained. "She had her purse with her and we found her driver's license in it."

Slumping down on the edge of a concrete planter box bursting with bushes, Belinda stared at Jeremy. She didn't say a word, but her hands trembled on her knees.

"Is there anyone you'd like us to call?" Reese ventured.

"No," Belinda said. Finally, she asked, "Where is my daughter now?"

"At the morgue," Jeremy said. "Dr. Beckwith, the coroner, will be contacting you about coming by to do a formal identification."

"Oh my God," Belinda said as she began to sob.

"I can escort you there when the time comes," Jeremy said. "And if you have other family members you'd like to go with, bring them along."

"My other daughters will want to be with me." Belinda's chin began to quiver, and Reese could tell she was about to fall apart. And who could blame her? The news she and Jeremy had delivered would be devastating for anyone.

"What about your husband?" Reese asked. "Would you like us to call him?"

"I'm a single mother," Belinda said. "I have no idea where Sabrina's father is these days. Could be Timbuktu, for all I know."

"You've suffered a serious shock," Jeremy said. "You'll find the number for the police department's Victim's Assistance Office on my card."

"All I want is for the police to find the bastard that hurt my little girl," Belinda said, her eyes narrowed.

"That's the goal," Reese said. "I realize this isn't the best time, but can I ask you a few questions? You might be able to help us."

"Who are you?" Belinda narrowed her gaze, looking at Reese as though she hadn't noticed her before.

"Reese Golden," she said, handing Belinda her business card. "I'm a private investigator, and I work with the police."

"I'll answer anything that might help."

"We understand Sabrina went with Violet Gentry to dinner on Friday night," Reese said. "Do you know if the two of them planned on meeting anyone else?"

"All Sabrina told me was they were going to eat at Sweet Clementine's," Belinda said. "The two of them love their food."

"Did Sabrina mention if they'd be discussing anything specific?" Reese propped one of her boots on the porch step.

Belinda shrugged. "Probably just gossip—who they were dating, recent fashion styles and frustration about their jobs. Typical girl stuff."

"I see," Reese said.

"Have you talked to Violet?" Belinda wiped tears away from her eyes, smudging black mascara. "She could probably tell you."

"Violet's missing," Reese said.

"She's been abducted," Jeremy added. "By the same person who hurt Sabrina."

Belinda's jaw dropped. "This can't be happening."

"I'm sorry to have to be so blunt," Jeremy said. "We want to get this guy as soon as we can."

"Were you close with Sabrina?" Reese asked.

"Of course," Belinda said, her voice threaded with grief. "We talked about everything. Just like I do with all my girls."

"Is there anything else Sabrina told you that could be important?"

Reese slid her hands into her vest pockets.

"Several days ago, Sabrina mentioned that Violet was worried about some guy."

"Someone she was dating?" Reese asked.

"Violet didn't know who he was," Belinda said. "She was upset because she believed he might be stalking her."

TWELVE

REESE'S ANTENNA PERKED UP. "WHY DID Violet think that?"

"According to Sabrina," Belinda said, "Violet caught the guy following her. But she drove around and managed to lose him."

"Did Sabrina ever mention what kind of car he had?" Jeremy asked.

"Violet told my daughter he was driving an old station wagon." Belinda wiped moisture from beneath her eyes. "She joked with Sabrina, claiming it looked a 1960s family station wagon. It was covered in bumper stickers with all sorts of end-of-the-world propaganda."

Like the one I saw in my vision. Reese shivered, believing more and more than what she'd witnessed came from otherworldly sources. Although it was difficult to honestly rely on such things.

"Propaganda?" Jeremy asked.

Belinda shrugged. "Things about the apocalypse and some new world order. Crazy stuff."

From his jacket pocket, Jeremy produced a small pad and made some notes. "Definitely a unique vehicle," he said.

"Did Violet ever give Sabrina a description of the guy?"

"Sabrina mentioned that Violet caught him watching her in Aunt Clara's Closet," Belinda said.

"The second-hand store downtown?" Reese asked.

Belinda nodded. "Violet mentioned he's a tall, hulking fellow with dark hair and pale skin."

"Mm-hmm," Jeremy said as he scribbled more notes.

"Do you suppose he was the guy who killed my little girl?" Belinda stood back up and placed her hands on her hips.

"It's possible," Jeremy said. "Either way, we intend to find out."

"Lord, help me," Belinda cried as she buried her head in her hands. "I just remembered—Violet told my other daughters about him. We should have reported him to the police."

"What did Violet say?" Reese asked.

"The girls started joking around and called him Violet's Vampire."

"Why?" Jeremy asked.

"I suppose because he lurked around in the shadows," Belinda said. "With Halloween not far off, that name seemed fitting."

Of course, everyone knew vampires were pure fiction, the fabrication of someone's overactive imagination. Nevertheless, Reese felt yet another shiver crawl up her spine, because anyone depraved enough to kill another human being should be feared. Once caught, they should be locked behind bars forever.

Belinda sniffed; her face swollen. "Have you talked with Violet's brother or her father? Surely, she told them about that creep."

"Tag's wife Sylvia is due to give birth soon, so Violet probably didn't want to worry the family," Reese said, recalling that many stalking victims decided to handle the situation themselves and suffer in silence, rather than go to the police or tell family. The police often didn't sympathize with them, either, because there wasn't much, they could do.

"This is so overwhelming," Belinda said as a fresh wave of tears filled her eyes. "If only . . . oh shit, I think I'm going to be sick."

Reese exchanged a knowing glance with Jeremy, and they edged back down the sidewalk toward his truck.

"Call if you need anything," Jeremy said.

"Right," Reese added.

Belinda flew inside the house, leaving the front door ajar. Retching sounds drifted outside.

"Poor woman," Reese said, wrinkling her nose. She recalled the abject despair she'd experienced each time she'd lost a family member. And, as she'd heard people say, you're never supposed to outlive a child—any parent's worst nightmare.

"God forbid we should ever have to go through something like that," Jeremy said. "It's bad enough to be in this line of work and see it so frequently."

"No kidding," Reese agreed. "I think I got my first gray hair when I turned 25. I'd only been on the force a few years."

"No way," Jeremy joked.

"Way," she said.

Jeremy drove Reese back to the police station where she'd left her truck. When they got out of his Trailblazer, he said, "I've got a hell of a busy day coming up."

"Same here," she added, thinking of the to-do list she'd started in her mind. First off, she wanted to start a suspect board in her office.

"I'm going to check to see if I can find an old station wagon, like the one Belinda described, registered to anyone in the local area," Jeremy said. "I've got a ton of other work to do, but I plan to devote my best efforts to finding Tag Gentry's sister."

"Finding Violet is my priority, too," Reese said.

"You'll be burning the midnight oil, won't you?" Jeremy asked.

"You know it," she answered.

"Do me a favor," he said.

"What?"

"As this case starts coming together, don't take any unnecessary risks. Okay?"

"I'll stay out of trouble," Reese said, hoping to remain good on her word.

"I appreciate hearing that," he said, shuffling from one foot to another. "I realize that we, ah, well . . . um . . ."

As he struggled for words, Reese did her best to supply them. "We're not officially dating?"

"Right, right," he said quickly. "I worry, and I want you to stay safe."

"It goes both ways," she said, then reached up to give him a peck on his whiskery cheek. When she pulled back, he frowned.

"Sweetheart, that's not a proper kiss," he said in a soft drawl. He swept her into his arms and made the kiss into a lengthy affair— one that left them both breathing heavily by the time they parted.

Reese rested her head on Jeremy's shoulder, her heart racing. He slowly stroked her hair, his fingertips brushing her cheek and leaving a trace of magnificent sizzling sensation. They stood together for a few moments, then slowly parted.

Holding her at arms-length, Jeremy asked, "What do you think?"

"I think I'd like more kisses like that, please," she admitted, her lips still tingling.

He chuckled. "We'll have to work on that."

"Definitely," she said.

"I'll see you later," he said.

"Sounds good." Still reeling from Jeremy's kiss, Reese watched his tall, broad-shouldered form as he sauntered toward the white cinderblock police station and went inside.

MR. BOJANGLES PADDED TOWARD REESE as she entered the house and set her purse on the table. He let loose a loud meow, announcing his pleasure at seeing her again. Or maybe he was scolding her for being gone too long . . . hard to say what that finicky feline thought.

"You're sure a loud customer, Bo," Reese told him. She grabbed a box of kitty treats sitting on the windowsill and sprinkled a small amount of the fish-shaped kibbles into a saucer. Bo leapt up to enjoy his repast.

Reese chose an apple from a wire fruit basket and munched on it as she headed into her office. As her computer booted, she brought up Violet's picture on her cell phone and emailed it to herself. She printed the snapshot and pinned it onto the large cork-board behind her desk chair.

With a black permanent marker, she wrote on the bottom of Violet's picture: **Abducted Friday, Sept. 14, Sweet Clementine's Restaurant in Meadowlark Valley, approximately midnight in old station wagon. Suspect is large, heavyset male, dark hair, light skin. Motive???**

Taking a seat at her desk, Reese spent the next several hours surfing through Violet's online social media, which had years of posts, photos and comments from numerous individuals.

Discussions ran in different directions. Violet talked with some people about range management and operations on the family's ranch. With others, she talked about hairstyles, clothing, food and shopping. A fan of selfies and other photos, Violet had posted a plethora of images from the last decade.

On Facebook, Reese noticed conversations directed toward Violet and Taggart's visits to local and county schools. Reading through the information, Reese realized the two were involved with the Wyoming Department of Agriculture's outreach.

The brother and sister team frequently gave presentations to local school students, promoting the Farm to School program that encouraged bringing healthy, locally produced food to school children and communities. Another goal educated children about where food comes from, how it is grown, and stressed healthy eating.

Nothing caught her eye, except a couple of off-hand comments from someone named Roman Jackrabbit, who made serious accusations about Gentry Ranch. About a week ago, ol' RJ had commented:

"How nice it must be to have inherited your spread from ancestors with blood on their hands—cattle barons who terrorized anyone who got in their way. You should be ashamed of yourselves."

Reese sat back; brows raised. Roman Jackrabbit, which probably wasn't a real name, sure had a bone to pick. She remembered studying Wyoming history, and the late 1800s range disputes that had erupted between influential cattlemen who belonged to the Wyoming Stockgrowers Association and small ranchers. They'd argued about water rights and other pertinent issues of the day.

That had happened a long time ago—who would be obsessed with a quarrel from a bygone era?

Clicking on the link to RJ's page, she found he had no friends listed, one photo of a sunset and nothing else. It appeared to be more of a placeholder than an authentic account.

Reese copied and pasted RJ's comment on a document, printed it out, then stood and tacked it onto her corkboard. On the threadbare Persian room-size carpet that had seen better days, she paced back and forth, allowing her mind to sort through possibilities.

THIRTEEN

Hours passed as Reese searched through Violet's social media accounts, as well as Tag and Sylvia's online presence. After poring over the Gentry Ranch's web page, she discovered one section outlined the ranch's founding, and another offered recipes for various meat cooking styles, like roasting, braising, grilling, etc.

Information about ranch events occupied an area, and a section detailed the Gentry's efforts at environmental stewardship of wildlife and other natural resources. The ranch's Facebook page displayed new windbreaks being constructed, haying season with bales littering fields, cows and calves, and even a photo featuring family members in a happy pose.

This is where Reese found another recent remark from Roman Jackrabbit, buried in a reply to Violet's comment about the great weather for turning bulls out into the cows' pasture.

"You are living on stolen land!" RJ said. *"Someday, you and your family will account for your sins."*

Reese sat back and rubbed the bridge of her nose. She'd stared for so long at the computer screen, her vision blurred. Checking the time, she noted it was 8 o'clock. Outside the window beside her desk, dusk had settled.

Jeremy called her a workaholic, but he seemed to suffer from the same condition. Yawning, she decided to close her eyes and sneak a quick nap. Placing her forearms on the desk, she pillowed her head. Every muscle in her body relaxed as she drifted off.

Before long, she felt a presence in the room. Looking up and brushing hair from her eyes, she spotted a shadowy figure standing in a corner by her rubber tree plant. As she blinked, it left through the front door of her office.

"Hey," she called out, certain she'd locked up earlier. "How'd you get in here! Who are you?"

Scurrying around her desk, Reese flew outside. The figure bolted down the sidewalk toward the park with Reese following. Before long, she reached the familiar stands of trees and shrubbery where she jogged each morning. She peered around, scanning the area for her uninvited visitor.

"Hello?" Reese called out.

How strange, she thought. There wasn't a soul around. September's lingering warmth usually attracted families to the park for picnic dinners. In the waning sunlight, kids would run around, either playing tag or maybe tossing frisbees to their dogs. Bicyclists loved this type of weather, too.

Then she saw the figure standing in front of the park's blue, glimmering lake. The shadowy individual stepped onto the water, then began walking across the lake.

"Walking on water?" Reese shook her head.

The figure turned around, transforming into Violet Gentry. "You're here," she said to Reese.

"What's going on?" Reese asked, puzzled.

"It's time," Violet told her.

"Time for what?" Reese asked.

"For you to find me." Violet, who wore a long dress made of crumbling dirt, tilted her head to the side.

Reese walked closer to the edge of the lake. "Where are you?"

"It's dark here." Violet looked around, grimacing. "And cold—really cold."

"Who took you?"

"I don't know," Violet said. "You've got to find me."

"I'm trying," Reese said. "Where do I start first?"

"To the north, you'll find the ancient bones."

"I'm confused," Reese said. "What does that mean?"

Violet's figure began to fade.

Frustration shot through Reese. "Come back, tell me more!"

Reese jolted awake. With an embarrassing snort, she awakened and looked around, finally realizing she'd been dreaming.

"Meow." Bo tilted his head and studied her.

"I'm wiped out," she told herself, standing unsteadily. "I should hit the sack."

Yawning, Reese recalled her nocturnal encounter with Violet. Chasing her out to the park had seemed so real, especially when the woman had talked to her.

"Find me to the to the north with the ancient bones."

"What did that even mean?" she mused. "If I didn't know better, I'd think I'd been hitting the sauce."

Bow started methodically licking his paws and wiping his face with then. He certainly wasn't worried about her wild imagination. Of course, as she reminded herself, he was only a cat.

After turning off her computer and the lights, she headed down the hall toward her bedroom. When something outside rattled, she froze for a second, then looked around, her gaze taking in every darkened nook and cranny. Pulling aside the front window curtains, she watched as a shadow moved past her porch and slid into the bushes.

Her skin prickled with awareness, and the sensation of being watched came over her. She shrugged into a sweater that she'd tossed on a chair, grabbed a fireplace poker, and stepped outside.

Veiled in glimmering moonlight, neighborhood homes sat with their lawns extended toward curbsides. Nothing moved, and it was quiet as a tomb. Nevertheless, Reese felt uneasy. The idea of someone skulking around her place was troubling.

Gripping her makeshift weapon, she searched the house's perimeter, studying bushes and flowers nestled at the base of the foundation. Nothing lurked in the alley or next to the sides of the house. Having made her way back to the front porch, Reese trekked down the sidewalk, instinctively heading toward the park.

Nothing disturbed the quiet, except for the lonesome hoot of an owl. Crickets, with their sonorous chirping, sang down by the lake. Reese nearly expected to see Violet materialize as she had in her dream. Of course, it didn't happen. Finally satisfied nothing seemed amiss, Reese stepped out into the street and began the journey home.

An engine gunned, lights flicked on, and a vehicle barreled toward her.

She jumped aside in time to avoid being flattened into a human pancake. Trembling and feeling faint, she tried to grasp the concept of what had just happened. She noticed the killer car had spun around and once again careened in her direction.

Breaking into a sprint, she headed down the street toward her house, breath bursting in her lungs. She jumped on the porch, hurled herself inside, locked the door, and deadbolted it. Gasping, she peeked out through the front window curtains to see if she'd been followed. Everything looked clear, so she hustled into her office and grabbed her cell phone.

Her first instinct was to call Jeremy.

"Reese, what's going on?" he asked in a weary voice.

"Someone . . . someone just tried to run me over."

Barely fifteen minutes later, Reese opened the door to Jeremy, feeling like an idiot that she'd called him in the first place.

"Are you all right?" he asked.

"I really am," she said. "I wish I hadn't panicked."

"Maybe I should take you off of this case," he said, consideration edging his voice as he walked inside.

"No, don't do that," she protested. She shut the door and locked it again. Moving aside the front window curtains, she glanced into the darkness, making certain no one lurked amidst the shadows.

"I did a thorough check before I came in. It's all clear." Jeremy settled onto the couch and ran a hand through his dark hair. He wore rumpled jeans and a T-shirt. Both looked like they'd been balled up and tossed on the floor.

Reese felt like she'd shrunk down to about one inch tall. She'd probably gotten him out of bed. Warmth crept up her neck. *Why am I acting like such a wuss?*

"What happened?" Jeremy pinned her with a concerned glance.

Reese sat down next to him. "I thought I heard someone outside my house. I decided to explore."

"And?"

"I looked around, but didn't find anything, so I took a short walk over to the park. I investigated, then began walking back home. I took a short cut across the street."

"Jaywalking, eh?" He gave her a crooked grin.

"Give me a break! Nobody was around and thought it would be safe."

"I'm joking, okay?" Jeremy hugged her and she leaned her head against his shoulder for a few seconds, realizing she'd overreacted. Suffering from nervous jitters didn't help matters.

"What happened next?" he ventured.

"This car flipped on its lights, gunned its engine, and headed my direction."

"Did you get a make or a model?"

"No, it was too dark and I was too busy running for my life."

"When did this happen?"

"Right before I called you." Reese took a calming breath, then added, "After the car came at me, I ran home and locked the door."

"I'm glad you called," he said. "Are you sure that you're okay? You're as pale as a ghost."

She nodded. "I'm just shaken up. I've got this creepy feeling someone's watching me."

"Well, hell," Jeremy said. "That's no good."

"I'm afraid our suspect knows about our investigation into

Sabrina's murder and Violet's disappearance."

"And now he's trying to put a stop to it," Jeremy said, his voice brimming with alarm.

"I'm afraid so."

"I really think you should stand down, Reese. You're not a cop anymore. You don't carry a gun and I don't like the idea of you being in danger."

"But—"

"Seriously, I appreciate all you've done." He kissed the top of her head. "And I know the department appreciates it, too."

"I'll be fine," Reese insisted. "You don't give me enough credit."

"I figured you wouldn't back out of this job," Jeremy said. "Guess I know you pretty well, huh?"

Reese sat up straighter, gathering her courage. "I got wigged out tonight, is all. It seems we're rattling someone's cage, even though we've barely started looking into this case."

"That shows we're already making progress," he said. "We just need to stay on top of things and remain wary."

Reese offered him a weak smile, not feeling so vulnerable with him here. He made her feel much safer, even though she'd experienced worse situations and had been perfectly capable of protecting herself.

"Thanks for coming over so quickly," Reese said.

"Any time," he said reassuringly. "I've got a police cruiser searching the neighborhood for any vagrants or signs of trouble. And I've got another officer posted outside to watch the house."

"That's not necessary," Reese insisted.

"I'm in charge, and I say it is," Jeremy returned in a firm, no nonsense tone. "If you want to stay on this case, you'll have to do things my way."

"Of course," she finally agreed, realizing Jeremy wasn't going to budge. In the grand scheme of things, this wasn't the hill to die on.

"Plus," he said in a gentler tone, "I couldn't live with myself if anything happened to you."

A shiver of a warmth raced up her spine.

"Just in case our perp decides to return, I think I should stay here, too," Jeremy said.

"That seems like overkill, you know. A waste of resources."

Jeremy lifted a brow, and Reese got the solid impression she'd be wasting her breath to protest any further.

"You really don't have to do that," she said.

"You're a civilian. How do you think the public would feel if they found out we hadn't protected you?"

"I'm a private investigator," Reese reminded him. "Of my own free will, I signed on to work this case."

"But you're assisting the MVPD," he said. "And the optics don't look good."

Reese stood and folded her arms over her chest. Was Jeremy only worried about the public's perception or her?

Far be it from her to create a PR nightmare.

This time, anyway, she'd let him have his way. It wasn't worth risking the loss of her police clearance. By now, she'd become totally invested in this case. She'd promised the Gentry's she'd do everything in her power to find Violet.

In fact, she considered it her sworn duty to do so.

"Since you insist on staying here, you can camp out on the couch," she told him. "If you get cold, there are blankets and pillows in the hall closet."

He leaned back on the cushions. "I'll be fine."

"Suit yourself," Reese said, then headed back to her room. Even though she'd had a brush with death tonight, it seemed ridiculous to have someone watch over her. She crawled into bed and stared at the ceiling, her mind racing.

A few minutes later, a knock sounded on her door. She walked over and opened up to see Jeremy standing there.

"I tend to get overprotective of the people I really care for," he said, his voice deep, and threaded with a serious note.

Reese relaxed. Once again, she'd overreacted and had behaved impulsively. "Sorry if I acted miffed. I got the wrong—"

Jeremy drew her into his arms, muffling her next words, and they kissed for a long time. The world fell away, and all Reese could think about was being with him. He made her feel safe, protected and needed.

When he finally pulled away and held her at arm's length, Reese asked, "What was that for?"

"For now," he told her. "Have a good night and sleep tight."

He sauntered down the hallway, then turned to give her a mock salute before heading back into the living room.

Reese crawled back under her bed covers, feeling like a teenage girl who had received her first kiss. It was a while before she dozed off. When she did, however, she slept soundly.

THE SOUND OF A VACUUM CLEANER awakened Reese. She blinked and rubbed her eyes, then sat up, noting her alarm clock said it was seven o'clock.

Confused as heck, she shrugged into her fuzzy pink bathrobe, stepped into her cowboy boots, and headed into the living room. Who in the world had decided to come into her house and play Mr. Clean? It sure couldn't be Jeremy. Or could it?

Maybe I'm dreaming again.

The vacuuming sound got louder and she winced, then went wide-eyed at the amazing condition of her place.

Now Reese didn't exactly think she was a sloppy housekeeper, yet she realized she could do a better job. As if elves had arrived in the night to handle the magical transformation, magazines had been straightened, blankets had been folded, and end tables had been dusted. In the kitchen, dishes no longer filled the sink and the counters gave off a spick and span shine.

Curtains had been opened and windows gleamed from the colors of the rising sun. Even Bo, who wasn't a fan of loud noises, lounged atop the couch, sound asleep.

Reese's nostrils flared with the scent of cleaning solution and fresh coffee.

Suddenly, a boy of about eleven or twelve walked past her, pushing her Dirt Devil across the carpet. He wore dark-rimmed glasses, sharply creased dress slacks, a plaid, short-sleeve shirt, and a bow tie. A determined expression creased his face.

She reached down and pinched herself.

Nope, not dreaming.

"Hey, who are you? What are you doing here?"

When he didn't answer, Reese noted he wore ear buds that were attached to a cord and cell phone tucked neatly into his shirt pocket.

Walking up to the boy, she pulled out one ear bud. "Hey, what's going on? Who are you?"

He switched off the vacuum and looked up at her apologetically. "Sorry, I was listening to a history podcast about the rise and fall of Rome. I'm Fox."

"Fox, who?"

"Fox Nesbitt, your brother," he answered. "Actually, half-brother."

Reese thought of Jesse, who had passed long ago in that awful car accident with her mother. Her heart squeezed and her mouth went dry. Surely the boy had the wrong address.

"You can't be my brother," she insisted. "By the way, how did you get in here?"

"It was easy," he said. "Your husband let me in."

Reese frowned, wondering what he was talking about, then realized what had probably happened.

"It must have been Detective Savage, and he's not my husband," she emphasized to Fox, realizing Jeremy must have brought the boy inside, then left for work. "I thought there was an intruder sneaking around my house last night, and he volunteered to keep watch."

"I've never heard of law enforcement doing that," Fox said, a suspicious glint in his eyes.

"Not typically, but he's a good friend," Reese explained. "He also posted a police officer out front, just in case."

"I didn't see any cop cars," Fox pointed out.

"They probably headed back to the station once it got light," Reese said with a shrug. "Tell me, why did you come here?"

"I *am* your brother," he insisted. "For some unknown reason, my parents never told you about me."

Who was this kid? He spoke like a college professor.

"What are your parents' names?"

"Cash and Tonya Nesbitt."

Reese shook her head. "Never heard of 'em."

"My mother left this for you." Fox walked over to the couch and picked up a backpack. After unzipping it, he removed a pale lavender envelope and brought it over to Reese.

After tearing it open, she withdrew a flowered notecard. As she did so, a snapshot fell to the floor. Icicles shot through her blood as she picked it up, perusing the very young version of her mother in a flowered sundress and a handsome, light-haired man wearing a cowboy hat, a western-cut shirt, and jeans.

She recognized her mother's distinct handwriting on the back of the photo. **Norah and Cash, 1985.** The smiling couple looked blissful, and Reese read hope and excitement in her mother's beautiful eyes. It broke her heart to remember how wistful and distant Norah had been to Reese as a child, no doubt disappointed by love.

Was Cash Nesbitt really Reese's father?

She had so many questions. Mainly, why he'd never contacted his family. And why hadn't he ever married her mother?

Reese turned her attention to the note. In loopy purple handwriting, it read:

Hi Reese,

I need you to watch Fox for me. Your dad's gone on another bender, and I've got to find him before he does something boneheaded. Hopefully it won't take me long to track him down.

You probably have questions. I don't blame you. Just know that Cash Nesbitt is your long-lost daddy and I'm your step

momma. We've never told you who we are because we didn't want to disrupt your life.

I'm desperate, so I'm begging you to be a good big sister to Fox.

Love, Tanya

FOURTEEN

"How do I know this isn't some sort of a scam?" Reese questioned Fox, the letter in her hand burning like a hot coal.

"Don't you believe what my mother said in her note?" Fox pushed his glasses higher on the bridge of his nose.

"My mom is in this photo, and I recognize her handwriting on the back of it," Reese said, "But I have no idea who Cash is."

"He's my dad. Your dad, too. When you moved back to Meadowlark Valley and they wrote that newspaper article about you, my mother explained everything."

"Like what?"

"She told me your mother and my dad were together a long time ago, and they had you and Jesse."

"You know about my little brother?" Reese's brows shot up. Jesse had become a secret part of her past—something she didn't like to share. He belonged only to her now, and he lived in a secret chamber of her heart. Along with everyone else she'd lost.

Fox nodded. "My father was a struggling country singer when he met your mom. They lived together for a while, but eventually he felt tied down and moved to Nashville to try and make it big."

Fox removed his glasses, polished them on his shirt, then put them back on. "Rather insensitive of him, if you ask me. Since I'm just a kid, despite my IQ, people don't care what I think."

"Did he ever become successful?"

"Unfortunately, not," Fox said. "He sings and plays guitar at country bars and drinks way too much."

"And your mother?"

"She travels around with Dad's band. She sings too, and drinks like a fish. I always have what I need, but I sense they're barely scratching out a living. I imagine someday when I get older, I'll have to take them in and support them." He gave a heavy sigh.

"Who stays with you when your parents are on the road?"

Fox shrugged and looked away.

"They leave you on your own?" Reese was floored.

"It's not that bad," Fox insisted, his eyes flashing. "In fact, when they're gone, the house is quiet and peaceful. It's never that way when they're around because they fight like cats and dogs. They throw stuff around and whale on each other. It's disgusting."

"I'm sure that makes you sad," Reese said.

"Of course, and mostly I'm sorry for those two. They're a couple of has-beens who never were."

"I take it you get yourself to school every day," Reese said, experiencing a pang of regret for being so rude to him. He'd obviously had a rough life, and honestly, seemed more responsible than his parents. He'd had to grow up way to fast, which was a darn shame.

"Heaven's no." Fox rolled his eyes. "I already graduated from Meadowlark Valley High and I'm taking online college courses from Duke University. My mother thinks I need to complete as many of those as I can before I actually attend classes in person. She's afraid the other students will bully me since I'm so young."

Reese tilted her head to the side, trying to guess his age. "How old are you?"

"Twelve and a half," Fox said, straightening his shoulders. "People say I'm a genius, but honestly, I simply love learning. It comes easy for me."

"Why were you cleaning my house?"

"To tell the truth, I simply can't study when things are disordered."

"You're saying I'm a slob?"

"No, no, I'm sure your job as a private investigator keeps you terribly busy. So, I thought I'd pitch in and lend you a hand. After all, since I'll be staying here, I decided I'd better earn my keep, as they say."

"I don't know where I'm going to put you," Reese said, wondering if she'd gone bat-shit crazy to even consider letting Fox remain here. "I need to get this misunderstanding straightened out before I can promise anything."

"No worries," Fox said. "I've already moved myself into your spare room."

"It's full of boxes," Reese said, shocked, as she hustled toward the small bedroom. She hadn't yet had a chance to sort through the mess since she'd moved back home.

As soon as she opened the door, she noted the stack of folded boxes in the corner. The single bed had been made up with sheets and blankets. The rod she'd purchased had been installed and a set of plaid curtains she recognized from her Denver apartment now hung on the window.

The Ikea dresser and desk she'd ordered had been put together and the spare rug that had been rolled up in one corner now covered the floor. She walked over to the closet and opened it. A row of nearly identical plaid shirts and dress slacks hung side by side. A large, rolling suitcase sat on the floor.

"Did you do all of this?" Reese asked, looking back at Fox.

"Your husband helped," Fox said.

"Like I told you before, Jeremy's not my husband."

Fox turned a dark shade of red. "My apologies. Is Detective Savage your boyfriend then?"

Reese narrowed her gaze, ignoring his question. "Just exactly long have you been hanging around my house?"

"My mother dropped me off about five this morning," Fox said. "I'm sorry if I interrupted you and Jeremy having sex."

"Oh, for Pete's sake!"

She was caught off guard by Fox's assumptions, and also wondered if it had been him skulking around her house last night. Probably not, however, because he'd claimed his mother dropped him off this morning.

"Oops, my mom says sometimes I talk too much," Fox said.

"Did you tell Jeremy who you are?"

"Of course," Fox said.

"What did he say?"

"He told me to watch over my big sister, and that he'd bring breakfast to us later."

Reese decided that when Jeremy heard Fox knocking at the door, he'd judged him to be no threat, and decided to let him in. Amazingly enough, she'd slept through all the commotion. She must have been exhausted, and Jeremy's presence had relaxed her enough to fall into a deep sleep.

Like tumbleweeds, thoughts rambled around in Reese's head. "I typically work from home, but I'll have to find someone to watch you when I go out on assignment."

"That's not necessary, I'm old enough to watch myself," Fox assured her.

"We'll see about that," Reese raked a hand through her mussed hair, realizing she must look like a zombie. The idea of leaving Fox alone terrified her, especially if he decided to organize her office. God forbid he move anything!

She met Fox's gaze. "Hey, stay out of my office, *capishe*? It's totally off limits."

"Sure thing," he promised. "I realize adults are peculiar about others rooting around in their work space."

"I'm not peculiar about it, there are important papers and files in there," Reese insisted. "I don't want you trying to organize them. You could throw important documents that I might need or forget where you tucked something."

"Cross my heart and hope to die," Fox said, making the motion across his chest. "Does that make you feel better?"

"Yeah, sure," she lied.

Studying Fox closer, Reese made out some of Cash Nesbitt's distinct features she'd noted in the photo—specifically his eyes and square chin. If that man was really her father, she had no clue what she would say to him. Truthfully, it was difficult to believe she had any relatives remaining in Meadowlark Valley.

Right now, all she could handle was the fact that the boy standing in front of her had been abandoned, and until she could figure out why, she would be responsible for him. She'd seen firsthand how the foster care system operated, so she didn't want to call the cops and get Fox tangled up in that mess. Especially if he was, in fact, her little brother.

"I imagine you need coffee," Fox speculated.

"That's not a bad idea," she said, relaxing some.

"There's a fresh pot in the kitchen that I just brewed," Fox said as he walked toward a mug tree. He poured a cup from the carafe and handed it to her, a huge grin on his face. "I've got scrambled eggs and toast in your microwave if you're hungry."

Reese closed her eyes as she sipped the warm, hazelnut brew. Amazingly, Fox cleaned, cooked and made damn fine coffee.

FIFTEEN

SEATED AT THE KITCHEN TABLE ACROSS FROM Fox, Reese studied him. She found it difficult to believe that he'd shown up here out of the blue, and that his mother expected her to keep an eye on him. Only in her dreams could something this bizzarro have happened, and yet, here she was, actually living through it.

As they polished off the breakfast he'd prepared, Fox explained he'd brought along a laptop computer in order to complete assignments for his online college courses. He added that he had everything he would need while staying with Reese, and promised he'd be no trouble.

"How long did your mom say she'd be gone?" Reese asked.

"She said if she found my dad right off the bat, it might only be a few days."

"Don't you hate that your mother left you with me?"

"Somebody's got to go and find my old man," Fox said with a shrug. "I can't drive yet, so I can't do it."

"What if he's not so easy to find?" Reese raised her brows.

Fox winced. "Then my mother said she might be gone a week or two—maybe a month. Or . . . or more."

Oh, boy.

"Does your dad leave like this very often?".

"He has a penchant for wandering off," Fox revealed. "He gets depressed about how his career in country music flopped, and he goes wandering."

"Are there certain places he winds up so your mother knows where to find him?"

"He has some favorite honky-tonks he likes to haunt."

"In town?"

"Yeah," Fox said. "Since my mother has to go on the road to try and find him, he must have branched out this time."

"Meaning?"

"He's probably hiding out in a nearby town."

"Which explains why it might take a while for your mother to find him," Reese said. She finished up her scrambled eggs and ate the last bite of her toast.

"Exactly."

The front door opened and Jeremy called out, "Hey, everybody."

"We're in the kitchen," she said.

Jeremy strode in through the arched doorway and placed a couple of grocery sacks on the table. He wore a black, button-down shirt, a corduroy jacket, and dark jeans.

"I thought you might want some snacks, Fox."

Fox dug through the items, making contented noises as he pulled out milk, bread, eggs, chips, cookies, and doughnuts. "Thanks, Jeremy! Reese's cupboards are pretty bare, so we really need the groceries."

"Don't get a sugar buzz," Reese warned.

"I'm smart enough to know not to eat too many sweets at once," Fox said.

Jeremy removed his cowboy hat, and gave them both a crooked smile. "I see you and Reese got acquainted," Jeremy said. "That's swell."

"Why didn't you two wake me up earlier?" Reese asked.

"No need to," Jeremy said. "Fox and I had everything handled just fine."

"Sure did," Fox said. He put another forkful of egg in his mouth.

Jeremy looked Reese up and down, then cleared his throat. His eyes crinkled with humor as he said, "Is that what all the private investigators are wearing these days? Fuzzy pink bathrobes and cowboy boots?"

"Oh, crap," she said.

"We've got a development in Violet Gentry's case, so you need to get it together."

Reese stood, drawing the robe tighter around herself and knotting the belt. "What's going on?"

"Her father's awake. He wants to talk to us."

"Did your crime techs get any fingerprints from the mur..." Reese glanced at Fox and trailed off. "Ah, from the scene they processed?"

"Uh-huh," Jeremy said. "The techs are searching all available databases for a match. We've also gone public and sent out a photo of Violet and Sabrina to the media, along with the general details of what happened."

"I hope somebody saw something or heard something that might help us," Reese said. "We need all the breaks in this case we can get."

"For sure," Jeremy said.

"I'll go get dressed," Reese said.

"Make it quick." Jeremy snapped his fingers. "Time's a wastin'."

"Sure, boss," she said, laughing.

"Jeremy's your boss?" Fox looked back and forth between the two of them, an inquisitive expression on his face. "I thought he was your boyfriend, you know, and that you guys were all lovey-dovey."

"Never mind," Reese said. "It's an inside joke."

"Oh, a joke," Fox said, chuckling. "I get it."

"What's Fox supposed to do while you're gone, Reese?" Jeremy asked.

"I can take care of myself," the boy reiterated.

"Sure," Reese said, not about to leave him home alone. "In case something comes up, I called and asked Mrs. MacGillicuddy, my neighbor, to come over."

"Mrs. Mah-what?" Fox shot to his feet; hands fisted at his sides. "I do not need a babysitter!"

"You can call her Mrs. Mac, and quit pouting," Reese said. "It's undignified."

"But—"

"My house, my rules," Reese interrupted, recalling her mom frequently using that phrase with her and Jesse. She felt a wee bit powerful uttering it herself.

"Whatever," Fox growled as he stormed toward his room. "I've got homework to do anyway."

Both Reese and Jeremy jumped when Fox slammed the door, which rattled in its frame. It sounded like a Wyoming twister had flattened the old house. Fox might be some sort of whiz kid, but emotionally, he was still an adolescent.

"Teenagers," Jeremy said, shaking his head. "Another reason having kids is off my list. You can't live with 'em."

"What did I do to deserve this, Lord?" Reese hustled toward her bedroom, then called over her shoulder to Jeremy, "I'll be ready ASAP."

"Sure, sure," Jeremy said jokingly. He strode into the living room and slumped down on the coach. "Pick up the pace; we don't have all day."

Reese showered and applied a dab of lipstick and mascara. In her bedroom, she dressed quickly, pulling on her jeans and a gray zippered sweat top with dark blue stars. She slid on her boots and grabbed her cowboy hat and headed into the front room.

"Presto, chango," she told Jeremy. "That fast enough?"

He lounged on her couch, one of his long legs crossed over the other, scratching Bo. Raising his brows, he studied her. "I'd say Superman's phone booth changes have nothing on you."

The front door burst open and Jane MacGillicuddy, her cropped, champagne pink hair in disarray, entered the room. A long western-print caftan, featuring cactus and wagon wheels, draped her tiny, 4 feet 11inch body. On her feet she wore pink leather cowboy boots covered in embroidered butterflies and daisies.

Jeremy unfolded his large frame and stood. He studied the

elderly lady, a smile playing at the corners of his lips.

"Mrs. Mac, I'd like you to meet Detective Jeremy Savage from the Meadowlark Valley Police Department," Reese told her. "We work together."

"Aren't you one good looking, tall drink of water?" Mrs. Mac said jokingly. "Where have you been all my life, honey?"

Jeremy gave Mrs. Mac a bashful grin.

"Nice to meet you ma'am," he drawled. "Thanks for helping out. I really need Reese's help today."

"No problem at all."

"Those are new boots, aren't they Mrs. Mac?" Reese asked her.

"Damn straight." Mrs. Mac tousled her short locks and posed several different ways to showcase her footwear "Paid a pretty penny for 'em on E-Bay, too. They match my hair real well, don't they?"

"Sure do," Reese agreed as she gave her neighbor a hug.

Mrs. Mac switched her huge leather cowhide satchel from one shoulder to the other. Narrowing her gaze, she looked around. "I suppose I'd better get to babysitting. Where is he?"

"Hiding out in his bedroom," Reese said, pointing toward it.

"I am not hiding out, and I don't need to a babysitter," Fox shouted loud enough for everyone to hear.

Mrs. Mac rolled her eyes and ambled toward Fox's door, belying her age, which most likely was around the mid-seventies. "Come on out, squirt," she urged. "It's not polite to keep an old lady waiting. Besides, I got something you'll wanna see."

"You can wait until the cows come home," Fox pouted.

"Well, then, I'll just take these here retro comic books back to my husband Herman so he can put 'em back up in safekeeping. He's been collecting them since he was a kid." Mrs. Mac snorted in derision, then pulled a handful of slim volumes from her purse. "I thought sure you'd get a kick out of looking through these. Let's see, here's one about Thor and his giant hammer. Here's another about Batman and we've got one about The Avengers . . . "

Fox cracked open his door and peered out, his expression inquisitive as he studied the old magazines in Mrs. Mac's hands. "Really?"

Mrs. Mac tilted her head at him. "I don't have any reason to lie to you, boy. Now come on out and have a look. I've also got a container of freshly baked chocolate chip cookies in my bag. Herm and I can't eat 'em all, and I sure don't want them to go to waste."

"Give me a few seconds." Grinning, Fox disappeared back into his room.

"How did you know comic books would break the ice with Fox?" Reese asked, both relieved and surprised as she grabbed her purse and keys.

"I had had three brothers, and Hermie and I raised two boys of our own," Mrs. Mac said. "Along the way, I learned a thing or two."

"Thanks for helping me out in a pinch," Reese said. "I'll be back as soon as I can, but I can't say for sure when."

"No worries," Mrs. Mac said, waving her wrist, which was encircled with a large silver and turquoise bracelet. "Take all the sleuthing time you need. Me'n the kid will be just fine."

"Will Herman mind if you're gone too long?"

"Nah," Mrs. Mac said. "He's busy watching the sports channel and gorging himself on potato chips."

"It was a pleasure to meet you Mrs. Mac," Jeremy said as he opened the front door.

"Later," Reese told Mrs. Mac, then left with Jeremy.

SIXTEEN

REESE SAT IN THE PASSENGER SEAT of Jeremy's Trailblazer as he drove to the hospital. He didn't talk at first; just kept his gaze on the road as they headed downtown. Reese wondered if something was bothering him, but she didn't ask.

"How did you sleep after last night's fiasco?" he finally asked.

"Fine, considering that it's not every day you're nearly run over." Reese figured his kiss had worked its magic, helping her to fully relax and forget about that killer car gunning for her. That kiss had gotten her thinking about other things, too, but she decided it would be best to mull that over some other time.

"That's good," Jeremy said. "The uniform parked out in front of your house said the neighborhood remained quiet all night. And I didn't hear a thing, either."

"Except for Fox, when he showed up this morning."

"Right, except for Fox," he reiterated.

"I suppose the jerk who tried to run me over figured I'd received the message loud and clear, and there was no reason left to hang around."

"I suppose."

Jeremy maneuvered his truck into a parking spot and Reese hopped out. He came around from the driver's side and took her elbow as they walked inside the tall building and rode in the elevator to the cardiac unit. Doctors and nurses dressed in scrubs walked up and down the sterile, brightly-lit halls.

They entered Wade Gentry's room, where Tag and his wife sat beside each other in orange vinyl chairs, whispering. In the bed, hooked up to various monitors, Wade Gentry slept, his chest rising and falling with even breaths.

Tag rose when he saw them. "Thanks for coming."

"Of course," Jeremy said softly.

Sylvia gave a little wave. "I hope you don't mind if I stay seated. It's getting harder and harder to maneuver myself these days."

"Please, stay comfortable," Reese said, her gaze passing over Sylvia's large baby bump, wondering what it would feel like to have a new life growing inside of her body.

Wade opened his eyes and glanced around. When he saw Reese and Jeremy, he pressed a button. As a whirring sound filled the room, he elevated the top of his bed.

"Dad," Tag said. "This is Reese Golden, the PI I told you about. And Detective Jeremy Savage from the police department."

Wade coughed, then in a dry voice said, "I can't believe this is happening. It was bad enough to wake up and discover I'd had a heart attack and surgery, but to find out my daughter's missing—it's devastating."

"I'm sure," Jeremy said in a sympathetic tone.

"We're doing everything possible to find her," Reese quickly supplied.

"Tag says you're the best, young lady," Wade said in a tired voice. "There's something you need to know, though. Hopefully it'll help."

"Sir?" Jeremy asked, easing closer toward the bed.

"Out at the reservoir that day, I wasn't alone. Some SOB rode a big chestnut horse through the bushes and scared the shit out of me. He sat in his saddle, covered in a long black coat, staring at me."

"Are you sure it was a man?" Reese asked.

"He was a big fellow with broad shoulders," Wade said. "I couldn't see his face well because of the hood, but he started cussing up a storm and telling me off in a deep, gruff voice."

"What did he say?" Jeremy asked.

"That I needed to pay for what my ancestors had done—stealing other people's ranches," Wade said.

"What happened next?" Reese asked, remembering the attacker in the surveillance video from Sweet Clementine's. It could have been him, judging from the physical description Wade had provided.

"Guess I panicked," Wade said with a sigh. "My chest started to seize up and I couldn't breathe. I started to sweat and I must've passed out. Next thing I knew, I was here."

"You received quite a shock that day." Tag placed a hand on his father's shoulder. "Fortunately, Reese and Jeremy were up fishing at the lake, too. They're the ones responsible for getting you help."

"There was another lady who found you first, Cricket O'Donnell," Reese said. "And we were able to get you medical help right away."

"I have a good idea who that fellow was," Wade said. "When Violet was up at Central Wyoming College a few years back, she dated a student from the Wind River Reservation. I swear he was the one who scared the bejesus out of me. I'm afraid he took Violet, too. Probably wanted revenge."

Reese and Jeremy exchanged glances.

"The person who took Violet also killed her friend, Sabrina Byrd," Jeremy said. "What's the name of the student your daughter dated?"

"An Indian by the name of Ned Spearhunter," Wade said.

"Native American, Dad," Tag said, sending Reese and Jeremy an apologetic glance.

Wade shrugged. "Damn it anyway, I keep forgetting all the newfangled ways of addressing people. Point is, I didn't like the two of them getting so serious. They come from different worlds. He grew up on the rez, and my girl grew up here in Meadowlark Valley. It never would have worked."

"Dad, I think you might be letting your imagination run wild," Tag said, his brow creased.

"Nah, I'm sure when that boy realized Violet's family owns a big spread, he figured out pretty quick that she stood to inherit a bundle."

"Now, Dad, we honestly don't know much about—"

"Tag, quit treatin' me like some old fool," Wade growled, a thread of annoyance in his voice. "I might have some age on me, but that also comes with wisdom and experience. I say that Indian boy was disappointed when he lost his chance to get at Violet's money."

"Do you believe Spearhunter was disappointed enough to commit murder if someone got in his way?" Reese asked.

"He was pretty hot under the collar when Violet told him she couldn't date him," Wade said, clutching his blue blanket with calloused hands. "She said the boy took it pretty hard, so she steered clear of him for a while."

"Was she afraid he'd hurt her?" Reese asked.

"She didn't say so exactly, but I sensed he made her uneasy," Wade said.

"Why do you think Spearhunter would have killed Sabrina?"

"Damned if I know," Wade growled.

"Did Violet ever mention someone was following her?" Reese asked. "Someone driving an old, beater station wagon?"

"No," Wade said.

"I'm going to pipe in here," Sylvia said. "I recall she talked to me about getting a new car because too many people knew what her truck looked like. Said it made her nervous."

Reese brushed a stray hair away from her face. "But she never specifically mentioned she thought she was being followed?"

"Never," Sylvia said. "I wondered at the time what she meant, but I didn't ask."

"Hmm," Reese said.

"Do you believe Spearhunter would retaliate against you or your daughter because you disapproved of their relationship?" Jeremy asked.

"Anybody's capable of doing terrible things if they get pushed hard enough." Wade sipped from a water bottle on a tray beside his bed, then wiped his mouth on his forearm. "I wouldn't put it past that boy to try and get revenge."

"Do you know if Spearhunter is living on the Wind River Reservation?" Reese asked.

Wade nodded. "Last time Violet mentioned him, she said he ran a trading post in Fort Washakie."

"I'll check into him," Reese said. After she paid a visit to Violet's high school boyfriend, Austin Buell, she'd check out Ned Spearhunter.

"Find my girl," Wade pleaded, tears glimmering in his eyes. "When her mom disappeared, I realized how much my family means to me. I can't lose her, too."

Reese and Jeremy talked with the Gentry family for a while longer about Dotty Gentry's disappearance, and how strange it was that there'd been no trace of where she'd gone or why. Local police and even the FBI had come up empty-handed.

"I think that's why people started the nasty rumor that my mother had an affair and took off with her lover," Tag snarled. "It satisfied their curiosity. But I know she wouldn't have done that."

"People say cruel things," Jeremy said.

Reese and Jeremy finally headed back to his truck and he drove her home. As Jeremy pulled in front of her house and parked, he turned to Reese and asked, "So, what's happening with Fox? What are you going to do with him?"

"I'm trying to figure that out," Reese said slowly, clutching her purse to her chest.

"Not that it's my place to tell you what to do," Jeremy said. "But for all intents and purposes, Fox's mother up and abandoned him. You should call Child Protective Services."

"His mother, Tanya, left me a letter claiming she's married to my father, Cash Nesbitt, and that Fox is my half-brother."

"Do you believe her?" Jeremy asked. "You said your mother never told you who your father was."

"No, but Tanya left me an old photo with the two of them in it," Reese explained. "At this point, I'm unwilling to call CPS and get Fox into the foster care system. It's a mess and always has been. I don't want to put him through all that if his folks are returning soon."

"Did this Tanya person say when she's coming back?"

"She claims Cash is on a bender, and she needs to find him. That's all."

"Something sounds awfully fishy to me," Jeremy said, frowning. "I wouldn't trust her or any bit of this situation. It could be a scam. And as charming as Fox might be, you're taking a huge risk buying into it."

"I'm going with my gut feeling on this," Reese said. "Fox might be obnoxious at times, but he's young, so that's to be expected. Unless he causes trouble, I'm going to let him crash at my house. Hopefully, the Nesbitt's will show up soon. They'd better be ready to explain all of this, though."

"If you get burned, don't say I didn't warn you," Jeremy said. "Meanwhile, I'm going to do you a favor and check on any recent cons or rip-offs going down in this neck of the woods. Crooks are getting pretty gutsy these days."

When his phone rang, Jeremy clicked it on.

"Savage here," he said. He nodded several times, then said, "Got it."

"What's up?" Reese asked.

"We've put out more information to the media about what happened to Violet and Sabrina, and we've given them access to the restaurant's surveillance video. An advisory has gone out telling folks to be on the lookout for old station wagon covered in bumper stickers and crazy manifestos."

"The car Violet thought was following her."

"Right," Jeremy said. "Anyway, Officer Berry said the department phones are blowing up. We're getting tips and leads, but nothing that's been deemed credible yet."

"Hopefully that changes," Reese said.

Jeremy rubbed the back of his neck. "Yeah, I hope so, too."

"I was too upset to tell you last night, but while I was surfing Violet's social media, I ran into somebody named Roman Jackrabbit," Reese said. "It's obviously a fake name, but they kept making comments about Violet's family stealing their property."

"That's similar to the accusation the guy on horseback shouted at Wade up at the reservoir," Jeremy said. "What do you make of it?"

"I've been researching Wyoming's historical land wars and how cattle barons often clashed with squatters."

"That was over a hundred years ago," Jeremy said.

"True, and these days, property lines are mostly well-defined," Reese said. "Here and there squabbles erupt, but they're usually resolved in court."

"Where are you going with this, Reese?"

She held up a finger. "What if there's an unresolved issue from the past that is eating away at our suspect?"

"It's possible," Jeremy said.

"Poor Sabrina caught this guy by surprise and paid for it with her life." Reese remembered seeing the woman's body in the back of the blue truck, then shook off the unpleasant memory. "By the way, have you gotten anywhere on Violet's cell phone records?"

"Not yet," Jeremy said. "The judge is taking his sweet time approving the court order to obtain them."

"A woman's life is at stake," Reese grumbled. "And the judge is probably out playing golf."

"What's your next move?" Jeremy asked.

"After I get in touch with Austin Buell today, Violet's high school boyfriend, I'm going to call Cricket O'Donnell to see if she'll meet me up at Fire Reservoir. I want to talk to her more about the morning she found Wade. Maybe if she has another look around it will jog her memory."

Jeremy nodded. "The guy Wade described sure seems similar to the guy we saw in the Sweet Clementine's surveillance footage."

"True," Reese said.

"Do you think that same guy tried to run you over last night?" Jeremy lifted a dark brow.

"Maybe," Reese said, her skin prickling with the memory. "He's probably heard by now that we are investigating the incident with Sabrina and Violet. Now he's trying to scare me off."

"I'm nervous about him going after you," Jeremy said.

"Me, too, but from now on, I'll be more cautious. His stupid stunt makes me more determined than ever to get some answers about this case."

"I'll have to say you've got some serious chops for this type of work," Jeremy said.

"Yeah, and I've earned them the hard way," Reese said. "Do you want to go with me today?"

"I've got too much to work on at the office or I sure would," Jeremy said.

"That's why I'm helping the department, right? You guys are stretched to the limit."

"That's a fact," Jeremy said.

"After I leave the reservoir, I'm heading up to Wind River Reservation to talk to Ned Spearhunter. See if he's got an alibi for last Friday."

"We should make him come down here for questioning," Jeremy suggested.

"I'd rather go up to the reservation," Reese said. "Before he has a chance to concoct an alibi or lawyer up."

"It's a long drive," Jeremy pointed out.

"It might be a matter of life or death for Violet."

"Yeah, I know," Jeremy said. "I also know once you've made up your mind, there's no stopping you."

Reese met his discerning gaze. "I've been there before. I know my way around."

"I figured as much," Jeremy said. "I'm concerned that if Spearhunter has something to hide, he could get angry."

"I can handle myself. You know this."

"You spending the night in Riverton?"

Reese shook her head. "Not with Fox here. I don't want to be gone that long."

"You'll be home late, then."

"It won't be the first time."

"Keep me posted." Jeremy's lips twitched. "You tend to get yourself into tricky situations."

"Ha, ha," Reese said. "Believe me, I won't be gone longer than necessary. I don't want Fox deciding to clean my office."

"What would it hurt? It'd keep him busy."

"I'm afraid he'll throw away something important."

"You think?"

"Let's just say I have my own way of filing things."

"Right, the XYZ system," Jeremy said with a chuckle.

"What's that?" Reese asked.

"Stacking crap on top of each other with no rhyme or reason," he explained.

Reese couldn't help but smile.

SEVENTEEN

SILENCE FILLED THE HOUSE when Reese entered. The couch, loveseat and recliners were empty, the living room carpet clear and end tables neat and tidy. Bo meowed when he spotted her, then stood and arched. He jumped down from the window sill, shimmied around her legs, then scampered off.

Mrs. Mac's comic books rested in a neat pile on the coffee table, but that was the only sign that she and Fox had spent time in here.

Laughter reached Reese's ears, drifting into the room like a distant echo. It had been a long time since her home had been filled with the joyous sound. Glancing toward the kitchen, with its clear counters and shining appliances, Reese noted the door to the backyard was open. Appreciation for the clean, uncluttered area sifted through her as she trotted across the tile and pushed open the screen.

Amidst the bushes and flower beds, Mrs. Mac tossed a baseball to Fox. With an eager expression, he held up a leather glove, nearly catching it. Unfortunately, the ball sailed past him. Grunting, he stumbled across the grass to chase it down.

Reese instantly recognized Jesse's old sports gear, and her heart squeezed. In her mind's eye, she saw her little brother playing catch, instead of Fox. Lord, she missed him. Warmth filled her face and tears threatened.

"You're home," Mrs. Mac exclaimed. "I hope you don't mind that I got into that box on the shelf in Fox's closet. Can you believe that kid's never played baseball? Every red-blooded American boy and girl should have a go at it, that's what I think."

Reese cleared her throat and forced back the surging emotion. "It's f-fine. And you're right. Look at how much fun he's having."

"Can you believe it?" A satisfied expression spread across Mrs. Mac's face.

"Hi Reese," Fox said, breathing heavily as he ran toward her clutching the baseball. "You were right. Mrs. Mac is a super babysitter."

Reese grinned, despite her momentary lapse of nostalgia. Fox was actually acting like a young boy, instead of a college professor. Amazingly, the word babysitter rolled off his tongue as if he didn't hate the implication any longer.

That was huge.

Watch out, Reese, Fox is growing on you. What if it turns out he's not really your brother?

"I'm glad you're enjoying yourself, kid." Reese surveyed the two unlikely companions, amazed at the friendship they'd formed already.

Fox fist-bumped Mrs. Mac and the two of them laughed conspiratorially.

"I've got to head out again," Reese said, supposing this is what it would feel like if she had a family waiting for her every day after work. "I won't be back until probably early evening. Will you two be all right?"

"I should say so," Mrs. Mac said, planting her fists on her hips. "We've got a lot more planned. Fox showed me how to use your TV's remote control, so we're going to watch a movie later on and order pizza for dinner."

"Yesss!" Fox said, pumping his fist into the air.

"What about Herman?"

"He'll be joining us," Mrs. Mac said. "I called him and he plans to shuffle over in a bit."

"I'll leave money on the counter—"

"Oh, pish posh," Mrs. Mac told her. "No worries. You just go take care of your gumshoe business."

Fox stepped back and tossed the ball to Mrs. Mac, who pitched it back to him. Again, he missed. A determined look in his eyes, he ran toward the fence to scoop it up.

"He'll figure it out soon enough," Mrs. Mac predicted. "It takes practice."

"You have a way with children," Reese said.

"I miss the days when my boys were young." Mrs. Mac said with a sigh. "They're all grown now and so busy with work, they rarely visit. Maybe someday they'll give me grandkids. Now that would be real nice."

"I owe you," Reese told her, touched by Mrs. Mac's honesty. It would be difficult to know your adult children were out there in the world, but didn't bother to come and see you.

"It's my pleasure," Mrs. Mac said, then made a shooing motion. "Now off with you!"

Reese headed back inside and made herself a bologna sandwich. After she'd eaten, she grabbed a Starbucks Frappuccino from the refrigerator and swallowed some of the cold brew. She surfed the internet on her phone, found a number for Austin Buell and called it.

"Hello?" A woman answered.

"I'm looking for Austin Buell," Reese said.

"I'm his mother," she said. "Unfortunately, he passed away last year."

"Oh, my deepest sympathies to you and your family," Reese said, truly sincere in her wishes. Austin was off of her suspect list.

"Th-thank you," the woman answered.

Reese took a moment to collect her thoughts, then looked up Catherine O'Donnell's phone number and called her.

"Hello?"

"Hi Cricket, this is Reese Golden. Would you mind meeting me at Fire Reservoir in about twenty-five minutes? I need to ask you some more questions about the morning you found Wade Gentry."

"Not a problem," Cricket said. "After I finish putting away some clothes I just picked up from the dry cleaner, I'll head up there. What's going on?"

"Meet me where you found Wade," Reese said. "I'll explain then."

Reese clicked off her cell, grabbed her purse and keys, and headed outside where she climbed into Betty. She started up the old Bronco, frowning when it took a bit longer for the engine to turn over. Backing down the driveway, she made a mental note to take the vehicle into the repair shop to be looked at.

Plugging in one of her mom's old country music cassettes, she began to hum. No wonder her mother had loved that style of music since that's what Cash played. Envisioning him serenading her mother on his guitar, she drove out of town toward the mountain peaks nestled together like giant stone buffalos.

The road to Fire Reservoir offered rugged beauty, fit for the canvas of any painter. Sandy gray-colored slabs of rock, like upturned tablets, sliced through the land. Scrub brush and tufts of grass clung to towering canyon walls that reached into the heavens, shading the narrow highway.

Despite September's grip, warmth continued to embrace the heights. Spiked purple wildflowers, along with cream and blush blossoms, thrust between rocky crevices. Autumn's cool nights had tipped aspen trees amber, and early snow storms had deposited patches of white along the summits. Evergreens remained as always, green, except for a few sections that displayed brown from beetle kill.

Reese turned down a dirt road leading to the reservoir. Dust clouds rose around her truck as she bumped down a road leading to the water. When the lake appeared, like a giant sapphire sea serpent coiled at the bottom of the bulky red bluffs, she drew in a breath. Always, she marveled at the beauty of this vista.

No wonder people continued boating on the mirrored surface even though the season had begun to wane. They were out to enjoy every last minute of this amazing weather before Old Man Winter set in. If she had her way, she'd buy some land nearby and build a house. That way, every time she wanted to relax, she'd set up a chair along the lake to fish or simply read a good book.

When she reached the dirt parking area, she pulled Betty in and switched off the engine. She hopped out and locked the door. Several other vehicles surrounded her, one being a giant motor home with a tiny dog sitting on the dashboard.

As the pooch watched her, she chuckled, then stuffed her keys in her back pocket. Like a blue tarp, the sky arched overhead, etched with white of clouds and a lone jet trail.

Wind blew hair across her face as she trekked toward the spot where she and Jeremy had found Wade Gentry. Seagulls wheeled overhead; black birds cawed noisily as they perched in tree branches. Added into the mix was the steady buzz of insects. Water lapped at the sandy shore, littered with driftwood, rocks, and even a bleached fish skeleton.

Nothing seemed out of the ordinary.

"Hi."

Reese wheeled around in surprise. Spotting Cricket, dressed in jeans shorts and a black T-shirt, she gulped down a breath of fresh air.

"Sorry," Cricket said. "I didn't mean to startle you."

"That's okay, I'm usually not so jumpy," Reese said, figuring her close encounter with a car last night had made her edgy. "Thanks for meeting me."

"It's a nice day to go for a drive."

Reese placed her hands on her hips and looked around at the cove. "Wouldn't you say this is where we found Wade?"

"Yes." Cricket lifted her brows. "You said you had questions for me?"

"What do you remember the morning you found him? Strange noises, sounds, anything out of the ordinary?"

"Nothing, really, but let me think." Cricket glanced around, a faraway look in her eyes. Then she snapped her fingers. "Smoke! I remember smelling that. At first, I thought it was lingering from the recently extinguished fires. Then I realized it came from something different."

"Like what?"

"Definitely tobacco," Cricket said. "My grandfather puffed cigars on special occasions, and that's what it smelled like."

"That's good," Reese said. "I really appreciate your time."

"Like I said, no problem," Cricket said. "But I've got to head out now. I've got a baby shower to attend."

"Be safe on the roads," Reese said as Cricket left the area.

Scouring the ground with a narrowed gaze, Reese headed toward a clump of bushes and tangled weeds. Lowering her gaze to study the marshy ground, she noted the mishmash of dead leaves, sticks, and slimy gravel.

A stale odor made Reese's nostrils twitch. Holding aside branches, she studied the place closer. Worn hoof prints dented the mud. Next to them, she spotted something else.

"Bingo," she muttered.

EIGHTEEN

After removing a blue vinyl glove from her pocket, Reese snapped it on and picked up a half-smoked cigar. A red label encircled the top, with the writing: Especial Romeo Cigarro.

Reese looked into the distance, letting the name of the brand sink into her brain. It was the same type of cigar she'd found near Sweet Clementine's.

She noted another important connection.

"Romeo," she murmured. "Romeo Jackrabbit, just like the name of the person who has been making threats on Violet's social media."

Had their suspect created a bogus online persona using a name from his preferred cigars?

Backing out of the bushes, Reese hiked over the scruffy expanse of sandy beach and up the hill to the parking lot. Climbing into her Bronco, warm from sitting in the sun, she removed a paper evidence bag from her center console and dropped in the cigar. Later, she'd drop it by Jeremy for DNA testing.

She fished the cell phone from her purse, looked up Fort Washakie and found the Sacajawea Trading Post, where Ned Spearhunter hopefully still worked. She punched in the number, and when someone answered, she asked for him.

"He'll return in about a half hour," the lady said. "Would you like me to leave him a message?"

"No, that's fine," Reese said. "What time do you close?"

"Not until 6 this evening."

"Thank you," Reese said. After clicking off, she punched in Jeremy's number.

"Savage here," he said.

"Hey," Reese said. "I'm at the reservoir and I found a half-smoked cigar butt in the bushes near Wade's fishing spot."

"Did it have a brand label?" Jeremy asked.

"Yes, Especial Romeo Cigarro."

"Just like the one you found in the bushes by Sweet Clementine's. It seems our perp has a penchant for dropping those at crime scenes."

"Maybe we can find out where those are sold."

"I've already got my people working on it," Jeremy said. "They're specially ordered from the Dominican Republic and there's a few places around the state where they're carried. Locally, the Wolf Smoke Shop in Meadowlark Valley carries them."

"Finally, a connection," Reese said.

"I'll try to get over to check their records," Jeremy said. "Get names of the customers who buy those."

"If you don't get to it, I'll do it tomorrow," Reese said.

"Sounds like a plan."

"Remember I mentioned Violet's social media was full of snarky remarks from someone named Romeo Jackrabbit?"

"I do."

"Maybe that means something. Like the guy who smokes Especial Romeo Cigarros is also Romeo Jackrabbit."

"Again, that's a stretch," Jeremy said, wariness edging his voice.

"Yeah, but it's not too far of a stretch," Reese said.

"Maybe," Jeremy said doubtfully.

"I'm headed up to the reservation now," Reese said. "With luck, I'll be able to catch Ned Spearhunter and have a chat with him. He still works at the Sacajawea Trading Post."

"He's there today?" Jeremy asked.

"Yep, I checked."

"Keep a low profile, you know, don't piss off anyone."

"Seriously, that's an insult," Reese shot back. "I handled some rough situations back in the day."

"I only—"

Wondering if Jeremy would always second guess her choices, Reese hung up, too quickly for him to reply. His mistrust of her abilities was annoying.

She dropped her phone back in her overlarge handbag, which contained almost everything she'd would need to survive a nuclear holocaust, should one ever occur. Upon realizing she wanted to set her cell's GPS in order to find the damn trading post, she groaned, yanked the device back out of her purse and plugged it in.

Firing up Betty's engine, she told herself to quit fretting about Jeremy and drove away from the reservoir. The dirt road caused a brown cloud to mushroom from beneath her tires. It didn't help one bit that she was driving angry.

"Did I just overreact with Jeremy?"

She shrugged, realizing that because she liked him so much, his opinion of her was very important. Getting uppity with him wasn't going to win brownie points, by any means. That is, if she wanted their relationship to continue, which she did.

Merging back onto the highway, she headed north. Thoughts of what she'd say to Jeremy when she saw him again taunted her as she plugged a country tape into the cassette deck. So that she couldn't brood, she began to hum. A wasteland of asphalt stretched between here and the Wind River Indian Reservation, so she settled in for a long drive.

LATE AFTERNOON SUN SLANTED ACROSS the Wind River Indian Reservation's rolling prairie as Reese drove toward her destination. Covered in scruffy brown grass, bushes, random patches of cotton-wood and Russian olive trees, the open territory offered a fantastic view. To the east, the Wind River Mountain Range rose in misty purple majesty. Bright yellow sunflowers bobbed their heads at the edge of the road.

Numerous houses and trailer homes of blue, white and tan appeared in the distance surrounded by blue-green sagebrush. Trucks and cars sat nearby. Some of the dwellings boasted fields of green exposing rounded bales of hay and farm equipment.

The seventh largest in the country, the Wind River Indian Reservation contained more than 2.2 million acres. Around 2,500 Eastern Shoshone and 5,000 Northern Arapahoe tribal members lived here. Wyoming's Wind River Country offered a historical and educational addition to the state's tourism.

"Here we go," Reese said to herself as the words Fort Washakie appeared on a hill in white lettering, along with a brown and white sign marking Sacajawea's grave site. In fourth-grade history, Reese's teacher had taught the students that the Indian maiden, at the tender age of 16, had served as a guide and interpreter for Meriwether Lewis and William Clark on their 1804 Louisiana Territory exploration.

Reese recalled visiting Sacajawea's grave long ago with her family. Decorated with bouquets of flowers from visitors, people continued to honor the young woman's bravery.

The city extended across the plains, edged by a lumpy brownish-green buttes, which also served as backdrop for a water tower. Reese drove over a bridge that crossed a river, then entered the house-lined streets. She slowed down for a shaggy white dog as it darted near the road, then wove its way back into the neighborhood.

A brick church, fronted by a statue of the Virgin Mary, caught her eye. The beauty of it washed over her. Directed by her GPS, she turned a corner, passing a school, a few businesses, and then she spotted the Sacajawea Trading Post.

Appreciating that it was a half hour before the store would close, Reese hustled toward the large timber building boasting a stone foundation. It displayed both an American flag and a

Wyoming flag at the entrance, and painted Native American patterns adorned the storefront.

After parking the Bronco by the boulder-lined front sidewalk, she entered the establishment. Shelves along the walls offered an assortment of Native American jewelry, blankets, pottery, clothing, T-shirts, mugs, purses and brilliant artwork. The log walls held painted animal skulls decorated with feathers, metal sculptures, and bright tapestries designed with colorful tribal patterns. At the back of the store, a museum offered information about the local tribes.

Reese approached a counter where a young man, his long dark hair pulled into a pony tail, talked with a lady who was purchasing a leather jacket. He wore a red and gray striped shirt, jeans, and a black leather vest. Around his neck dangled a leather thong holding a carved wooden turtle.

Reese browsed through a display while the man was occupied, choosing a pair of turquoise and brown fleece leggings featuring buffalo silhouettes. She decided they'd make a nice addition to her wardrobe for the impending cold winter nights.

When the man at the counter was free, Reese advanced toward him, noting his name tag identified him as store manager, Ned Spearhunter.

"Good afternoon," he said to her with a smile.

"The same to you," she said as she handed him the leggings.

"These are nice for our cold spells," he said, folding the leggings. "Are you from around here?"

"Meadowlark Valley," she said.

"That's a long drive," he said. "What brings you this way?"

"Thought I'd try my hand at some gambling," Reese lied.

"Of course, at the Wind River Casino in Riverton," he said.

Reese nodded. "I took a side trip out here."

"Welcome to the Rez." He rang up Reese's purchase on a cash register, and Reese handed him her credit card. Finished, he dropped the leggings in a paper bag and handed them to Reese along with her card.

"You look familiar," she said, putting away her card.

"Okay," he said with a shrug. "That happens."

"I bet I know why, too," Reese said. "Did you date a girl named Violet Gentry? She's a good friend of mine. I'm pretty certain she showed me a picture of the two of you at Central Wyoming College."

"Yeah, I took some business classes there. That's where I met her."

"Small world, isn't it?" Reese said.

"Yep." He chuckled. "I took a lot of flak for being a college boy. My friends called me an Apple, red on the outside but white inside. They stopped joking around when I didn't leave the Rez."

"Have you seen Violet lately?" Reese asked.

"It's been years," he said. "In fact, I haven't thought about her in a long time."

"She mentioned her father being upset about the two of you dating."

"Her old man wasn't too keen on me," Ned agreed. "Thought I was a dirt poor Indian out to steal Violet's inheritance."

"Did that make you angry?" Reese asked.

"Sure, but I figured it wasn't worth getting worked up about. Can't change some people's opinions about our way of life up here. Besides, Violet and me had nearly called it quits by the time her old man got wigged out."

"There weren't any hard feelings when you parted?"

"We had a couple of arguments, but nothing awful. We both realized it was best that we part."

"Why?"

"She planned to transfer to the University of Wyoming to finish up her ag degree. CWC is only a two-year school."

"Right, right," Reese responded. "By any chance, were you in Meadowlark Valley last Friday evening?"

"No reason to go down that way," he said, his voice taking on an irritated edge.

"Where were you?" Reese asked.

Ned frowned as he folded his arms across his chest and pinned her with a suspicious stare. "Why do you want to know? What's with all the questions?"

At that moment, a young woman in a maternity top and jeans walked out of a back room. Long dark hair flowed down her back. Her pierced ears displayed studs, hoops and jade earrings.

"He was with me," she said. "My parents had us over for dinner, then we wound up staying the night."

"And you are?" Reese asked.

"Ned's wife," she said. "Billie."

NINETEEN

"I KNOW YOU MUST RESENT ALL THESE QUESTIONS," Reese said. "Violet's missing and I'm working with the police on her case. I'm a private investigator."

Reese removed a business card from her purse and set it on the counter. Both Billie and Ned studied it.

"You figured an Indian guy from the reservation would probably be guilty, huh?" Billie scoffed.

Ned placed his hand on his wife's arm. "Billie, don't—"

"I'm tired of people thinking that because our skin is brown that we're violent," Billie frowned.

"That's got nothing to do with it," Reese said. "Violet's family is worried. I'm following up with everyone Violet knows."

"Uh, huh," Billie shot back in a loud voice.

"What's all the commotion about?" An elderly man wearing a flannel black and white checkered shirt, jeans, and a leather vest came out of a back room. His dark hair was shot with gray and he walked with a limp.

"This lady is asking questions about where Ned was Friday night, Dad," Billie said.

"It's all right, Jim," Ned said measuredly to his father-in-law. "We're handling it."

"My apologies for upsetting anyone," Reese said.

"What's the issue?" Jim asked, placing his work-worn hands on the counter.

"A girl Ned used to date a long time ago went missing last Friday," Reese explained. "I'm working with the police in Meadowlark Valley to try and find her."

"I see," Jim said. "My daughter and Ned stayed at my home that night. We were celebrating my birthday."

"Sorry for the trouble."

"No problem," Jim said. "Excuse me though, I'm sorting through our stock and I want to finish up."

"Of course," Reese said.

With a nod, Jim limped into the back room.

"You should have told me why you were here in the first place," Ned told Reese. "You didn't have to sneak around. I don't like hearing that Violet's in trouble, either."

Billie looked up at her husband and leaned closer to him. "Ned's not the type to take revenge," she said, pressing a hand to her rounded stomach. "He's a good man."

"I meant no disrespect," Reese assured them. "I only want to find Violet, so I'll be on my way."

"Sorry to be so defensive," Billie said, the anger on her face fading.

"In your shoes, I'd probably react the same way," Reese admitted

"I hope you find Violet," Ned said.

"Too many women go missing up here," Billie said. "It's terrible. It destroys our families."

"It's devastating for families everywhere when someone goes missing," Reese said. "Thanks for talking to me."

She lifted a hand in farewell, then walked back through an aisle of merchandise and left the building. That confrontation turned out to be a bit uncomfortable, but she'd gotten the information she needed. She'd talk to Jeremy about Ned, but in her opinion, he could be crossed off the suspect list.

Outside, she hurried to her Bronco, climbed back in, and headed home. The western sun slanted through her windshield, so she slid on sunglasses and pulled down her visor to cut the glare.

She managed to find a decent radio station with a talk show, then settled in to the sound of conversation and humming tires. Politics weren't her thing, nevertheless, she listened to the host and his callers discuss current events. Before long, the voices on the program faded into background noise as Reese tried to piece together the puzzle of her current case.

Violet knew someone had been following her—someone Sabrina's sisters nicknamed "Violet's Vampire" because of the way he dressed. The guy drove an old station wagon covered in bizzarro bumper stickers and doomsday proclamations. She bet the same guy killed Sabrina, getting her out of the way so he could take Violet with no witnesses.

The Gentry family claimed that Violet didn't have any enemies, at least that they knew of. She was respected in the community and involved with charitable activities. Since Violet's abductor had also threatened Wade Gentry, Reese decided that's where the link must exist.

Then there was social media's Romeo Jackrabbit and with all those comments about the Gentry family stealing ranch land. Reese decided it might be time to conduct historical research. Like many other long-time ranchers in Wyoming, the Gentry's had established firm Wyoming roots in the late 1800s.

Apparently, whoever was after the Gentry's was going to extreme measures to get their attention. Did the family have skeletons in their family closet? Was Violet's kidnapper the same person who had nearly run her over?

Outside, the wind had picked up to a solid speed. It slammed against her truck, rocking it back and forth. Gripping the steering wheel, Reese fought to stay in her lane. At least the mighty gusts propelled her truck forward. With any luck, it wouldn't guzzle as much gas.

"And maybe donkeys fly," she said with a snort.

INDIGO SHADOWS DRAPED MEADOWLARK VALLEY when Reese rolled to a stop beneath her carport, and turned off the Bronco's engine. It made an unusual clicking sound, alerting her once again to the need to get the truck serviced soon.

Mrs. Mac must have turned on the porch light, which glowed like a beacon. As she entered the house, Reese heard muffled TV voices, as well as soft snoring. Leaving her purse on the table, she entered the living room.

Mrs. Mac stretched back in a recliner, a blanket pulled over her lap and shoulders. Apparently sensing Reese's presence, she flipped down the footrest and jumped to her feet.

"Back off or I'll carve you up like a Thanksgiving turkey!" She waved around the gleaming butcher knife clutched in her hand.

"It's just me," Reese said, backing up.

Mrs. Mac blinked and lowered her weapon. "Thank goodness. I swear I heard something bumping around outside."

"When?" Reese's stomach flip-flopped.

"Not too long ago." Mrs. Mac set down the knife, parted the front room curtains, and peered out. "I swear I saw someone sneaking around, hiding in the shadows."

Reese eased up next to her and looked out. "I don't see anyone now."

"Thankfully, neither do I," Mrs. Mac said. "Since crime around town has increased, I've been keeping a closer eye on things."

"Where's Fox?"

"In bed," Mrs. Mac said. "I must have worn him out with the baseball."

"You're a life saver," Reese said.

"That's what neighbors are for," Mrs. Mac said. "There were many times that your grandparents watched my boys."

"I'll probably need your help tomorrow," Reese admitted, wondering if Jeremy might be right about her keeping Fox. How long would she need to rely on Mrs. Mac to stay with the boy when she went to work?

"I've got nothing else on my agenda," Mrs. Mac said, patting Reese's arm. "You're a working girl. You can't drop everything and take care of a child."

"It is difficult."

"When you called and told me about Fox, I was flabbergasted." Mrs. Mac shook her head. "I can't believe his mother would have the nerve to assume you'd be able to take in her son."

"She claims he's my little brother."

"I suppose that's a mess you'll have to sort through as soon as what's-her-name returns."

"Tanya."

Mrs. Mac patted Reese's shoulder. "She's lucky you have such a big heart."

A loud thump sounded on the porch. Reese and Mrs. Mac exchanged startled glances, then hurried toward the door. When Reese peered out, she spotted a fiery object sitting on the floorboards near a planter.

"Holy Moses!" Mrs. Mac backed away, her eyes wide with fright.

Reese streaked into the kitchen, grabbed the fire extinguisher from beneath the sink, then ran onto the porch. Pulling the extinguisher's pin, she aimed the nozzle, and squeezed foam onto the small, orange-red blaze. After a few back-and-forth swipes, the flames seemed to be out.

A toxic odor assailed her nostrils, and she wrinkled her nose. "Pee-yew!"

"Whatever that is, it smells hideous," Mrs. Mac said.

"Like a rotten cigar or worse." As if a heavy fog had rolled into the area, smoke still lingered. Reese grabbed a metal plant stake from a dirt-filled flower pot, and poked the charred remains. She watched them long enough to ascertain the fire had indeed gone out.

"Looks like manure," she observed, frowning at the black and brown mess nestled in a paper bag. She'd need to scrape and repaint the floor boards, but otherwise, there was no damage to the porch.

"I just knew someone was snooping around out here." Mrs.

Mac moved closer, her expression troubled. "Why on Earth would someone do this?"

What a vindictive act. Then again, she was tracking a killer. If he was responsible for this, he hadn't left a note, but, once again, she got the message.

"I think it has something to do with the case I'm working on," Reese commented.

"What do you mean?"

"Someone's pissed at me, and this is their way of telling me to back off."

"Oh, I get it." Mrs. Mac met Reese's gaze. "And are you going to do that? Back off?"

"Hell, no," she said. "I must on the right track."

"But that means someone's watching you." She shivered. "Scary."

Reese shrugged. "That goes with the territory."

"You're braver than me for sure," Mrs. Mac said. "Will you be all right or do you want me to stay over here the rest of the night? Herman will volunteer to stay too, once I tell him what happened."

"No, but thanks. I'll be fine."

"And Fox?"

"The timing is bad for him to be here," Reese said. "But I can handle this."

"I'll suggest he call his mother tomorrow to see if she's coming home soon."

"That's a good idea," Reese said. "If it's possible for her to come and get him, it would be best."

Mrs. Mac went inside briefly, then came out with her purse hanging from her shoulder. "Let me know what time you need me to come over tomorrow."

"Will do."

Yawning, Mrs. Mac walked next door to her tidy, red brick home. She glanced around warily, then went inside.

Reese trekked to her carport and grabbed a metal snow shovel. She cleaned up her porch, dropping the mess into a large metal bucket. Back inside, she checked all the doors and windows, making sure she'd locked everything up tight.

Carefully, she peeked inside of Fox's room. He'd plugged a night-light into one of the electric sockets. Soft luminescence revealed his small form stretched out on the bed, covered with a quilt. His even breathing and peaceful expression told Reese he felt safe.

Protectiveness surged through her.

Mr. Bojangles slept near Fox's feet, curled up in a ball. He'd obviously made another friend, and had quickly changed allegiances.

"Traitor," Reese whispered, a smile curving her lips.

Weariness sifted through her as she headed to her room. Honestly, how could a mother simply up and leave her child with a stranger? Poor kid. She dropped her purse on a chest and withdrew her phone. Sitting on her bed, she punched in Jeremy's phone number.

"I'm home," she said when he answered.

"What's the word?" he asked.

"Spearhunter's got a solid alibi," she said, not bothering to mention the porch fire, otherwise Jeremy would threaten to pull her off the case again. "He and his wife, Billie, were with family all Friday night."

"It was worth checking out," Jeremy said. "Now that we know Spearhunter's accounted for, can you check out that tobacco shop tomorrow? It opens at 10 a.m."

"Obviously you didn't make it down there," Reese said.

"That would be correct."

"No problem," she said, making plans to call Mrs. Mac in the morning and ask her to come early in the morning to babysit again.

"How'd Fox make out today?"

"It was like he had a stick up his butt until Mrs. Mac got a hold of him. She had him out throwing a baseball and eating pizza. That old gal has a magic touch, I tell you."

"That's good to hear."

"Definitely, since I'll need her help until Tanya or Cash Nesbitt show up."

"Hopefully soon."

"Right. Otherwise, I'll need to make permanent arrangements for Fox."

"Like what?"

"I don't know yet," Reese admitted. "I'll have to put some serious thought into that."

"Stop by my office tomorrow when you finish up with the tobacco shop," Jeremy said.

"Will do." Reese disconnected. Sleep called to her, but she had some research to conduct before hitting the hay. Her stomach growled, calling for food first.

She wandered into the kitchen, stuck her nose into the refrigerator and did a thorough sweep. Her mouth dropped. To her amazement, milk, eggs, bread, and butter, along with other items like fruit, meat, and yogurt had been stocked on the shelves. Apparently, Fox and Mrs. Mac had done some shopping. Typically, Reese didn't keep much food in here besides a can of opened cat food, and diet drinks.

Spotting a pizza box, Reese pulled out a piece, grabbed a can of diet lemon-lime soda and headed into her office.

TWENTY

Reese immersed herself in Wyoming history while navigating her computer around the internet. Information flashed rapidly across her screen while she surfed. She lost track of time while studying the state's lore, most of which she'd learned in school.

In 1803 the United States purchased the Louisiana Territory from France, which included most of what would eventually become Wyoming. John Colter explored Wyoming in 1807, putting Yellowstone on the map. Fort Laramie, a fur trading post, came along in 1834, eventually becoming a military outpost and a stop for emigrants bound for Oregon, California and the Salt Lake Valley.

Native Americans saw more of their lands encroached upon as 1867 brought the Union Pacific Railroad. By 1869, women earned the right to vote. Famous outlaws like Butch Cassidy and the Sundance Kid robbed trains and cowboys tended cattle on vast parcels of territory.

The Johnson County War caught her eye—a range conflict that waged from approximately 1889 to 1893. A number of events took place, leading to large cattle ranchers facing off with smaller settlers about land, livestock, and water rights. Shootouts and murders erupted. In order to end the violence, President Benjamin Harrison ordered the United States Cavalry to intervene.

Nate Champion, Joe Elliot, John A. Tisdale, and many more names peppered her reading material. A rancher named Anson Gentry also became involved in some of the dustups, claiming squatters had settled on his land, and had rustled some of his cattle. Possibly he was a distant relative of Wade Gentry, and had gained a reputation for accusing small ranchers of various infractions.

ALTHOUGH THE LAND WARS HAD OCCURRED more than 100 years ago, Reese suspected that the individual causing the Gentry's such grief right now might be obsessed with that issue. It seemed possible that he'd been lurking on Violet Gentry's social media accounts as Romeo Jackrabbit and that he smoked Especial Romeo Cigarros.

One of his online comments echoed in her mind: "How nice it must be to have inherited your spread from ancestors with blood on their hands—cattle barons who terrorized anyone who got in their way."

Why would someone get hung up about an incident that happened so long ago?

Underlying greed, jealousy, heartbreak, and other strong emotions typically drove people to extreme lengths. Sometimes, their reasons simply didn't make sense.

On the Gentry Ranch's website, she looked through the different pages, trying to spot something that might appear offensive. She searched for information about each of the family members, which brought up material about local and national awards, including the family's involvement with charitable activities, and their agriculture honors.

A while ago, Wade Gentry had received Rancher Daily Magazine's Top Producer of the Year Award. He, along with Tag, had been the keynote speakers and presenters at the conference held in Chicago. At other sessions and meetings, Violet had taken the lead in presenting facts about the Gentry's ranching operation, along with the handling of cows, horses, and other livestock.

The accolades filled pages. Bottom line, when family members spoke to the media or commented in articles, they each emphasized family relationships, consideration, and God's blessings as key to their success. Fertile fields and crop yields were secondary to everything that went into their success, they claimed.

Sitting back in her chair, Reese closed her eyes and rubbed her forehead. Weariness drifted through her body. She couldn't decide if her studies would be profitable or if they'd been a waste of effort.

Only time would tell.

Poor Violet.

She'd been missing since Friday, and now it was past the critical 72 hours point, making the chances of finding her alive slim. Reese felt like she been grasping at straws. Jeremy and the police officers he'd assigned to work Sabrina's murder case hadn't been any more successful at uncovering leads, either.

Frustrated, she shut down her computer and checked the doors and windows again. All seemed safe. After getting ready for bed, she crawled under the covers, her nerves tensed. Over and over in her mind, she thought, *Violet, where are you? Who took you and why?*

Unfortunately, tossing and turning kept Reese alert and wide awake. First her foot itched, then her arm. Warmth blossomed throughout her body, so she kicked off the blankets. When her toes tingled with cold, she replaced the covers. Maybe she couldn't sleep because her traitorous cat had deserted her.

Darn it anyway. She had too many ideas ricocheting through her mind.

"Crap," she mumbled, rolling over on her side to check her ancient digital alarm clock. A red 2 a.m. glared across the night table, taunting her until she felt like screaming. She got up and headed back to her office where she used a sticky note to write a message to herself about things she wanted to check on.

Finished, she padded back to her bedroom and crawled into the sack. Staring at the ceiling, she thought of more things she needed to do. Gusts of wind began to howl, knocking around the house like wild horses galloping across the prairie.

"That won't help me sleep," Reese said to the darkness.

Whenever the wind blew, she envisioned the damage it might cause, and the nightmare of having to turn in a claim to her insurance company. The idea of downed fences, ripped shingles and lawn furniture blown to Nebraska made her wince.

Lord, please bless the poor soul who'd placed garbage dumpsters along the curb. If the wind had its way with the unwieldy containers, last night's leftovers might get splattered across the street, a veritable feast for wandering dogs and cats.

At last Reese's mind stopped spinning and she drifted off. A sensation of falling vaulted through her, ending with a frightening jolt. Darkness, like thick black velvet, surrounded her. Clammy sensations raised goosebumps on her flesh, and she shivered.

Within the light of a flickering candle flame, Reese saw a crying woman, her head buried in her palms.

"Who are you?" Reese asked.

The woman stopped sobbing and looked at Reese.

"It's me, Violet." She ran her hands up and down her body and cried out. "What's happening to me?"

Reese studied Violet's attire, a dress made up entirely of dirt, moss, and spears of grass. Reese recognized it—she'd seen it before.

"You're missing," Reese told her. "I'm trying to find you."

"Why?" Violet ran a muddy hand through her dark, tangled hair.

"Someone took you."

"I don't understand." Violet began to pace. Dirt crumbled from her clothing and piled on the floor. "Why can't I come home?"

"I have to find you first." Reese moved closer to the woman, but she held up a hand.

"Stop, you aren't allowed here," she warned. "I'm too far away."

"Where are you?"

Violet looked around. "Somewhere cold and dark."

"Your family is waiting for you," Reese said. "Try to remember where you were taken. Help me get to you."

"Hurts so bad," Violet said, closing her eyes.

"What?"

"My head." Violet said. "I hit it when I fell."

"Who took you?" Reese insisted.

"It's a big mess," Violet said. "I think I'm dying."

"No, you can't!" Reese cried. "You've got to hold on."

"It's no use," Violet interrupted, fresh tears streaking down her dirty face. "I'm too far north. I'm freezing. And I'm hungry."

"Reese," someone called, but it wasn't Violet.

"Huh, what?" Reese muttered, then smacked her dry lips.

In a whirling frenzy, she felt herself lifted up through the darkness and tossed out onto a prairie covered in tall grass, and rusty-brown bluffs. A dark purple and gray storm brewed over the distant mountain range. To her dismay, the scene melted and ran like a water color painting in the rain.

The blare of her alarm clock cut through time and space.

Reese sat up, pale morning light streaming through her windows. Fully dressed, Fox stood beside her bed, his hands pressed over his ears.

"Where is that infuriating noise coming from?" he shouted.

Reese punched off the alarm button. The noise stopped.

"Don't get your panties in a twist, it's just my damn clock," she growled.

"My mom swears a lot," Fox said. "My dad, too."

Reese ran a hand through her tussled hair, realizing she probably wasn't giving a very good impression. "Adults do that."

"I bet you need coffee," Fox suggested. "There's a full pot ready in the kitchen. I made it from the bag of Starbucks brand in your cupboard. I figured that's your favorite."

Reese yawned. "It sure is."

"I've also made eggs and toast for breakfast."

"I don't eat this early." Reese imagined Fox banging around in her kitchen, getting into her stuff and making a huge mess.

"Suit yourself." Fox spun on his heel and left Reese's room.

"Man, I need more sleep," she complained. It was six in the morning, so she'd maybe gotten three or four hours of sack time. Unbelievable. It was high time someone invented a coffee IV drip.

Dragging herself out of bed, she removed her nightshirt and put on a pair of blue leggings, a matching top, and sneakers. For months now, her dreams had become more vivid, which made her wonder what was going on.

They seemed especially significant whenever she was working on a missing person's case. Almost as if she had an astral connection to the victims. The trouble was, the disjointed ramblings of her unconscious mind didn't make much sense.

The ancient Greeks may have believed dreams were from divine sources, but Reese believed that sometimes, they came from a darker, more sinister place. That might be a good question to ask her friend Kiki, who had studied things of that nature.

If Kiki couldn't help her, she'd better make appointment with a therapist. Post-traumatic stress disorder did terrible things to people, if that was her problem. She didn't have time to fall apart or she wouldn't be able to work.

Concerned that she'd have to go see a shrink in order to deal with her disturbing dreams, she headed into the kitchen. Fox sat at the table with a coffee cup, reading the newspaper. To her surprise, the kitchen was neat and tidy, and the dishes he'd used were washed and sitting in the dish drainer. No chaos, no mess. Even her disloyal cat sat in his window seat watching birds fluttering around in a tree, his tail switching back and forth.

"Bo seems happy as a clam," she commented. "He usually wants a scoop of wet food in the morning."

"I fed him already," Fox said. "Hope you don't mind."

"Uh, that's fine," she said, feeling a tad useless at the moment. "You drinking coffee?"

Fox scrunched up his face. "Nope, hot cocoa. Mrs. Mac got me a box of the instant kind when we stopped by the grocery store."

"That's good," Reese said as she poured herself a cup of java and began to sip. "My mom used to say coffee stunts a kid's growth."

"A myth," Fox said. "People used to fear caffeine would affect calcium absorption, but the studies on that subject are inconclusive."

Reese held up a hand. "Okay, okay, I get it."

Fox pursed his lips.

"You ever jogged before?" she asked him.

"No, why?"

"Because I meet my friend Kiki every morning at the park and we go running."

"You do whatever you need to," he said. "I'll be fine here."

"I'm not leaving you alone. So, let's get going."

Groaning, Fox stood. "I'll go grab the baseball and glove in my room, if you don't mind."

"Sure, that'll keep you busy."

Arms crossed over her chest; Reese waited for him to return. She couldn't help but wonder what this day would bring.

TWENTY-ONE

"I GREW UP HERE," REESE TOLD FOX as he studied the houses lining either side of the street, his gaze skimming over trees, hedges, flowers, and other signs of life.

"This is a very quaint old neighborhood," Fox said. "I like it here. And although your home is structured for a 1940s family, I find it quite cozy."

"My grandparents left it to me when they passed on," Reese said.

"How old are you, anyway?" Fox raised his brows.

"It's not polite to ask someone's age," Reese responded, feeling like an antique for even having to say that.

"I'm only checking," he said nonchalantly, as if he'd pointed out that the sky was blue.

"Why?"

"A woman's fertility decreases after age 30," he said, looking her up and down. "I thought you should know that in case you ever want to get married and have children. I'd say the sooner the better."

Reese's face grew warm, and she struggled with how to respond. Finally, she asked, "What does it matter to you?"

He zipped up his jacket and smoothed down his collar. "I thought it might be fun to have nieces and nephews. Being an only child, I find myself alone frequently. It's also not easy for me to make friends. Having more family around would be nice."

"I'll keep that in mind," Reese said, feeling somewhat guilty she couldn't promise to make him an uncle. "Thanks for the reproduction talk, though."

"You're most welcome," he responded.

Reese honestly felt sorry for Fox Nesbitt. He seemed well adjusted and brighter than most crayons in the box. Nevertheless, those attributes didn't make up for the loss of companionship and love, which he obviously craved.

He didn't appear to be living the easiest life, even though he was a giant pain in the butt. If he actually was her half-brother, she'd need to learn to accept his eccentricities. Which, she realized, wouldn't be awful. He made life . . . interesting.

At the park, Reese found Kiki standing on the grass near a children's swing set. She wore a raspberry-colored jogging suit that complemented her dark, curly hair. Hands on her hips, she stretched from side to side, watching as Reese and her small sidekick approached her.

"Hey you," she said to Reese. "Who's your little friend?"

"This is Fox Nesbitt," Reese said. "Fox, this is my friend, Kiki Morningstar."

Fox extended his hand. "Pleased to meet you Ms. Morningstar."

As the two shook, Kiki's brows arched in obvious surprise. There weren't too many kids who exchanged pleasantries with adults, Reese figured. Fox had impeccable manners. No wonder her friend was caught off guard.

"Call me Kiki," she said.

"Kiki it is then," he agreed, pushing his glasses further up the bridge of his nose.

"Are you visiting Reese?" Kiki asked him.

"He's ah, um . . ." Reese stammered, trying to think of a way to explain the situation.

"Ah, hem," Fox said. "I'm Reese's little brother, actually half-brother. We have the same father."

"Really?" Kiki met Reese's gaze, her mouth open, a million

questions no doubt filling her mind. Reese had told Kiki she didn't know her father's identity because her mother had never told her. Norah had gone to her grave, keeping his identity a secret.

"I'll stay right here tossing the ball," Fox offered. "You two go do your morning jog. I'm sure you have a lot to talk about."

As Fox tried tossing the baseball into his glove, he dropped it, scrambling to chase after it. Kiki stifled a giggle.

Reese kept an eye on Fox as she and Kiki began jogging on the well-worn path around the lake. Buttery yellow and rust-colored leaves rustled in the morning breeze, making last night's windstorm seem like a figment of her imagination.

"What's the story?" Kiki finally said, brushing stray curls behind her ears. "I'm dying to know."

"It's crazy." Reese wished she could enjoy the shafts of warm sunlight washing over her skin. However, inner conflict made her uneasy. The idea that a murderer lurked nearby, keeping an eye her and her house guest, doubled her concerns.

"We're the crazy sisters, remember?" Kiki said with a chuckle.

"Right," Reese agreed. "We'd better slow down, though. I won't be able to tell you otherwise."

Reese slowed to a walk, and Kiki followed suit. After catching her breath, Reese explained how Fox had shown up on her doorstep.

"What was in the note his mother left for you?" Kiki asked.

"Tanya guilted me into watching him," Reese said. "She claims that he's my half-brother. His dad, Cash Nesbitt, who is supposedly my father, took off on an alcoholic rant. She insisted she had to go and find him."

"How long will she be gone?"

Reese shrugged. "Tanya didn't say."

"How could she trust a total stranger with her kid?"

"That's the weird part," Reese said. "Tanya, Cash's wife, or my step-mother if this story is true, didn't seem to have any qualms about up and leaving him."

"Mamma Mia," Kiki exclaimed. "Do you believe her?"

"My mom obviously knew Cash because Tanya left me a photo showing them together. So, I believe there might be some truth to what she's saying."

"Isn't that something," Kiki said. "It'd change a lot of things."

"Jeremy warned that it might be some sort of scam," Reese added.

"There is a strong chance he's right," Kiki said.

"I understand why Jeremy would think that," Reese said, "but gut instinct tells me otherwise."

"What about Fox?"

Reese glanced over at him. He continued tossing the ball, occasionally catching it. When he did, a huge grin spread across his face. He might be a nerd, but he was growing on her.

"For now, I'll keep him with me," she said.

Kiki shook her head. "I think you should call Child Protective Services."

"Jeremy thinks I should, too."

"So?"

"I won't do it," Reese said. "At least not right now. The system is messed up and I don't want to get him caught up in it. If he really is my little brother, I feel like I might be his only stable relative."

"You've got a point," Kiki agreed. "Who watches him when you have to work?"

"Mrs. Mac," Reese said. "She's a real character, but she's good with him. And Fox likes her."

"That's a relief."

"Meanwhile, I'm stumped on my current case."

"You're working for Tag Gentry, right? I remember when you texted me and said you're looking for his kidnapped sister."

"That's right," Reese said. "I probably shouldn't even be out here. I ought to be trying to crack this."

"Exercise has a way of greasing the wheels, so to speak," Kiki said. "It clears the cobwebs from the mind and helps you think."

"I sure hope so," Reese said. "By the way, how's your shop doing?"

"Decent enough," Kiki said. "I've got a big sale starting Friday. I want to move out some old inventory and make room for the new. Need any candles or windchimes?"

"I think I'm good," Reese said. "If you have any peppermint essential oil, set a bottle aside for me, though."

"Will do," Kiki said. "I imagine you won't be coming for my meditation classes while Fox is staying with you."

"Nope," Reese said. "Unless he wants to tag along, which I highly doubt."

"Yeah, he'd probably think it was dumb."

"While I've got your ear," Reese said. "I wanted to ask if you know anything about interpreting dreams."

"I took some classes about it once. What kind of dreams?"

"Ever since I started my PI business, I've had some really vivid dreams about my cases," Reese explained.

"Vivid as in how?"

"Disturbingly vivid, I guess you could say."

"Are they like premonitions?" Kiki asked, then clarified by adding, "Do they predict future events?"

"That's the thing, I can't tell. It confuses me as to whether they are warnings about what's happening, or if it's my mind supplying ideas about what I *think* is happening. Or will happen." Reese shook her head. "I don't know, but they're driving me nuts."

"Are you having dreams about Violet Gentry?" Kiki asked.

"Yes," Reese admitted. "And she's always wearing a dress made out of dirt."

"Dirt? Wow, okay," Kiki said. "Does she speak to you?"

Reese nodded. "And I ask her questions. For example, in the dream I had last night, I asked where she's at. She said it's cold and dark. And she said she thinks she's dying."

"Holy smokes," Kiki said. "Do the dreams make you feel that even though Violet's been missing for a while, that she's still alive?"

"That's the impression," Reese admitted. "I also felt a sense of urgency."

"Maybe you've developed the ability to sense what others feel, especially when you're tracking a missing person," Kiki said. "You've become an empath."

"An empath? I've heard of that word before."

"An empath prefers to be alone, which is one of your traits. You also have the uncanny ability to interpret when someone's truthful or not, and you trust your intuition, which a lot of people think is impulsive."

"Jeremy tells me that all the time," Reese said.

"It's not a bad thing," Kiki said. "You pick up on irregularities quicker than others and you care so much you can easily use up your energy. Which you do, because you often seem to be running on empty."

"I suppose," Reese said.

"Read up more about empaths when you get a chance," Kiki suggested.

"Yeah, I'll do that."

"I've got a professor friend at UW that also might be able to answer some questions for you if you make an appointment." Kiki glanced down at her watch. "Let's take one more lap around the lake, running this time."

"All right," Reese said.

They'd nearly finished the lap when Fox dropped his baseball and mitt and screamed, "Ouch!"

Reese and raced over to him with Kiki on her heels. She lifted up the hand he held out to her. A red welt formed on his skin.

"A bee did it," Fox said.

"Are you allergic to bee stings?" Reese's heart thumped in her chest as she considered the possibility. Kiki picked up the baseball and the glove as Reese nudged Fox toward the sidewalk.

"No," Fox said. "It hurts, though. Really bad."

"I'm sure it does," Reese said.

"I reached down to get the baseball and the little butthead stung me," he said.

Relieved she wouldn't have to rush Fox to the hospital, Reese said, "We'll put some baking soda and water on it. That's what my grandmother used when a bee stung me once."

"Do you have lavender essential oil at your house?" Kiki asked, coming up alongside them.

"I do," Reese said.

"It's my favorite oil for treating bug bites and stings," Kiki said. "You can apply it right on the skin. It'll soothe the area and take away the pain."

"Thanks, Kiki," Reese said as she collected the sports gear from her friend. "I'll call you later."

"Take care, you two." Kiki raised her hand in farewell, then turned around and began walking toward her house.

THE LAVENDER OIL DID THE TRICK, and before long, Fox was lounging on Reese's couch, immersed by a game he was playing on his laptop. She called Mrs. Mac and asked her to come over in a half hour. While Fox remained distracted, she hurried through her shower and dressed in jeans, a black graphic T-Shirt that read, "Boss Lady," and a plaid blazer, since the days were getting cooler.

After rolling on socks, she slid her feet into her grandpa's worn, comfortable boots. Smiling, she thought of him and his constant wisecracks and tidbits of wisdom. In her mind, she could hear him say, "Reese, my girl, go make yourself a good life. Don't sit around waiting for it to happen."

"I'm doing my best, Gramps," she murmured, wishing he was here to see her with her own business. Damn, she wished her entire family could see it. Why couldn't people you love be around forever?

If she believed the religious training she'd had while growing up, she should rest assured that she would see them again. Hopefully, there really was something beyond the earthly realm.

While applying a dash of makeup, she heard the front door open and Mrs. Mac's voice rang out as she greeted Fox. Reese grabbed her purse and hustled out into the living room, noting that her neighbor had taken a seat by the boy, observing as he demonstrated how to play his computer game.

"Get going," she told Reese, making a shooing motion with her hand.

"Thanks," Reese said. "I've got a long day ahead."

"Take all the time you need," Mrs. Mac assured her. "Herman's even coming over later with our cornhole board so Fox here can learn a good, old-fashioned game. Not a newfangled online one with those computer animated avatars."

"I like computer games," Fox commented.

"It's good to get outside and breathe some fresh air," Mrs. Mac said.

"Did you tell Mrs. Mac about your bee sting?" Reese asked.

"Yes," Fox said, glancing at his palm.

"And he'll be right as rain," Mrs. Mac said, running a hand through her cropped pink hair. "He's a tough guy. And he's going to call his mother today to see when she might be coming home."

"I'll see you all later." Reese went outside into the bright autumn sunlight. She hopped in her Bronco and drove down to the Meadowlark Valley Police Station. Yet another day had begun in her search for Violet Gentry.

TWENTY-TWO

REESE PARKED IN FRONT OF MEADOWLARK VALLEY'S white cinderblock, two-story police station. She walked past several blue and white squad cars, pushed through the glass entrance door and went inside.

The familiar waiting area held a black leather couch, a couple of mauve chairs and an artificial Ficus tree. She walked toward the office area where several workers sat at desks, concentrating on computer screens. TV monitors hung on walls. Filing cabinets, printers, and book shelves jam-packed the area. After working with Jeremy on several police department cases, the city's cop shop had become a familiar place.

Wearing his typical dark blue polo shirt emblazoned with the Meadowlark Valley Police Department logo, Steve Daniels, the Administrative Coordinator, nodded in her direction.

"Hi Reese," he said.

"Hi," she echoed.

He started to say something else, but before he could speak, Jeremy called out, "How's it going?"

Reese spotted him striding down the corridor toward her.

"Not as good as I'd like," she said, instantly regretting her lack of reassurance. "I'm sure things will pick up soon".

"Did I give you the smoke shop address?"

"I already know where it is," Reese said. "My grandfather used to go there for his cigars back in the day."

"Okay."

"Where are you off to?" Reese noted Jeremy had his keys clutched in his hand.

"There's been a robbery at the Morgan Falls Bank. I'm headed over there."

"That's where Sabrina Byrd's mother works, isn't it?"

"One and the same," Jeremy said. "In fact, it was her that called it in."

Reese shook her head. "It's like we live in the Wild West."

"Yeah, except we can't shoot the bad guys." Jeremy shoved his keys in his pocket, then draped his arm around Reese's shoulders and walked outside with her. "The robber threatened one of the tellers that he'd kill everyone if she didn't hand over the money in her drawer."

"What did she do?"

"Belinda said the teller kept her cool and did everything the robber asked," Jeremy explained. "It was so early, there was only one customer in the bank."

"Where was the security guard?"

"He wasn't there yet."

"That's unfortunate."

"The robber didn't get away with much."

"Yay for that."

"Get this, though. When Belinda gave me the description of the guy, I was floored. He wore a black hooded coat and a black mask. Just like our suspect from the restaurant video."

"Maybe they are one in the same," Reese said.

"Could be. Anyway, I'm going to get the bank staff's statements, then check their security footage. If the perp drove off in a vehicle, I might get a license plate."

"Let's hope so," Reese said.

Jeremy gave Reese a brief kiss, then both of them headed to their vehicles. When Reese climbed into Betty, she fired up her engine and drove away. That weird rattle had disappeared, so her confidence about the truck's performance improved. Maybe she wouldn't have to call the repair shop, after all. The sound could have been a weird fluke.

THE WOLF SMOKE SHOP RESIDED IN A HOLE-IN-THE-WALL spot downtown between two larger brick buildings. Reese eased Betty into a two-hour parking spot. She got out, put on her hat, and strode up to the storefront window which was plastered with cigar advertisements, and neon lights.

Natural American Spirit, Samson, and CAO represented only a few of the brands available for local cigar aficionados. Reese walked up a couple of cement steps and opened the door. A bell attached at the top tinkled brightly, announcing her entrance.

The long, rectangle space, floored with old black and white tile, had held a pharmacy here back in the day, according to Reese's grandfather. The shelves and counters, which had no doubt offered all styles of remedies and medicines, now held stacks of cigar boxes.

The smoky scent took her back in time to trips here with Gramps. She remembered staring at the rows and rows of color-ful boxes as he purchased his favorite brand. He hadn't been a big smoker, but on special occasions, he'd light one up to celebrate.

Memory supplied the pleasant scent Reese always associated with her grandfather's occasional indulgence of smoking his Tatiana cherry-flavored cigars.

"May I help you?" someone with a clipped, British accent asked.

Reese spotted a man dressed in a gray wool blazer and a tan turtleneck standing beneath a wooden ceiling fan at the back of the store. A dignified-looking gentleman, his dark hair bore streaks of silver and Reese imagined he must be in his late forties to early fif-ties. It seemed like he would be at home in the finest restaurants of Europe or vacationing at an exclusive ski chalet in France.

"Yes," Reese said as she walked toward him and handed him one of her business cards. "I'm working with the police on a missing person's case. Violet Gentry? You may have read about it in the newspaper or heard it on the news."

"Everyone has," he said emphatically. "Terrible businesses that, both a kidnapping and a murder. So difficult to believe it's happened in a peaceful place like Meadowlark Valley."

"It is," Reese said.

He moved aside and pointed toward a poster bearing Violet's photo and the pertinent information regarding her case. "Her brother's been most persistent posting these around town. The poor man. I most certainly hope you find her."

"That's my goal," Reese said.

"How can I help you?" he asked.

"I understand you carry the Especial Romeo Cigarro brand."

"Indeed," he said, reaching under the counter and pulling out a gold and red box, which he placed on the counter.

Reese studied the label. "Do they sell well?"

"Not particularly," he said. "It's a cheaper, less-refined brand."

"But there are a few people who purchase them?"

"Yes," he said.

"On a regular basis?"

"More or less," he said. "I know better than to ask why you need to know about them. It's police business, isn't it?"

Reese smiled. "Would you by chance remember who purchases them?"

He pulled out a piece of paper, wrote down three names, then handed it to Reese. "I hope this helps."

"Thank you," Reese said as she took it and moved away from the counter.

"Cheerio," he said.

Outside, Reese kept an eye on the cars cruising back and forth in the street as she got back into her Bronco. Everybody seemed to be in such a hurry as they went about their business. Her heart pounded with impatience as she thought about Violet.

She, too, needed to be in a hurry to resolve the mystery of the woman's disappearance. And she was. Unfortunately, working cases with the police cramped her style. It seemed she had to color within the lines more than if she'd been investigating on her own.

Seated back in her truck, she fished her phone from her purse. Using her people finder app, she looked up the addresses of the individuals who purchased Especial Romeo's. Both lived only a short distance away. Choosing one name, Cyrus Ledbetter, Reese backed out of her parking spot and drove to his home.

She chewed her lower lip, feeling like she could make better use of her time. Unfortunately, right now, the cigar lead was all she had. Maybe Jeremy would be successful checking out the bank's security video. If he could get the plate number of the robber's vehicle, it would be great.

Ledbetter lived on the outskirts of town in a modest-looking white farm house flanked by an old garage with lift-style doors. Surrounded by tall cottonwoods and elms, it boasted a small amount of fenced property holding an older model van, a kiddie pool, and an open-air shelter. All of the neighbors were spaced generously far apart.

Reese rolled into the gravel driveway and stopped. Stepping out of her truck, she headed up to the porch and knocked.

An older woman in a blue housedress dotted with tiny daisies opened the door. The front room beyond her looked like it had been furnished in the 1950s, featuring a long, turquoise couch, two matching chairs, and vintage blonde end tables. Paintings of colorful, geometric shapes covered the walls. A retro turquoise vinyl dinette set filled in an eating area.

"If you're selling something, we're not buying," the woman announced in a nasal tone.

"No, nothing like that." Reese handed her a business card.

"Humph," the woman muttered as she glanced at it.

"I'm looking for Cyrus Ledbetter?"

With a flounce, the woman turned around and hollered, "Cyrus Dale Ledbetter, where the hell are you?"

"What d'ya want now, Ma?" Came the answer from a back room.

"There's someone here to see you," she shouted.

A stocky young man with pale, shoulder-length hair drove his wheelchair up beside the woman. Two small potbellied pigs with black spots trotted alongside him, snorting and squealing. A musky scent permeated the space, which no doubt emanated from the porky pair.

"Shh, you two," he said, leaning over to pet their hairy white backs.

"Have you fed them two today?" the woman asked. "That's probably why they're makin' such a ruckus."

"Yes, Mom, I fed them." Cyrus met Reese's gaze. "You're here to see me?"

"I understand you've purchased the Especial Romeo Cigarro brand of cigars from the Wolf Smoke Shop downtown."

Reese immediately realized he couldn't be her perp, so she decided to make up a harmless story about her reason for coming here.

"Yes, so what's this about?"

"I'm compiling a survey for the company," Reese said. "We're asking people what they like the best about the cigars."

Cyrus scratched his head. "Well, first off their cheap."

"What about the taste?"

"I wouldn't know," Cyrus said. "I feed them to my little friends here, Tootsie and Roger. They're my emotional support animals."

"Land sakes, boy!" his mother said. "I told you not to feed those things to your pigs. It ain't good for 'em."

"The vet says they need lots of fiber in their diets," Cyrus insisted.

"Like alfalfa!" She smacked the side of his head. "Don't do it anymore. Got it?"

"Yep." Cyrus turned to Reese. "Did you need anything else?"

"I appreciate your time," she told him, watching as he returned to the back room. Tootsie and Roger obediently trotted after him.

"My boy lost the use of his legs in a car accident," Mrs. Ledbetter said. "He didn't let that get him down, though. He's a big-time cartoonist."

"That's wonderful," Reese said.

"Ever heard of the Tootsie and Roger cartoon strip?" she asked.

"I don't usually read the comics page," Reese admitted.

"Have a look at it sometime," Mrs. Ledbetter said. "It's down-right funny."

"I'll do that," Reese promised. "Take care, now."

"You, too." Mrs. Ledbetter backed inside of her home and closed the door.

"Crapola, that was a major strikeout," Reese mumbled as she headed toward her truck.

TWENTY-THREE

THE NEXT ADDRESS REESE ARRIVED AT turned out to be a stately, butter-colored Victorian style home located on a large corner lot downtown. Constructed with grand style, perhaps a century ago, it boasted three floors, which included a tower and two balconies. Bordered by lush evergreen bushes, trees, and flower gardens, the old home spoke of elegance from a bygone era.

Tall, narrow windows and ornate gingerbread trim offered both vertical and horizontal details. Carved columns, gables, scrollwork, spindles, and brackets covered the exterior. Truly one of a kind, it would have been difficult for anyone to duplicate this style of architecture. It might be similar, perhaps, but never exact.

After parking along the street, Reese got out of her truck. She strolled past a large sign planted in a cluster of rose bushes that read, Cozy Mansion Bed and Breakfast. Red, yellow, and dark purple daylilies flanked each side of the porch as she walked up several steps and opened the door, which bore an OPEN sign.

Shortly after entering, a tall, willowy woman with brown hair scooted back from a desk and stood. Smiling, she approached Reese, her black silk pantsuit making a whooshing noise as her legs brushed together.

"Hello, do you have reservations with us?" she asked.

"Actually, no, I'm not here to stay," Reese explained as she handed over one of her business cards. "I'm conducting a survey for the company that manufactures the Especial Romeo Cigarro brand of cigars. I received information that an H. G. Culpepper who lives at this address orders them."

From the corner of her eyes, Reese swiftly absorbed her surroundings—a large foyer with wooden floors and a majestic matching staircase with carved balustrades. Antique carpets with matching runners. A marble fireplace, old-fashioned landscape paintings with thick gold frames, a stained-glass window, and ornately carved tables laden with Boston ferns.

"That would be me, Hortense Grace Culpepper." She smoothed down stray hairs that had escaped her bun. "I provide them for our customers. People often like to enjoy them in our drawing room after dinner. Perhaps with a glass of sherry or a fine whiskey."

"I see," Reese said. What a nightmare it would be to try and track down all the individuals who had smoked the cigars over the years.

"Is something amiss?" Hortense asked.

"Do you keep a record of who smokes them?" The question seemed far reaching, even in her own mind.

"Heavens' no," she said. "I never even considered doing that. And I'm not a smoker, so I've never touched them."

"I'm sorry to have wasted your time," Reese said.

"Wait, perhaps my sisters could help you," Hortense said. "Tilly, Tansy, come out here."

"We're right in the middle of making blueberry muffins," a woman shouted.

"Please," Hortense emphasized. To Reese, she explained, "Tilly and Tansy are my twin sisters. They help me run this place."

"It's beautiful," Reese said. "I'm sure you need all-hands-on-deck to keep it in good running order."

"Indeed," Hortense said. "We also hold weddings, business conventions, and other receptions here. If you're ever looking for a venue, please consider us."

"Of course," Reese said.

Tilly and Tansy appeared wearing matching gray jumpers, pink aprons spotted with creamy batter, and pink tennis shoes. While their sister Hortense cut a tall, statuesque figure, they were much shorter, with curly gray hair and matching wire-frame glasses.

"Hello, I'm Tilly," one of them said with a grin. "I prepare the meals here."

"And I'm Tansy," the other twin said. "I make up the beds and do the guests' laundry if needed."

"Will you have a special diet request?" Tilly placed her hands on her hips. "It's no problem to accommodate you."

Hortense handed Tilly the business card and said, "Reese is conducting a survey."

"For TV?" Tansy placed her hands on either side of her cheeks and grinned. "I have so many favorite shows. I could never decide on the best one."

"She's not here to ask you about your TV shows," Hortense said impatiently. "It's for the company that makes those cigars we provide for the customers."

"Oh, that's disappointing," Tansy said.

"I'll be writing a report that details what smokers enjoy the most about the cigars," Reese said. "Also, if they have any suggestions to improve their flavor. Have the customers ever made comments about them?

"No," Tilly said.

"Customers haven't told me anything either," Tansy said. "I tried them though, and let me tell you, I nearly choked to death."

Tilly put a hand on her chest, brows raised. "Those things cause cancer!"

"Since when did you start smoking?" Hortense asked.

"I started and quit the same day," Tansy told her sisters. "Those things taste rotten, so you don't have to worry on my account."

When Reese's cell phone jangled, she cursed inwardly for not shutting off the ringer. Recalling that her phone number had also been listed for people to call in tips about Violet, she removed it from her purse.

"Excuse me, ladies," Reese said to the sisters. "I need to get this."

"Of course," Hortense said.

Reese stepped a few feet away and answered, "Hello?"

"Is this Reese Golden?" a man asked.

"Yes," she said.

"I'm staring at Violet Gentry," he said. "She's at the Harvest Festival."

Reese's heart leapt, and the blood in her veins seemed to pump faster. "It's serious business when someone goes missing. You're not playing a prank, are you?"

"I should say not," he said. "This is Amos Townsend."

"You're on the city council, aren't you?"

"That's right," he said. "I represent Ward Two."

"Where's Violet at, and what's she wearing?" Reese asked.

"She's hanging out by the Cowboy Kissing Booth," he said. "She's wearing a University of Wyoming hoodie, and jeans."

"Thanks," Reese said.

"Anything to help," he said.

"I have to run, ladies," Reese told Hortense and her sisters. "I appreciate your input."

"Of course," Hortense said.

"Any time," Tilly said.

"Come back when you can stay," Tansy added.

Reese hustled out of the bed and breakfast and back to her truck. She called Jeremy, but he didn't answer, so she left a message on his voice mail.

"Amos Townsend spotted Violet at the Harvest Festival by the Cowboy Kissing Booth," she told him. "I'm going to check it out. Come find me when you get this."

She jumped into Betty and drove to the annual affair located at the Cooper Farm just outside of town. Her heart drummed with anticipation and her right foot pressed too hard on the gas pedal.

Hopefully, a cop wouldn't pull her over.

RECENT RAIN HAD LEFT THE FARM'S parking area full of muddy potholes. Although Reese tried her hardest to dodge the craters, the Bronco continued thumping through them. Pretty certain that the truck now wore splotches of dripping brown on the sides, Reese found a spot and parked.

Sliding down from the driver's seat, she stepped out onto the grass and did her best to walk around the brownie batter sludge. At a small wooden shack painted with cornstalks, she paid for her entrance ticket, and stepped into a world of autumn activity.

The aroma of popcorn, hot dogs, and roasted peanuts permeated the air. It took her back to the days when she'd attended the festival with her mom and little brother. What fun she and Jesse had had sprinting from booth to booth, trying to decide what to try first. Meanwhile, their mother followed patiently, reminding them not to wander away and become lost.

Fast forwarding to the present day, Reese's gaze slid past trees bursting with rust and lemon-yellow leaves, ridges of sunflowers nodding their large heads, hay bales, pumpkins, and baskets brimming with decorative squash and Indian corn. Voices of the young and old, combined with blaring country music, made for a loud commotion. Reese studied the different venues, desperately seeking the Cowboy Kissing Booth.

A photo booth for families, pony rides, a floating duck game, face painting, pumpkin tossing, sack races, and food vendors blurred together as she searched. Parents strolled by with kids in tow, talking, laughing, and issuing instructions to their offspring.

At last, Reese spotted her destination over by the hayride wagon. Three muscular guys in western wear and cowboy hats posed next to a blue booth, which advertised one kiss for $5, two for $10 and three for $15. All proceeds went to the local animal shelter.

Reese studied the line of people, seeking Violet. She noticed that whenever ladies went behind the curtains with one of the country hunks, they came back out laughing as they clutched foil-wrapped chocolate kiss candy.

"Clever," Reese muttered, easing her way through the crowd.

At last, she was rewarded for her efforts when a dark-haired woman in a UW sweatshirt walked out from behind the curtains. Her cowboy hat shaded most of her face, but her build looked familiar.

"Violet," Reese called out, walking toward her. "I need to talk to you!"

Violet bolted into the corn maze, flying past the wooden sign. Either side was flanked by scarecrows attached to fat wooden posts, and they seemed to give Reese mocking stares.

"Oh crap, a runner," she growled.

She raced after Violet, observing when she brushed past a corner teeming with tall, crackling cornstalks. A sign read, "Watch for flying monkeys."

A group of people moved into her way, blocking her progress. Two children, two ladies—the younger one harnessed with a baby carrier—and a very tall man. Reese could hardly make her way past them.

Finally, she squeezed by, only to be met with a beaten dirt path shaded on all sides by more tall, leafy cornstalks that nearly blotted out the sun. At the end of the corridor, the trail split into three different directions. Violet was nowhere in sight.

Should I go left, right, or straight ahead?

Corn mazes used to be a fun challenge as a kid. This time? Not so much. Which way had Violet gone?

With no clear answer, Reese headed down the trail to the right. Her nose started to burn, and twitch. Her eyes watered.

"Just what I need, an allergy attack!"

Ignoring her symptoms, she forged on, making her way past other people being entertained by the twisting, turning path. A little girl with curly flaxen hair flew past Reese, screaming and laughing. She wore a black long-sleeved shirt, black tights, and a bright pink tutu skirt that flounced as she ran.

Mere seconds later, two little boys appeared, also screaming and laughing as they ran lickety-split after the girl. It seemed safe to continue, so Reese hustled farther down the path, passing by another scarecrow holding up a message board.

"Lost? Wait and we'll be by soon to help," the sign read.

Running through rows of corn would never be on Reese's top ten list of fun things to do. Since the stalks blocked air movement, warmth crept its way through the stagnant air. Perspiration pooled on Reese's body and dotted her forehead. Queasiness nearly stole her determination, and she felt dizzy. Her eyes watered and itched.

Along with her allergic reaction, she felt ready to give up. Straight ahead, through her bleary eyes, she saw someone wearing brown and yellow. She hustled toward the individual.

Grabbing an arm, Reese growled, "Violet, for Pete's sake, stop running!"

"My name isn't Violet," the woman shouted, spinning around to glare at Reese. She had dark hair styled in a similar manner as Violet's, but her heavily made-up face told the truth.

Reese didn't recognize her. The fact that she'd been chasing after someone she didn't need to lanced her gut, and she felt sick. She couldn't blame Amos Townsend for making the same mistake she had.

"I, I thought you were someone else," Reese said, wishing she could melt into her boots.

"Obviously," the woman said, yanking away from Reese's grip.

"Why did you run from me?"

"I thought you might be a cop."

"Why is that a problem?"

The woman sneered at Reese. "Wouldn't you like to know."

"I don't carry a badge," Reese said. "You're safe."

The woman's lips twitched as she looked around to make sure no one else was watching. She reached into her pocket and held up a joint between her thumb and forefinger.

"Now leave me alone." The woman tossed strands of hair over her shoulders. "I've got to go back and find my friends. They probably think I left without them."

"I wish you would have talked with me in the first place. It could have saved us both a lot of trouble."

"Oh, well," the woman said. "It sucks to be you."

She ran off down another path of the maze.

Reese rubbed her watery eyes, then removed a tissue from her purse and blew her dripping nose. Another group of kids scrambled past her, slopping through a mud puddle and about knocking her on her can.

Reese wiped dripping moisture from her face.

"Nah, nah, nah, nah, nah, nah," a little boy in a red sweatshirt taunted her.

"Nah, nah, nah, yourself," Reese called out.

Laughing hysterically, the kid took off after his friends, no doubt believing his antics were amusing.

Bone weary, Reese headed down another dirt trail, hoping she'd manage to locate the exit to this wacky maze. She'd wasted more time on this goat rope than she wanted to admit, which did not make her happy.

Clues to Violet's whereabouts were evaporating as quickly as she found them. Trudging along the endless path was giving her a massive headache. Even the dry, drooping cornstalk leaves seemed to be scornful of her. She vowed never to eat another kernel of corn, even if her life depended on it.

When she turned a corner, she came upon a young man and a young lady smooching. She stumbled to a stop and they abruptly parted.

"Excuse me," she said as she backed away, feeling like the biggest dum-dum on the planet. "I'm totally lost."

"Don't worry, I know the way out of here," the guy said with a chuckle. Taking his girlfriend's hand, the couple walked down another path, with Reese plodding along behind. After a couple more twists and turns, afternoon sun backlighted a large field of waving grass, beyond which the festival was taking place.

TWENTY-FOUR

SPOTTING JEREMY PACING BY THE COWBOY Kissing Booth, Reese hurried toward him.

"Where were you?" he asked, looking a tad annoyed.

"Chasing a ghost through the corn maze," she said. "It wasn't Violet. Looked like her from a distance, but no dice."

"I didn't get your message right away or I'd have been here sooner," he said, weariness threading his voice. "It took longer than I expected at the bank."

"What about the robber? Did you get a look at the bank's security video to see what kind of vehicle he drove?"

"His getaway car was a big chestnut horse."

"You've got to be kidding," Reese said.

"It's no joke," he confirmed.

"Wade's visitor at the reservoir rode a chestnut horse."

"It would be remarkable if the bank robber turned out to be our suspect in that case."

"And now he's in the wind again." Reese rubbed the back of her neck, trying to massage away the tenseness. "Could this day be any less productive?"

"Don't say that out loud and tempt the fates," Jeremy said.

Reese's phone rang and she removed it from her back pocket. "Reese Golden," she answered.

"Hello, this is Dirk Phillips from the Wolf Smoke Shop," he said.

"We spoke earlier about the Especial Romeo Cigarros."

"Yes," Reese said.

"My apologies for not giving this name to you earlier, but I remembered there's another individual who purchases that particular brand."

"Is that so?"

"Frida Crawford gets them," he said. "Last week, she came in and bought a new box."

"Thanks for following up with me," Reese said.

"You're most welcome," Dirk said.

Reese clicked off the call, then looked up Frida's address on her phone. Spur Road was outside of town, and the idea of driving all the way out to heck and gone on another wild goose chase didn't sit well with her. Nevertheless, she couldn't pass up an opportunity that might produce a lead.

"What's up?" Jeremy asked.

"It was Dirk Phillips from the cigar shop," Reese said. "Frida Crawford just got a box of cigarros last week. She lives way out in the boonies not far from the Gentry Ranch."

Jeremy glanced down at his wrist watch. "I've got to get back to the station to write up my report. Otherwise, I'd drive out there."

"I'll take care of it," Reese said.

Discussing their current case, the two started walking from the festival grounds and out into the parking lot.

When they reached Reese's truck, Jeremy said, "By the way, I finally got Violet's phone records, which have nothing in the way of a lead that we can follow up on."

"Crap," Reese said. "And horses don't have license plates, so we can't follow up on the bank robber, either."

"I've got a couple of officers patrolling the neighborhood the bank robber disappeared into. They're going to knock on a few doors, see if anyone noticed which direction he went."

"Maybe we'll get lucky," Reese said, doubting any useful information would come their way.

"Neeta Poole also emailed me a copy of the restaurant's security video," Jeremy added. "I'm going to watch it again. Maybe we missed something; a detail or a clue."

"Let me know if you come up with anything."

"Sure." He looked her up and down. "How are you holding up?"

"I'm fine," she said.

"No more threats?"

Reese shook her head. Working on this case really made her feel uneasy, especially with Fox staying at her place. Yet, she didn't want to admit that to Jeremy. She'd gotten spooked when someone had tried to run her over, but felt okay now. By choosing a career as a private investigator, she'd taken the risk of potentially being targeted on different cases.

"I worry about you," he said.

"I promise you, Jeremy, I'm okay," Reese said. "I can't help that sometimes I'm defensive about what I do, but I worked hard to learn the ropes of this job, and to be able to hold my own."

Jeremy took her hand and kissed the back of it. "Stay safe, and don't take any unnecessary chances. I like having you around."

"The same goes for you, Detective," Reese said. "I like having you around, too."

Jeremy gave her an encouraging grin, then sauntered away. Reese watched him for a few seconds, realizing that the two of them were growing closer with each passing day, then climbed into her Bronco. She switched on the engine and drove away from the Harvest Festival. Since it was sliding into late afternoon, she decided that after visiting Frida Crawford, she'd head home.

If they were fortunate, maybe Jeremy would find another clue on Sweet Clementine's security video. Admittedly, they'd been in a hurry when they watched it in Neeta's office earlier in the week. They'd also been distracted, knowing the police were processing the scene of a homicide right outside of the restaurant.

Driving down a gravel road, Reese studied the country homes, barns, and other outbuildings scattered across the prairie, which was ringed by jagged peaks. Fenced pastures held cattle and horses, munching away on clumps of grass. Fields of dry cornstalks stretched into the distance like ragged soldiers.

At one farm, someone in a large green tractor tilled the ground, possibly in preparation for planting hard red winter wheat, which would be harvested come July. No doubt the farmer wanted to get the task finished before the first frost, which in Wyoming, could happen any time now.

A shaggy, black and white dog decided Reese had gotten too close to its territory. It jumped from the front porch of a house and ran down the lane barking. Reaching the end of the road, it slid to a stop and watched warily as she drove past.

Reese spotted the sign for Spur Road in the distance. When she reached the turnoff, she drove past a few older houses and double-wide trailers. She scanned the numbers on the metal mailboxes until she saw Frida's address.

Turning down the graveled drive, she passed a two-story home surrounded by black, broken tree stumps and overgrown grass. A dingy cantaloupe color, the design looked like something constructed in the 1960s. Broken windows and doors hanging on hinges indicated the place was abandoned.

Beside the house sat a shed covered with a bent, corrugated metal sheet. Grass and weeds clogged the perimeter of the leaning structure, which housed a rusted, broken-down ancient car. Dead trees encircled the vignette, the branches stretching across the roof like brittle, blackened fingers.

Rounding a corner, she came upon a gray one-level, stick built home with blue shutters and a porch. New sod had been laid up to the edge of the foundation and several saplings, staked for support, dotted the yard. The gravel drive ended a short distance from the residence where an oversize two-car metal garage sat. Nearby, the sun glimmered off of a shiny black GMC Sierra Denali and a luxury travel trailer.

Everything appeared to be in great shape, so Reese guessed

Frida Crawford had recently acquired the additions. She parked Betty and walked up to the front door. Aside from the flower pot full of dry, withering yellow chrysanthemums, and a large wooden bear sculpture, nothing else sat on the concrete porch. She rang the doorbell, stood back, and waited. When no one answered, she tried again, then knocked. The only thing she heard was a buzzing motor sound coming from somewhere nearby.

Deciding no one was home, Reese surveyed the small farm area that held a chicken coop and a pasture with a few Guernsey cattle. One of them hung its head over the fence boards, chewing its cud while it watched her.

"How now brown cow," Reese teased as she walked toward it. It mooed, tossed its head, and continued chewing. While patting the bovine, she spotted a metal barn nestled at the bottom of a hill. A couple of horses stood in the adjacent penned area. Nearby, penned goats chomped on grass.

As she hiked down to investigate, a flock of tiny birds sitting in an overgrown bush took flight, obviously frightened by her appearance. Several crows in the tree next to it remained, staring down at Reese with dark, baleful eyes.

Those black critters seemed to be perched everywhere she went these days.

She made clicking sounds to the horses. "Aren't you two beautiful?"

Nickering, the horses trotted over to the fence and Reese reached out to stroke their muzzles. The velvet sensation brought back memories of when she'd worked on a dude ranch as a teenager during the summer. She'd started as a stall cleaner, then became a groom, working her way up to become a trail guide, tacking up horses and guiding visitors.

"I wish I had some treats," she said, admiring their colors—a dappled gray and a chestnut.

Chestnut?

That was the color of horse ridden by the unfriendly rider who had approached Wade Gentry. And it was the color of horse ridden by the bank robber today. That didn't mean anything, really. Chestnut was a common horse color, yet it piqued her interest and got her thinking.

Ch-chunk!

When the unmistakable sound of a shotgun being racked assaulted Reese's eardrums, she froze, and held up her hands.

TWENTY-FIVE

"YOU'RE TRESPASSIN'," SOMEONE WARNED IN A gravelly tone. "I didn't mean to cause any trouble," Reese said, turning around slowly.

The voice belonged to a tall, thin woman with a leathery face and two thick, iron gray braids. She wore a flared jeans skirt, boots, a black turtleneck, a knitted sweater vest, and a beanie hat topped with a floppy pom-pom. Her piercing blue eyes bored into Reese as she glared over the shotgun barrel.

"What did you come here for?"

"I'm looking for Frida Crawford," Reese said, on edge, and wondering what to expect to happen next.

"I'm Frida," she growled. "What's it to ya?"

"I'm a private investigator," Reese said. "I'm conducting a survey for the company that manufactures Especial Romeo Cigarros."

"You don't say?" Frida narrowed her gaze.

Reese stared at the shotgun, imagining the giant sinkhole one of its bullets could make in her chest. "Uh, can you put that thing down?"

Frida continued glaring down the barrel at her. "How do I know you aren't a burglar stakin' out my place?"

"I've got business cards that prove who I am," Reese quickly replied. "If you're okay with me getting one out, I'll give it to you."

"Go on," Frida said with a nod. "Don't make any sudden moves and I won't shoot."

Peachy, Reese thought. Carefully, she reached into her purse and removed one, handing it to Frida.

With a sour look on her face, Frida read it. She lowered her weapon.

"I promise, I didn't mean to startle you," Reese emphasized, finally able to breathe freely without the shotgun in her face.

"Well, you did."

"I rang your doorbell and I knocked," Reese said. "When no one answered, I assumed you weren't home."

"Yet you busted your butt to come down here and fool with my horses?"

"I love horses," Reese said. "I live in town so I can't have any. Yours caught my eye and I couldn't resist."

Frida pressed her lips into a thin, disapproving line. However, she relaxed her shoulders, and she seemed less upset about Reese's intrusion.

"Did you see the bear statue sitting on my porch?" Frida asked.

"I did," Reese said.

"I design those for craft shows and special orders," Frida said. "I've got a woodshop at the back of my garage over yonder. I've been working out there all day with my chainsaw."

"That must be the noise I heard," Reese said.

"What d'you want to know about those cigars?" Frida asked.

"The company wants me to study customer satisfaction and to see if anyone has suggestions about improving the flavor," Reese said.

"Hmph," Frida said. "I don't smoke the suckers."

"Oh?"

"My boy Wyatt smokes 'em," Frida said. "I like to keep them around for him."

"I see," Reese said, her interest piqued. "Does he live here?"

"Yes," Frida said, then added quickly, "on occasion. I haven't seen him in close to six months or so. He travels for work."

"What is his profession?"

"Investments of some sort," Frida said. "I don't make much from my chainsaw art, but Wyatt is generous. He makes sure I have everything I need. I figure he must be pretty successful, considering all the help he's given me."

"Do you know if he'll be coming home any time soon?"

Frida's gaze took on a suspicious gleam. "What's with all the questions?"

"I'd like to stop by another time to talk with your son about the cigars," Reese said. "I won't get paid if I don't have survey results. You know how that is, making ends meet and all."

"Sure, yeah, I get it." Frida sighed heavily. "My whole life I've had to rob Peter to pay Paul. Wyatt's financial help the last few years have made a huge difference. I don't live like a pauper no more."

"When do you expect him home?" Reese pressed.

"Hell, I have no idea," Frida said. "That boy shows up whenever he feels like it. He never tells me."

"Kids are a handful, am I right?" Reese decided to try and relate to Frida's mothering challenges. "They march to be the beat of their own drum."

"They sure do," Frida agreed. "You got any rug rats?"

"Not yet," Reese said. "But I've had plenty of experience helping with my little brother, er, brothers. I understand what they're like."

In the back of Reese's mind, she thought about Fox. She couldn't be certain he was her brother, but she also couldn't rule it out yet.

"Have you heard that old poem that goes, 'Snakes and snails and puppy dog tails, that's what boys are made of?'"

"A long time ago," Frida said.

They both chuckled, and Frida leaned her shotgun against the fence.

"In order to raise boys, you have to be a special kind of crazy," Frida said. "From the time Wyatt was little, I insisted he follow my rules, but he hated 'em. He would act out and do crazy shit like smash his toys if he didn't get his way. I'd put him in time out, and he'd sulk. When he got in school, he hated doing homework. He'd piss and moan whenever I made him finish assignments."

"I get the impression that raising Wyatt was like trying to break a wild horse," Reese said.

"That's putting it mildly," Frida said.

"Being a mother is difficult." Reese folded her arms across her chest. "You feel ultimately responsible for another human being's life."

"That's a fact," Frida said. "And I wonder if I was too hard on him. He created imaginary friends who he claims told him to do bad things, like play with matches and fry snakes on the electric fence."

Reese winced. "He sounds like a typical kid to me."

"I reckon. And I did my best raising him alone."

"His father wasn't in the picture?"

Frida shook her head. "I remember Wyatt getting so upset when other kids had their dads, but his pa was gone. I figure he blamed me that his dad ran off."

"I'm sure as he got older, he understood," Reese said, fishing for more details.

"In the end, it seemed like I could never give Wyatt enough love and that I couldn't do anything right for him."

Reese remembered struggling with troubled emotions after her grandparents took over raising her at age 12. She regretted that she hadn't made it very easy on them. They had shown incredible patience to keep her in line and help her remain focused on the important things in life.

"Growing up isn't easy," she mused. "The teenage years can do a real number on a kid's self-image. Raging hormones and social media don't help."

"Thank goodness Wyatt's gotten past all that now." Frida tucked strands of loose hair behind her ears.

"You have an amazing view out here," Reese said as she looked around. "How long have you had this place?"

"My whole life," Frida said.

"Really?"

"Yep, my great, great grandpappy immigrated to Wyoming from Quebec, Canada in the 1880s. He could only speak French, but he was a hard worker and he hired out as a ranch helper. Later on, he started his own homestead with a tiny log cabin, a barn, and a chicken coop."

"Sounds like he was determined," Reese said.

"That he was," Frida said. "Unfortunately, Grandpappy gave up his original homestead during the Johnson County War. He got in the way of those big cattle barons that were taking up all the land. They accused him of being a squatter, and of rustling their cattle. They nearly hanged him."

"That's awful," Reese said, recalling what she'd read about that incident. It was a terrible blotch on Wyoming history. She also recalled the comments on Violet's social media made by Romeo Jackrabbit, accusing the Gentry's of stealing their land.

In her gut, she sensed a connection of some sort, but nothing she could nail down.

"Grandpappy left the territory before things got really bad," Frida continued. "Otherwise, he'd have probably ended up dangling from the end of a rope. He moved his family farther south, down here, away from the trouble."

"How terrible that he lost his land," Reese said.

"He decided that was the best thing to do," Frida said, obvious pride shining in her eyes. "He valued the lives of his family more than saving his homestead."

While Frida continued to stroll down memory lane, recounting her family's history, Reese scanned the rolling farmland. Most of the acres had been cleared, but sagebrush, clumps of tall grass, trees, and bushes edged the periphery.

"Over the years, my family has gradually sold off parcels of Grandpappy's land to pay bills," Frida said. "This place is all that's left."

"I see," Reese said.

Frida picked up her shotgun and eased toward the metal garage. "If we're through here, I need to get back to work."

"Thanks for your time," Reese told her.

"Good luck writing your report."

"My what?" Reese floundered for a second, then remembered her excuse for asking about the cigars. She laughed unsteadily. "Of course, the report."

Frida's brows drew together, as if she'd picked up on Reese's absentmindedness. Did she suspect Reese had another reason for coming here today? She didn't say anything, so Reese did her best to cover up her blunder.

"I got so caught up in your story," she quickly rambled. "I kind of lost track. My bad. If Wyatt comes around, give me a call. I'd like to get his opinion on those cigarros."

"Will do," Frida promised.

Reese headed back to her truck, noting that Frida kept an eye on her as she climbed into Betty and drove away. Glancing in the rearview mirror, she spotted Frida gripping her shotgun, grimacing at her.

TWENTY-SIX

VIBRANT AUTUMN COLORS SPLASHED the rustling tree leaves as Reese observed the countryside through her open window. Nature's symphony never got old. Humming insects and resonating birdsong, along with the comforting sights and the sounds, filled her with peace.

Only the purple clouds mounded on the horizon marred the afternoon, indicating the pleasant weather could change soon. Moisture wouldn't be a bad thing, Reese decided. Wyoming's dry climate could always use a douse of H20. Inhaling another whiff of the fresh air that also ruffled her curls, she detected the dampness of oncoming rain.

Shafts of late afternoon sun trickled across haystacks and old log buildings. Edging the road like fine lace, colorful wildflowers trembled in the breeze. A church with faded white paint reminded her of her childhood, and how she'd always been fascinated by the three wooden crosses planted nearby in the blue-green sagebrush.

Her gaze drifted toward four deer grazing in a field beneath several large cottonwoods. Tempted by their wild beauty, she slowed down. One of the does looked up, watching her with large black eyes.

Scruffy looking with chunks of fur on their hides, Reese realized the animals had shed their summer coats, and had grown in thicker winter ones. This shaggier covering would absorb warm sunlight and hold more body heat to guard them from freezing temperatures.

In the distance, she spotted the outline of Bluff High School, which sat on a neglected asphalt road. Built in 1924, the turn-of-the-century-style red brick building boasted three floors. Local kids had received their secondary education there, until the new facility in town had been built. According to the old timers, the school had apparently been quite a grand dame when first constructed.

These days, it had a general look of abandonment. The darkening skies and ominous rain clouds gave it a sinister appearance. She wished someone would take on the task of renovating and repurposing the place. Unfortunately, historical preservation societies often didn't have the money to spare for those projects since they operated mostly on grants, loans, and donated funds.

Overgrown with weeds and tall brown grass, the once-green, manicured lawn had gone native. Graffiti painted near the double door entrance had never been erased, and the puffy black letters surrounded in white spelled out, "No more thought control!"

An ancient bus sat adjacent to the building, serving as a reminder that the school had once hosted important daily activity. The vehicle's tires had been slashed, so it slanted onto broken chunks of pavement. It looked lonely and lost. Sitting next to it sat a rusty station wagon, covered in stickers and spray-painted handwriting.

"What the heck?" Reese slowed down and turned off on a side road, her blood pumping as she remembered the description of their suspect's car.

She traveled down a bumpy dirt road and pulled into the cracked parking lot covered in potholes and choked with weeds. Overshadowing trees spread their branches across the area, blocking out the waning sunlight.

She honestly didn't want to go into that place alone, yet curiosity won. The overwhelming urge to explore took control. If Violet's attacker was lurking around in the empty building, she wanted to find him. After parking Betty beside the station wagon, she shoved her keys in a back pocket and grabbed her cell phone.

A few raindrops splashed on her face as she got out of her Bronco. The thought of getting caught in a downpour didn't thrill her. Blessed with an inquisitive nature, however, Reese felt the urge to press onward. She examined the station wagon's license plates, which had been pieced together with metal strips. The front one said, "Peace," and the back one said, "Out."

"Crap," Reese said. How in the heck did this joker drive around town with fake plates and never get stopped by law enforcement?

Glancing through the dust-streaked windows at the mess inside, she noticed heaps of random clothes, along with food wrappings, soda cans, and other trash. When her gaze landed on a bloody rag, Reese froze. She tried to open the doors, but they were all locked. Whipping out her cell phone, she snapped pictures of the vehicle at different angles.

The hair on the back of her neck prickled, and she sensed someone watching her. Replacing her cell in her pocket, she looked up. On the second floor, a figure in a long, black hooded jacket watched her from a window.

When he moved away, Reese hustled toward the building. Door by door, she checked for any way to enter. Broken windows were plentiful, but none that would allow her to climb inside.

Behind the school, she hurried toward a set of concrete steps leading up to a double door entrance. Climbing them two at a time, she found one side had been wedged open.

Pulling out her cell, she called Jeremy.

"What's up?" he asked.

"I'm at the old Bluff High," Reese said breathlessly. "I think Violet's abductor is hiding out here."

"The abandoned school outside town?"

"Yes."

"I'll send out a squad car. I'll be right behind them."

"Good," Reese said. "But I'm going in."

"Wait till we get there," Jeremy cautioned.

"I'm afraid he'll run."

"If you find him, what are you going to do?" Jeremy made a frustrated sound. "What if he's got a gun?"

"Just because I don't have a weapon, it doesn't mean I can't handle a perp," Reese shot back.

"But—"

She hung up and slid her phone back into her pocket. Now wasn't the time for Jeremy to get all macho on her. While she appreciated his concern, she believed his feelings sometimes overshadowed his common sense. She had a responsibility to her client, Tag Gentry, and to the police department, to do her job.

She entered the cold, dark school, brushing past overturned furniture, books, and scattered papers. Cracked plaster walls rose on either side, broken gray tiles littered the floor, and the dirty, streaked windows allowed in only filtered light.

Shuffling through the hallway debris, she peered through several open doors. All the classrooms were littered with broken student desks, chairs, and other random furniture. Blackboards displayed a film of white chalk dust, and one bore a game of hangman. Walls held torn maps and crooked-hanging posters

Homeless people apparently made this their occasional camp site because makeshift beds of rags and old blankets lined the walls. Fast-food wrappers, soda cans, and water bottles gave Reese images of people shivering in the cold, eating unhealthy meals, although they'd probably been grateful for what they could scrounge.

A small jump rope with red plastic handles, a tattered doll in a broken carriage, and a set of jacks cluttered one area. Reese shuddered, thinking of the displaced kids who had once called this place home. Meadowlark Valley's community services had improved vastly in recent years. Hopefully individuals in transition could now find better accommodations than this place.

Dust from the filthy interior tickled her nose. Sneezing and coughing, she approached a smashed wooden table that appeared to have come from a library. It wasn't too difficult to break off one of the legs. Holding it over her shoulder like a baseball bat, she resumed searching.

Her quest took her around the entire main floor and through the office area, the large cafeteria, the auditorium, bathrooms, and another room with torn, blue vinyl couches that had probably held the teachers' lounge.

Climbing stairs to the second floor, she kept a cautious watch, then searched a couple more rooms. From the corner of her eye, she caught movement. Spinning around, she saw a tall man with black hair, dark, soulless eyes, and a scar across his forehead. His lips curled, revealing sharp, filed teeth.

Like a wild animal.

He reached out to grab her, but she swung the table leg, smacking his midsection. Emitting a groan, he backed away from her. He tripped on a chunk of tile and tumbled to the floor, sending up a cloud of debris.

Dust tickled Reese's nose.

Overwhelmed by a fit of sneezing, she stumbled backward. Quick to take advantage, the guy pushed to his feet and began running. Reese followed him to the stairwell and scrambled down the steps after him.

His head start and longer legs got him to the first floor faster. By the time Reese made it, he was nowhere in sight. Impatience lanced through her as she searched for him.

As she walked past a doorway that held a stairwell leading down to the basement, she heard heavy footfalls. She raced down to the lower level, sneezing again as the dank atmosphere closed around her. Small basement windows lining the top of the walls allowed in only weak sun, so she pulled out her cell phone and switched on the flashlight app.

I can't see squat.

A second later, her eyes adjusted to the dimness. Her progress was slow, considering she had to scoot around piles of boxes and old furniture. A gigantic steam boiler with its boxy metal body, snaking pipes, and valves took shape. Reese realized this must be the school's maintenance area.

She encountered a tile wall that supported dented metal lockers. Across from those, along the top of the walls, were rusted and broken shower heads. Apparently, this is where gym classes cleaned up after games, or after students sweated through P.E. It also stunk to high heaven.

Gripping the table leg tighter, she stepped up a concrete ramp and passed through a doorway. A large, tiled room stretched ahead. Banks of long windows up along the ceiling allowed in more light, which revealed the large, empty swimming pool.

She walked along the deck of the pool, checking behind boxes and large wooden crates. At the sound of running footsteps, she glanced through another doorway just in time to see her target dart up another staircase. She sprinted after him, but the toe of her boot snagged on something.

Grabbing the wall to steady herself, she glanced down. Her eyes went wide when she realized she'd tripped on a skeletal foot, which was attached to a human skeleton wearing tattered jeans shorts, a bra, and a pink tank top. The white bones splayed out next to a dirty, stained mattress, one of the wrists attached via handcuffs to a radiator grate.

TWENTY-SEVEN

IGNORING THE SQUEAMISH STAB TO HER STOMACH, Reese pursued the guy out of the basement and up the stairs to the first floor. She spotted him as he rocketed around a corner and pushed through the set of double doors that led outside.

Reese took off after him. By the time she caught up, he was speeding through the parking lot. Rain steadily fell to the ground, splashing on the dusty weeds and dirt. It was soaking him, and it was soaking Reese.

"Stop," she cried at him, tossing aside the table leg.

He gave her only a quick glance, then unlocked the driver's door of his car, then got in. His vehicle roared into life and tore off down the road.

Digging out her keys, Reese flew toward her Bronco, jumped in and sped after him. When he reached the end of the dirt road, he turned left, with Reese right on his tail.

Puffs of smoke shot out from the station wagon's exhaust pipe, producing a cloud of grayish-black smoke. Reese blasted through it. She figured the jerk must be floor-boarding his gas pedal.

As rain pelted the windshield, she switched on her wipers. Each time she caught up to the guy, he accelerated and zipped ahead, pushing on toward a recreational area. *How in the world did his old hunk of junk hold together?* Wind began whipping through the area, shaking trees and bushes in a gyrating dance.

Heart hammering in her ears, Reese navigated the twists and turns, keeping an eye on the ever-worsening weather as well as the car ahead of her.

The road slanted uphill past reddish Sherman granite boulders shaped like giant chunks of Tootsie Roll. Piles of them slanted into rock formations, protruding through the yellow aspen leaves and spires of green spruce. Remembering the Native American lore attached to this place, Reese thought about their belief that playful spirits had stacked the rock, mimicking the look of stone pillars. In the distance, cliff ledges outlined a valley of brownish green.

"Crap," Reese shouted as she drove past a sign indicating they were entering Takkoa Recreation Area. Located on the northern edge Medicine Bow National Forest, there were numerous ways leading around the stone pinnacles. Within the mish-mash of roads, it would be too easy for her to lose this speed demon.

Teeth clenched, she pushed Betty to her limit, coming up along-side of the station wagon. The suspect kept looking over at her, his face lined with furious resolve. That look of hatred—and his dead eyes—would be forever etched in Reese's mind.

"Get over," she growled, doing her best to try and steer him onto the road's shoulder. He might have a gun, Reese recalled Jeremy warning her. Obviously, he didn't, otherwise he would have used it by now.

Farther and farther, he pushed into the recreation area, once known as a hiding area for outlaws. Since not much of the terrain had changed in all these years, it remained a good place to lay low. Even though small clearings held picnic tables, fire rings, and camping sites, they were deserted this close to the end of tourist season.

Reese stopped trying to force the guy to pull over. He obviously wasn't going to do it. Determination coursed through her and she continued riding his bumper. As long as she had this jerk in her sight, she'd stay on his tail.

No way would he slip through her fingers.

As the sky drew darker with thick storm clouds, visibility became more difficult. She strained to make out shapes, perspiration coating her brow. Her nerves felt taut, like a rubber band stretched to its full capacity.

A ravine formed to the right, the edges covered in sagebrush and deep grass. Only a trickle of silver moisture ran along the bottom. At one time, it must have held a much larger body of water, perhaps a stream, since a stone and wood bridge crossed over the banks. If this storm turned into a gully washer, it would fill quickly.

A heavy-duty bump in the road lifted her up, then down hard on her seat. Her teeth clattered together, knocking the breath from her. Her scrambled mind took a second or two to clear. When she returned her gaze to the road, the station wagon had disappeared.

"Son of a banshee!" Reese slowed down, studying the bushes for movement, hoping to see movement that would indicate which way the station wagon had turned. Not even a stick moved.

Rain sluiced down as if someone had thrown a bucket of water across her truck. She could barely make out an intersection of three dirt roads up ahead surrounded by granite boulders. Hesitation gripped her.

Which way should I turn?

"Here goes nothing," she said as she went down the left side, hoping like hell she'd chosen wisely. The bumping rattled her skull, but she didn't see the station wagon. Hope dwindled within her; defeat taking its place. After another half hour of following the twisting road, trying to see through the pouring rain, she finally admitted she'd lost this round.

Thunk, thunk.

After that warning sound, the Bronco's engine cut out, leaving Reese stranded in the middle of the road. She did her best to remain patient for a second, then she tried restarting the engine.

It made a sound like a dying moose.

Reese slammed her hands down on the steering wheel. "Betty, don't do this to me!"

She waited another second, then tried again. It was no use. The engine was dead, dead, dead.

The sound of a revving engine exploded. She looked up in time to see the battered old station wagon bearing down on her. The guy had probably been watching her from behind trees or rocks. With Betty out of commission, he'd taken his cue to come after her.

"Come on, girl!" Reese tried starting the engine again. "You can do it!"

She was about to bail from her Bronco and run when Betty finally turned over. Reese hit the gas and lurched forward, right before being rear ended. Now, with the old station wagon on her tail, Reese flew down the road like a madwoman.

Checking her rearview mirror, she noted that the station wagon had disappeared again. A mixture of relief and disappointment shot through her. This guy obviously knew this territory well. Once again though, he was in the wind.

When her cell rang, she pulled over to the side of the road and took a calming breath. Phone in hand, she looked at the number. *Jeremy*. He'd probably give her hell.

"Hey," she answered, the relentless downpour pounding in her ears.

"I'm sure you realized you were breaking and entering private property when you went into the old high school, right?"

"First off, the back door was already open when I got there."

He grunted noncommittally, then asked, "Where are you? Wait, I'm actually afraid to find out."

"Wow, you're a real grumpy ass today, aren't you?" Reese's blood began to boil.

"Sorry, I didn't sleep well last night." He gave a heavy sigh. "And like always, you never, ever listen to me. You went into that place after I told you not to."

"It was good I did," Reese insisted.

"What did you find out?"

"Looks like our suspect has been using the school as a hideout," Reese said. "He got away from me though, and took off in that rust bucket he drives."

"Where are you?"

"I followed him up to Takkoa Recreation Area, but he gave me the slip. Now it's raining cats and dogs, and I'm freezing my butt off."

Reese didn't mention that he'd nearly rammed into her bumper at top speed.

"That's rough terrain up there."

"Betty's in good shape," Reese lied. "She can handle it. But I had hoped our suspect's old rattle trap would give out. I was wrong."

"He didn't have any weapons?"

"No, and I got a good look at him," Reese added. "I can give a description to your police sketch artist."

"License plates?" Jeremy asked.

"They're fake, so that's not going to help us," Reese said. "I can't believe this dude hasn't been pulled over by now."

"Shit."

"My thoughts exactly," Reese said.

"Head back to the school," Jeremy said. "Me and a couple of uniforms are searching the premises. I'll send a police car to scout the recreation area. Maybe they can turn up something."

"Check out the basement by the pool," Reese said. "You'll find human remains down there."

"God, is it Violet?"

"No, it's a skeleton," Reese said. "It's been there a while. I believe it might be one of our perp's victims, though. Something tells me he's been kidnapping women for a while."

"A serial killer?"

"Maybe."

"Hell, just what this community doesn't need," Jeremy said in an ominous tone.

After hanging up, Reese made a call to Mrs. Mac to let her know she was running late. Mrs. Mac reassured Reese everything was fine, and urged her to, "Take care of the bad guys."

She fired up Betty and started back down the road, driving cautiously. It wasn't easy to navigate the terrain in the downpour since a thick fog draped the trees, rocks, and even the road ahead. Making it worse, rain slashed relentlessly across her windshield; her wipers barely able to make a dent in the sheets of water.

REESE AND JEREMY STOOD BESIDE THE skeleton in Bluff High School's basement. The odor of musty basement and human remains made her nose twitch.

In the background, technicians hung yellow caution tape and collected evidence. It was a typical crime scene, like any other, yet Reese felt humbled and deeply sad as she viewed the area where a woman had lost her life. It made her want to solve this case more than ever.

"Is that an ID bracelet?" Jeremy asked.

Narrowing her gaze, Reese leaned over and studied the silver chain clasped on the skeleton's right wrist. "It is," she said, taking a pen from her pocket and lifting up the face plate. "It's a medical one. It says Gina Miller, Type 1 diabetes."

Jeremy placed his fists on his hips, scowling. "That name sounds familiar."

"Isn't there a Miller Ranch nearby?" Reese asked. "At least I think I remember one from when I was a kid."

"That's right," Allison Berry, one of the police officers said as she walked up beside them. "They usually sell pumpkins in the fall. I remember my folks taking my sister and I out there to buy a few for carving."

Jeremy nodded. "I read a newspaper story about one of Rafe Miller's daughters going missing a couple of years ago. I was working as a police officer in Sage at the time, but it caught my eye."

Reese pulled out her cell phone. Logging onto the internet,

she brought up several stories about the incident. "Her name was Gina, and her father mentioned he was worried because she was a diabetic and needed her meds. He said the family had looked everywhere for her."

"Looks like she's been here all along," Officer Berry said in a sober tone.

"What sick bastard would do this?" Jeremy looked away for a few seconds.

Reese could tell he needed to collect himself. As moisture formed in her eyes, she realized she also needed a second. To distract herself, she clicked on one article and began to read. Buried in the paragraphs was a comment from Gina's sister.

"Georgia Miller, Gina's sister, said Gina believed she was being stalked before she disappeared." Reese held her phone toward Jeremy and he studied the article.

"Gina claimed the stalker drove a beat-up station wagon," he said.

"It has to be the same guy who took Violet." Reese frowned. "God, to think I was right on that sucker's tail. And he got away."

"We need to talk to Gina's sister," Jeremy said. He pulled out his cell and got busy searching for something.

Reese stood quietly as he placed a call.

After a second, he said, "Georgia Miller? My name is Detective Jeremy Savage from the Meadowlark Valley Police Department." He paused, then added, "Yes, it's an update about your sister. Uh, huh. You teach at Pronghorn Elementary? We'll be right over."

"Henry," he addressed one of the workers as he put away his phone. "See that ID bracelet on the body? I want you to put it in an evidence bag then give it to me."

"Sure," Henry, a tall, lanky fellow with large ears said. Dressed in his official technician attire and blue latex gloves, he removed the bracelet from the skeleton's wrist, dropped it into a clear evidence bag, wrote on it with a black marker, then sealed it.

"Here you go," he said as he held it out to Jeremy.

Reese took it from him and dropped it into her purse for safekeeping.

"Let's head over to the elementary and pay Georgia Miller a visit," Jeremy said. "We'll see if she recognizes the bracelet."

TWENTY-EIGHT

As Reese talked with Jeremy about recent case developments, she glanced out at the sagebrush-covered prairie. The storm had lifted, and now warm sunlight slanted through Jeremy's SUV windows.

Before long, the air became muggy and hot. Jeremy switched on the air conditioner. Welcome relief in the form of cool air washed over Reese. Around here, it wasn't unusual to experience extremes in temperature. One minute you could be chilled to the bone, and the next, roasting like a potato in a hot oven.

Reese pinched the bridge of her nose with her thumb and forefinger, trying to ward off a headache. Those dreams she kept having were wearing her out. Maybe a therapist could recommend some mind exercises that would help calm her vivid imagination. Then, maybe she could get some decent sleep.

"Are you okay?" Jeremy asked, looking over at her for a second.

"Sure," she responded. "I'm probably juggling too many projects."

"My offer to pull you off of this case still stands."

"No, I'm fine," Reese insisted, appreciating his concern.

He smiled at her, and she smiled back.

"I did some digging around and believe our suspect may be responsible for several abductions and murders in the state," he continued. "Eyewitnesses have spotted an old station wagon, just like his, close to the crime scenes. Also, there have been sightings of a large man who fits our suspect's description."

"It probably was our perp, and thanks to me, now he's in the wind again."

"You did your best."

"It wasn't good enough," Reese said, disappointed by her failure to catch this creep. "Every minute that passes lessens the chance of us finding Violet alive."

Jeremy pressed his lips into a firm line. "Believe me, that's constantly on my mind."

"Did you find out anything else?"

"Over the last two years, there have been three abduction cases. Daughters and wives of ranch owners have gone missing."

"I wonder if Wade Gentry's wife, Dotty, is one of his victims, too."

"It's possible, Jeremy said. "Although in most cases, a few days after the women go missing, the ranch owners received ransom notes warning them not to involve the police and demanding money in return for their release. Afraid for their loved one, many of the ranchers followed the directions."

"Were any of the kidnapped victims returned?"

"Unfortunately, not," Jeremy said. "After the money was paid, the victim was never seen again."

"How awful," Reese said.

"It's pretty obvious the victims have been killed and dumped somewhere, but none of the bodies have ever been found," Jeremy said. "And somehow, this guy's managed to elude law enforcement."

"If he's our guy, he's taken three other women besides Violet, then?"

"Three that we can document," Jeremy noted. "There may be more we don't know about. That number doesn't include Gina Miller, if she was actually murdered by our suspect."

"I hate that murderers are able to escape justice."

"That is an unfortunate fact of life," Jeremy said. "But that's why we wear the uniform. We've sworn to bring perpetrators to justice."

"Have you heard anything from the Gentry family recently?" Reese asked.

"Tag's been relentless about trying to find his sister," Jeremy said. "He's organized neighbors and community members to scout the area around the mall and the woods beyond. The police were pretty involved the first couple of days and sent out their K-9s to search, but they've pulled back a lot of the assistance—money and resources, you know."

"That's too bad," Reese said.

"Tag's volunteers are still out there though, checking every nook and cranny. They've even set up a command center at the Morningside Baptist Church where volunteers are processing leads, making calls, and sending out posters with Violet's picture."

"Seems he's determined to find Violet," Reese said. "I don't blame him."

Jeremy reached up to rub the back of his neck. "It's a damn shame that things like this happen."

"I'd move heaven and earth to find my family member if they'd been taken," Reese said.

"Which is pretty much what Tag is doing," Jeremy said. "He's even reached out to a couple of friends with private planes and helicopters who are scouring the mountains for any sign of Violet or the station wagon."

"Somehow our suspect manages to stay under the radar," Reese said.

"I wouldn't put it past him to have hideouts in caves or other abandoned buildings besides the high school."

"Violet's social media accounts have random comments from a person named Roman Jackrabbit," Reese said. "He keeps talking about how ranchers have taken advantage of Wyoming's homesteaders, stealing their land. Seems real pissed about it. I'm thinking he's probably our guy."

"Sounds like he's referring to the Johnson County War where Wyoming cattle barons squabbled with small homesteaders and accused them of being squatters. Things got out of control and some folks were even lynched." Jeremy shook his head. "But hell, that happened more than a century ago."

"Maybe something triggered our suspect and now he feels justified in righting all the wrongs that were committed back then."

"That seems like a real stretch," Jeremy said.

"I've seen stranger things," Reese said.

"Me too, so I'm not completely discounting the idea," Jeremy said. "When we get done talking to Georgia Miller, let's go back to headquarters. I've texted Peter Briggs, our sketch artist. He'll stay until we get there so you can give him a description of our suspect."

"You'll release the sketch to the media right away?"

"That's the plan," Jeremy said.

Reese knew time was of the essence. Sharing that update with the media could prove powerful. Community members would know to steer clear of him, and their potential tips about where they'd seen him would be invaluable. Often, that information led to the bad guys getting caught.

"It'll probably take a bit for Peter to come up with a rendering. You okay with that?" Jeremy met her gaze, then turned back to look at the road.

"I called Mrs. Mac to let her know I'll be really late tonight," Reese said.

"Good," Jeremy said. "Speaking of Mrs. Mac, how's she getting along with Fox? And how are you getting along with him?"

"He's a different kind of kid, as you know. His mind is like a steel trap."

Jeremy chuckled as he pulled off the highway and turned down a bumpy dirt road. Both sides of it were surrounded by farm houses and fields that showcased spotted cows and sleek horses munching on rangeland grass.

"Any word from his mother?"

"Not yet. Mrs. Mac was going to encourage him to call Tanya today."

"You think she's coming back?"

"It hasn't been that long since she left."

"She never should have left him with you," Jeremy said. "It was irresponsible."

Reese nodded. "How did she know I wouldn't turn him into CPS?"

"She took a big risk," Jeremy said.

"She's either a ditz or she was really desperate," Reese said. "That's another reason why I can't ship Fox off anywhere."

Jeremy looked at her with raised brows.

"He needs someone stable and dependable in his life," Reese said.

"Do you really think he's your half-brother?"

"I go back and forth about that." Reese chewed her lower lip momentarily. "But the possibility exists."

A sign alongside the road announced the upcoming town as Pronghorn Creek, population, 250. Before long, another sign displayed a crosswalk emblem. A neighborhood of modest, older bungalow style homes spread out over a few blocks. Smack in the middle sat a quaint, white church with a steeple.

"I've never been here before," Jeremy said. "Don't blink or you'll miss it."

He turned down another road that passed a small, dusty shopping center offering a country store, a post office, a farm implement business, and a few other places. Further down the lane, a square, pale brick building appeared with a rugged mountain backdrop composed of autumn's signature brown, green, ocher, and rust colors.

The school, surrounded by large old trees and bushes, sported a tall pole featuring both the Wyoming flag and the United States flag. Nearby sat a yellow bus, along with a few other cars.

A gravel playground area featured a sturdy swing set and slide, climbing equipment with attached monkey bars and a durable outdoor activity center. A seating spot, designed to look like a covered wagon, complete with large wheels, rested near a tall cottonwood.

Reminiscence welled inside of Reese, and she felt a smile tug her lips. "When I was a kid, maybe fourth grade, a bus brought my class out here for a mayday celebration. We actually danced around a maypole with colorful streamers. The teachers grilled hotdogs and hamburgers so we could have a picnic."

"Gotta love those childhood memories," Jeremy said as he pulled into an asphalt parking area near the front entrance.

Reese and Jeremy got out of his truck and walked up to the building.

Tall, old-fashioned front windows rested on either side of an engraved sign that said, Pronghorn Elementary, 1885. A couple of golden-orange leafed chokecherry bushes grew on either side of the stoop, dark, drying berries clinging to the branches.

"It's late for a teacher to be at school," Reese said, glancing at her watch, noting that it was almost five in the afternoon.

"Georgia said she's checking papers and preparing lessons for tomorrow's class," Jeremy returned. "Since she's the only teacher out here, I'm sure she's pretty busy."

"Makes sense," Reese said.

"She's anxious to talk about her sister," Jeremy said. "After all this time, she figured the police had forgotten her case."

"I don't blame her," Reese said.

"I think she wanted me to tell her our news over the phone, but you know I hate doing that," Jeremy said. "It's a cold, cruel way to tell someone their loved one is gone."

"I agree," Reese said.

Jeremy held the front door open and Reese entered. The large, well-illuminated room held shelves full of books and cupboards. A whiteboard, along with an interactive Smartboard, covered a portion of the front wall. A clock, several charts, children's artwork, and educational posters provided decoration. In a corner nearby sat the teacher's desk and her computer. The surface was covered in papers, books and a couple of apples. A metal cart held a number of lap tops, no doubt for the students' use.

A girl with brunette pigtails sat at a desk, her gaze curious as it passed over Reese and Jeremy. Probably in third- or fourth-grade, her pink tie-dye T-shirt bore a splotch of something purple—possibly grape jelly from a peanut butter sandwich. With her pencil poised in the air over a workbook, she continued to stare.

"Hello," Reese said. "We're looking for Ms. Miller."

"I'm Georgia Miller," a dark-skinned woman with long ebony hair said as she walked toward them. She pulled on a lavender sweater, then smoothed down her blue dress. Around her neck hung a red lanyard bearing an ID badge.

"Danielle," she told the little girl, "You can go home now."

"But I'm not done with my math homework," Danielle said.

"It's all right, honey," Ms. Miller told her. "You can finish that tomorrow."

"Okay." Danielle closed the workbook and tucked it inside her desk along with the pencil. She glanced at Reese and Jeremy again as she went over to a cubby, withdrew a jacket, and put it on. Grabbing a backpack, she slung it over her shoulders. "Bye Ms. Miller."

"Bye now," Georgia told Danielle. Once the little girl had left, Ms. Miller turned to Reese and Jeremy, an anxious gleam in her eyes. "You have news about my sister?"

TWENTY-NINE

"**T**HAT'S RIGHT." JEREMY HANDED HER ONE of his business cards, then nodded at Reese. "This is an associate of mine, Reese Golden."

"It's nice to meet you," Georgia said, her voice shaky. "What's going on?

Jeremy looked around. "Is there anywhere we could sit down?"

"Y-yes," Georgia said, pointing toward a small, half-circle shaped table. "You can take seats here. Hope you don't mind the tiny chairs."

Jeremy and Reese squeezed into the student-sized seats. Georgia sat across from them, making herself comfortable in the teacher's place.

"This afternoon, we found human remains we believe are Gina's," Jeremy said in a sober tone.

Tears welled in Georgia's eyes and she began sobbing. "After all this time, it doesn't seem real."

Reese reached out and patted Georgia's hand, realizing it was small comfort, but she wanted to offer it anyway.

"Until forensic testing is conducted, we can't be certain," Jeremy explained.

"I understand," Georgia said. "I've believed for so long she might come back someday. If you've found her, though, now it's real. Wh-what makes you think the remains are G-Gina's?"

"We found this." From her purse, Reese removed the evidence bag containing Gina's medical ID bracelet and placed it on the table.

Georgia covered her mouth with trembling hands. "My parents got that for her when she was diagnosed with diabetes. She always wore it."

"I'm so sorry," Reese said as she put away the evidence.

Jeremy frowned. "Until we get the coroner's official report, we can't say for certain it's your sister. We'll let you know one way or the other."

"If it's her, at least we know she's gone to be with the Lord." Georgia sobbed a bit, then said. "For two years, we hoped and prayed she'd come home to us. It's been terrible. Not that this news takes away the pain, you know? But at least we can have some closure."

"What about your parents?" Reese asked. "Would you like us to let them know?"

"They're gone." Georgia wiped tears from her cheeks. "I think they both died from broken hearts after Gina disappeared."

"Do you have other family?" Jeremy asked.

"My brothers live back east," Georgia said. "If it's really Gina you found, I'm sure they'll come home to help me lay her to rest."

"No doubt," Reese said.

"I can't imagine how my sister must have suffered," Georgia said, fresh tears streaming down her face. "Without her insulin, she couldn't have lasted more than a week or so."

"At least she's at peace now," Reese tried to reassure her.

"Where did you find her?" Georgia asked, rubbing her temples.

"At an old abandoned high school right outside of Meadowlark Valley," Jeremy said. "It appears she'd been held there for a while."

"She was kidnapped?" Georgia asked.

"We believe so," Jeremy said,

"Do you know who took her?" Georgia asked.

"We have ideas, but nothing for certain," Jeremy said. "We need to review the police file on Gina's disappearance."

"I know this is a difficult time," Reese said. "But maybe you can help us catch this monster. Would you mind if we ask you a few questions?"

"Whatever it takes," Georgia said with renewed determination in her voice. "I want to see this person behind bars for the rest of their life. I can't fathom the thought of someone else becoming a victim like Gina."

"What was going on with your sister before she disappeared?" Reese asked. "Do you recall anything specific?"

Georgia pulled a tissue from her pocket and dabbed her nose. "I'd just started teaching here at Pronghorn. Gina was working at the flower shop in in town, Blossoms, Etc. Our brothers, Garret and Gunnar were away at college. Everything was good."

"Did you and Gina grow up here in Pronghorn?" Jeremy asked.

"Yes, our parents owned a ranch near here. All four of us kids grew up loving that place, riding horses and sitting on hay bales in the moonlight. We attended school here at Pronghorn, and I think that's why the district hired me to teach. The students and their parents are all my neighbors and friends." She shook her head. "I'm sorry, I'm rambling."

"We understand," Reese said. "This must be a terrible shock."

"What happened to your family ranch?" Jeremy asked.

"Mom and Dad were terribly upset when Gina went missing. They lost all interest in running the place any longer, so they sold it about a year later. They moved to town to live with me, but both of them got sick and passed away within months of each other." Georgia blinked a few times. "You see, Pronghorn Creek is a quiet, peaceful farming community. People don't go missing or get murdered. At least, we never expect things like that to happen."

"Let's go back to before Gina disappeared," Reese said. "You said everything was going well."

Georgia took a deep, shuddering breath and continued. "It was a great time," she said. "There was one thing bothering Gina."

"What?" Jeremy asked.

"This jerk wouldn't leave her alone. We used to joke about him and what a numbskull he was, pining over her like a lost puppy."

"Who was the guy?" Jeremy leaned forward, apparently eager to catch every word and detail.

Georgia laughed in a sad, reminiscent tone. "The guy told Gina his name was Roman Jackrabbit. Can you believe that? Did he really think we would believe that was real?"

The fine hair on Reese's neck felt electrified when Gina said that name. It gave her a weird feeling to know that a guy named Roman Jackrabbit had been making a nuisance of himself with Gina Miller, too.

"To top it off, the guy drove an old beat-up station wagon covered in crazy stickers and window clings. Stuff was even handwritten all over the vehicle. Statements about end of the world, blah, blah, blah." Georgia looked down at her hands. "We laughed about him. Thought he was a nut bag. What if he resented us teasing him, and to get even, he took her?"

"You can't blame yourself for what happened," Reese said.

"I still feel guilty," Georgia replied.

"What did he look like?" Jeremy pulled a notebook and a pen from his jacket.

"Real tall, probably over six feet," Georgia said. "He had dark hair and dark, brooding eyes. Almost evil, I'd say. He used to hang around the flower shop, waiting until Gina got off of work. She refused to go anywhere with him. He was too creepy."

"You told the police about this guy?" Jeremy asked.

"Of course. They searched for him, but never found a trace. And we searched for Gina everywhere. Put up posters all over the county and went on TV to beg for her to come home."

"You did all you could," Reese said, thinking about Tag Gentry who was now searching for his sister, just as Georgia had.

"I don't think the police did, though," Gina said. "Taking into account her past, I'm afraid they believed she'd run off somewhere again."

"Again?" Jeremy asked.

"At 16, she got messed up with drugs," Georgia explained, glancing out the window as if remembering. "And she kept running away. For some reason, my sister was a troubled teenager. Mom and Dad did everything they could to help her. They sent her to a therapist and even a recovery clinic."

"That must have been so difficult," Reese said.

"It was," Georgia admitted. "My sister made it to 10th grade, but dropped out after that. Despite all of our efforts, she was always depressed. Later, a doctor diagnosed her with Type 1 Diabetes, and she got medication. For a few years after that, things seemed better for her. She got clean and healthy. The sweet Gina I knew as a kid made a comeback."

"Going back to this Roman Jackrabbit, did the flower shop owner ever see him?" Reese asked.

"Angela Riley used to own the place," Georgia said. "She gave a description of this Jackrabbit creep to the police, too."

"Where is she now?" Reese pressed.

"She closed down her shop shortly after Gina went missing. The place was having a hard time staying afloat. Angela claimed she couldn't stand to stay in business any longer since she was the last person to see Gina alive. She said she felt awful about what had happened. After the police questioned her, even though they didn't accuse her of anything, it seemed like she fell apart."

"Is Angela around?" Jeremy asked.

Georgia shook her head. "Last I heard she'd moved to Florida to be by her cousin. Both of them are widows, so the two decided to buy ocean-front condos near each other."

"Did you ever run into this Jackrabbit guy after your sister disappeared?" Reese asked.

"Maybe, but I can't be sure." Georgia began to fiddle with her lanyard.

"What do you mean?" Jeremy asked.

"The autumn after Gina disappeared, I believed someone might be stalking me, and I was afraid it might be him. Daylight Savings had moved the time back, so it was getting darker and darker by the time I left the school each evening. I could have sworn someone—maybe this Jackrabbit guy—was stalking me in the bushes. I feared he would come for me next."

"Did you report that to the police?"

"Yes," Georgia said. "But the police station out here is small. They sent out an officer to look around the school, but didn't find anything. He suggested maybe I'd been hearing a wild animal rustling in the bushes. We get a lot of those around here—bears and foxes, and the like. We even had a mountain lion in someone's backyard once."

"What happened after that?" Reese asked.

"I made sure to keep the school doors locked when I stayed late. I also started carrying a weapon."

Georgia got up and walked over by a poster board featuring information about geology. Nearby, books about rocks and soil were displayed next to different types of geodes. Georgia clasped her hand around one and brought it back to the circular table.

"Did you ever have to use it?" Reese asked,

"One time," she said. "I'd stayed late to grade papers and it was dark by the time I got ready to leave. I heard something in the bushes near the school. I said really loud, 'I'm warning you, don't come any closer. I've got a gun and I'm not afraid to use it.'"

Georgia sat down and placed the rock on the table. "When the bushes rattled again, I threw the rock. I competed in the shot put in college, so I know my aim is good. I'm certain I hit something that night because I heard a loud grunt."

Jeremy picked up the chunk of what looked like quartz and examined it. "I think this might be a bit of dried blood right here," he said, pointing at a sharp, ridged area.

Reese leaned over to study the cream-colored rock. "How can you tell?"

Jeremy removed a pen from his pocket and used it to locate a fleck of dried substance. "See?"

"Uh, huh," Reese said.

"Or it might rust-colored dirt. I won't know unless I send it to the lab to be sure. If that's okay." He looked at Georgia with raised his brows.

"Of course," she said. "Whatever you need. I sure hope I hit the dirtbag and made him bleed."

Reese remembered the scar she'd seen on the suspect's forehead when she'd run into him at Bluff High School. Had Georgia put a dent in his skull that day?

"There's one more thing I've never shared with anyone," Georgia said. "My mother only told right before she died."

"What's that?" Jeremy leaned forward.

"The kidnapper sent a letter to my parents, telling them if they paid $500,000, Gina would be returned. They weren't supposed to involve the police, though."

"Did they pay the ransom?" Jeremy asked.

"Yes," Georgia said in a sad tone. "They followed the kidnapper's instructions to leave the cash in a duffel bag on a bench in our little park in town. But Gina never came home, like the kidnapper promised. Maybe it was because they had already talked to the cops."

"That might not have made any difference," Reese said.

"I don't know," Georgia said. "If only we'd known then what we know now."

"Did your mother keep the ransom note?" Jeremy asked.

"Actually, she did." Gina went to her desk and pulled out an envelope. She brought it back over to the table and handed it to Jeremy, then took a seat again.

Jeremy studied it, then held it up for Reese to see.

"There's no postmark," he said.

"Maybe the kidnapper hand-delivered it," Reese suggested.

When they lived on their ranch, my parents had a metal mailbox at the end of the road. Everyone who lives in the country has a set up like that."

"This isn't going to tell us much." Jeremy withdrew the letter and held it up. "Especially since it's typewritten."

"What about fingerprints?" Reese asked.

"Maybe, but it's a long shot," Jeremy said. "And if our suspect has never been arrested before, his prints won't be in the system."

THIRTY

REESE AND JEREMY HEADED BACK to the old high school to get her truck, making a quick stop at a fast-food drive through.

"Yum," Jeremy said as he munched on his burger. "I love eating a 99-cent heart attack for dinner."

Reese swallowed a French fry and said, "Except that now the cheapest burgers are about five bucks."

"True." Jeremy crumpled a paper wrapper and tossed it in the back of his Trailblazer.

Reese looked over her shoulder at the drift of fast-food paraphernalia. "Bad detective! You need to do some house cleaning."

He shrugged. "Eventually. It's not high on my priority list."

"What did you think about Georgia Miller?"

"She seems genuinely disturbed by her sister's disappearance. I feel sorry for her."

"Me, too," Reese said. "I'm she'll always be haunted by what happened."

"I can't believe her parents paid the ransom for Gina," Jeremy said.

"You never know what you'd do in their situation," Reese said. "They were only trying to do the best thing to get their daughter back."

"Sometimes I really hate this job," Jeremy said. "Especially when we find out how low some people will go for greed, revenge or, well, you name it."

"I know, it kind of makes you doubt that God exists, when he allows such terrible things to happen."

"God doesn't allow evil things to happen," Jeremy said. "That's good ol' Satan taking control of people and promising them power and riches if they cheat, lie, steal, and kill. It's an age-old story."

Reese narrowed her gaze at him. "Since when did you start going to church?"

"My mom made me go as a kid," Jeremy said. "When you spend as many years as I did in Sunday School, you learn a few things."

"You don't talk much about your parents," Reese said.

"My mom and dad are cool, salt of the earth type of folks. But they wanted more for me than being a cop. They're disappointed."

Reese studied the expressions crossing Jeremy's face: sadness, regret, then determination.

"What did they want you to do?"

"My dad had his heart set on me becoming a doctor or a lawyer. That wasn't for me." Jeremy cleared his throat. "I got a bachelor's degree in psychology. When I graduated, I applied for the police department. After I got accepted, I attended the Wyoming Police Academy in Douglas. I never looked back. Law enforcement is in my blood, I guess."

"Why do you say that?"

"My grandfather served in Cheyenne as a police officer his entire life. I always looked up to him and wanted to be like him."

"What about your dad? Did you ever want to work in his profession?"

"No. He drove a garbage truck for 30 years, which didn't exactly suit me." He rubbed his neck, then placed his hand back on the steering wheel. "Don't get me wrong, Dad made an honest living and he's a good man—a good father, too. I just had other dreams."

"And your mom? What did she want for you?"

"She only wanted me to be happy. My mom isn't the type to make waves, but I know she worries about the risks I take."

"Family dynamics," Reese said, thinking about Cash and how easy or difficult it might be to accept him as her father.

"Once we find Violet, everything should settle down and we can take a break," he said. "I know you've been burning the midnight oil, just like me."

"You believe we're going to find her?" Reese asked.

"One way or another," he said, "especially with you on the job."

"I'm glad you have faith in me," Reese said. "I can always use the ego boost."

Jeremy met her gaze. "Are you having doubts?"

"I've got a million loose ends tangled up in my brain right now," Reese said. "Somehow, I need to piece the right ones together."

"It'll happen," Jeremy said. "We're going to get this loser off the street once and for all."

"I sure hope so," Reese agreed.

Jeremy turned down the road that led to Bluff High School. He pulled into the parking lot and stopped. By now, lavender twilight covered the surrounding prairie and rolling hills.

"I'll meet you at the station," Jeremy said. "Pete's there waiting for us, so don't dawdle."

"Sure, Dad," Reese said mockingly.

Jeremy scowled. "I'm your co-worker, not your dad."

Reese frowned. "Lord, please save me from mansplaining."

"What the hell is that?" Jeremy asked.

"What you just did."

"Huh?"

"I can't believe you've never heard of that term."

"I'm too busy to worry about the latest buzz words." Jeremy's brow wrinkled, and he really did look clueless.

"You're a good cop, so I forgive you." Chuckling, she pecked his cheek, then got out of Jeremy's Trailblazer and headed toward her truck.

As she hopped inside and started her engine, she envisioned their suspect's facial features, along with his malevolent expression.

He wasn't pleasant to look at, especially since she knew that behind his dark gaze, the devious mind of a murderer lurked.

An uneasy tremor lanced through her.

He must be possessed by a demon in order to kidnap young women and murder them in cold blood.

AT THE POLICE STATION, REESE AND JEREMY entered the cubicle office of Peter Briggs, Meadowlark Valley Police Department sketch artist. Leaning back in his chair, his feet propped on his desk, he talked on the phone.

The walls held shelves lined with awards and trophies, along with a graduation diploma from Grand Canyon University. Framed pencil sketches of individuals filled the wall behind him, their faces expressive and detailed.

When Peter noticed the two of them, he said polite goodbyes and put down the receiver.

"Hello," he said in a deep voice as he stood and shook their hands. Short of stature, he wore a dark blue pinstriped suit and sported a dark brown beard and mustache. His handsome face, marked with dimples, lit up when he smiled.

"It's nice to meet you," Reese said.

"You must be Reese Golden, our local PI," he said, lifting his bushy brows.

"And you must be Peter Briggs, the cop shop sketch artist."

"Guilty as charged." He chuckled. "Detective Savage has told me all about you."

Reese shot Jeremy a wary look. "Hopefully only good things."

"Indeed," Peter said as he nodded at Jeremy. "He's been very complimentary of you and your abilities."

"Thank goodness for that," Reese responded. "I don't want my image to suffer, you know."

Peter pointed toward a couple of chairs on the other side of his desk.

"Please, sit down," he said.

"I don't want to be in the way, so I'm going to scoot." After winking at Reese, Jeremy left the cubicle.

Peter collected a drawing tablet from a cupboard and reseated himself in his office chair.

"I understand you got a good look at the suspect we believe is responsible for Sabrina Byrd's murder and Violet Gentry's kidnapping," Peter said.

"That's a fact," Reese said. "We also believe he may be connected to other kidnapping cases in the county."

"Nasty business," Peter commented, shaking his head. "What can you tell me about this man? Specifically, his facial features, and approximate age."

"He's tall with dark hair, probably around 30," Reese said as she reflected back to when she'd seen him at the old high school. "He's got a square jaw and brooding eyes. His complexion's pale, and across his forehead, there's a white scar."

Peter pushed a large, spiral bound notebook toward her.

"Have a look at these head shots," he said. "When you see people with facial features like the suspect, show me. I realize the guy was coming after you, so it might not be easy to remember every detail. But do your best."

"You bet," Reese promised.

She turned the book around to see it better, and began to page through the photos. When she saw one that had facial details similar to the suspect's, she flipped the book around toward Peter.

"This guy has the same square chin and face," she said. "His lips are thin, like the suspects. And he's got that five o'clock shadow going on."

With his tablet pen, Peter began to draw.

"Something else about this guy that's really weird is that his teeth look like they are filed into points," Reese said. "It makes him look feral, like a wild animal."

Nodding, Peter continued to sketch.

Reese pointed out a few more photos of men who resembled

the suspect, and explained what it was about them that seemed significant. Peter studied the photos, then continued his work, quickly rendering a drawing.

"What do you think?"

Peter pushed his tablet toward her and she inhaled, realizing he'd drawn a nearly identical rendition of their suspect. The eyes, the brows, the nose, and mouth, then the facial features blended together with skillful touches.

"That's amazing," she told Peter.

He shrugged. "It's nothing, really. You have to realize that I've been at this a long time."

"Incredible," she said.

"Right off the top, what do you like or dislike about this?"

"Let's see, I believe his face needs to be thinner," Reese said. She pointed to the cheek area and traced the area's contour.

Peter worked on the tablet some more, then urged Reese to examine his work.

"The guy's nose is bigger," she said.

He corrected that feature.

"Better," she said as she studied the sketch again.

"What type of clothing did he wear?"

"Although other people who got quick glimpses of him thought he was wearing a cape, it's actually a hip-length black, hooded coat," Reese explained. "It's no wonder they saw him as some sort of bogeyman."

Peter tapped the screen with his pencil. "His teeth are peculiar."

"Do you suppose he had them filed down like that?"

"Maybe, but a dentist surely wouldn't agree to do it."

"Right, it doesn't seem too healthy." Reese mulled the idea over in her mind, then a light bulb flashed. "Do you suppose he's wearing dentures, like something Hollywood actors might use?"

"A definite possibility," Peter said, then snapped his fingers. "I've seen those hideous things advertised online for Halloween costumes. They're cheap and easy to come by."

"Exactly," Reese said.

Peter scribbled something on his tablet, then used his pencil to add more detail to the suspect's teeth. When he'd finished, the man sported a ghoulish set of fangs.

Holding up the sketch again, Peter asked, "Thoughts?"

"That's him almost to a T," Reese said, her blood running with what felt like tiny shards of ice.

Jeremy appeared in the doorway. "Thought I'd check in."

Reese turned to look at him. "Peter's drawn our suspect perfectly."

Peter handed the tablet to Jeremy and he studied it.

"Let's get this out to the media ASAP," he said. "Then I'm calling an emergency press conference. This S.O.B is about to go down."

THIRTY-ONE

A N HOUR LATER, THE MEADOWLARK VALLEY Police Department's conference room was filled to the brim with media, their video cameras poised on tripods to document the upcoming session. Voices from clusters of people reached out in a low hum.

Reese walked to the front of the room, absorbing the tenseness that seemed to vibrate from everyone. The florescent lights gave the place a cold, austere vibe. She took a chair next to Sylvia and Wade Gentry, who were seated in the first row.

"Thanks for calling to let us know about this presser," Sylvia said. "Although we're dodging the paparazzi and their millions of questions."

"That must be unpleasant," Reese said.

"I realize they're only doing their jobs, but it makes me crazy," Sylvia said, rolling her eyes.

"Damn vultures," Wade barked. "They don't have a compassionate bone in their bodies. How would they feel if one of their family members had been kidnapped?"

Sylvia patted his hand and he quieted down.

Reese's gaze swept the room, taking in white walls, brown carpet, rectangular tables, and chairs. A utilitarian clock hung on the front wall, along with a Smartboard that generated a blue screen with a time and date readout: 7:30 p.m., Wednesday, September 19.

For five days, or approximately 120 hours, Violet Gentry had been missing. The vital 72-hour deadline, the period in which law enforcement preferred to find a missing person, had been breached. Reese's skin prickled.

Had she lost her edge? Would they be able to solve this before it was too late?

Shaking off her unease, she turned to Sylvia and Wade again. "I realize reporters' questions can be harrowing, but otherwise, how are two holding up?"

"I can barely sleep," Wade admitted in a tired voice. "I just want my daughter home."

He set his jaw and looked grimly toward where Jeremy, Tag Gentry, and several police officers were milling around, talking with one another.

"That's understandable," Reese sympathized.

Sylvia patted her tummy. "At least junior has decided to wait for a while longer before making his arrival."

"That must be a big relief," Reese said.

"With Violet missing, who would feel like celebrating?"

Reese had to agree.

A dark-skinned young woman stepped up to a lectern. Dressed in a white blouse, a blue jacket, and matching slacks, she adjusted the microphone, then said, "Thank you for being here on such short notice. I'm Carol Moreland, the Meadowlark Valley Police Department PIO. I realize it's late, but we've got an update on the Violet Gentry case, which, as you know, ties directly into the Sabrina Byrd case. Please take a seat so we can get started."

When everyone seemed settled, Carol tucked strands of black hair behind her ears and resumed.

"As we've already shared with the media, on the evening of Friday, September 14, in the parking lot outside of Sweet Clementine's restaurant, two women were assaulted by a large man wearing a dark, hooded jacket. The first woman, Sabrina Byrd, was murdered and her body stowed in the bed of Violet Gentry's light blue 2000 Ford Ranger. The suspect then attacked and abducted Miss Gentry. This information was obtained from surveillance footage we received from Sweet Clementine's owner, Neeta Poole. Our dedicated police officers, detectives, and administrative staff have worked tirelessly to determine the whereabouts of Violet Gentry and her abductor."

Several people thrust their hands in the air, obviously eager to ask questions.

"Detective Jeremy Savage and his people have taken the lead on this case," Carol explained. "He'll give his statement first, then he'll take your questions."

The hands were lowered and a few murmurs of disappointment rippled around the room.

Carol moved away from the lectern and Jeremy took her place. Taller than the PIO, he had to adjust the microphone, then he began to speak. "I promise I'll be brief and to the point. As Carol mentioned, it's late and I'm sure we all want to finish work and get home." He cleared his throat. "Since the incident last Friday, our investigative team has sought leads to identify of the suspect and where he might have taken Ms. Gentry. The parking lot surveillance video captured footage of him, unfortunately, we weren't able to clearly identify what he looked like until a short time ago."

"That's the sketch of the dark-haired man you recently emailed to all news outlets?" a reporter asked.

"Correct," Jeremy said. "One of our team members encountered him briefly and was able to give a description to our department sketch artist, Peter Briggs."

"The perp got away?" the reporter asked.

Murmurs of disappointment rippled through the crowd.

"Unfortunately, yes, despite all efforts to apprehend him, he managed to flee and is currently at large." Jeremy clicked on the Smartboard and surfed through a couple of documents, then brought up a .jpeg of Peter's sketch. He also brought up a .jpeg of Violet hiking on a local trail, her smile engaging.

Wade and his daughter-in-law inhaled sharply. Sylvia grabbed Wade's trembling hand and held onto it. Both had tears in their eyes.

"We're asking for your help on this," Jeremy continued. "Our goal is to find Violet Gentry before any more time passes. Please distribute this rendering far and wide on your stations, your social media, and your newspapers. Urge community members to call the department if they see him or his vehicle. Warn them not to approach the suspect, as he is highly dangerous and we believe he may be suffering from some sort of mental disorder. There is no telling what he might do if he felt threatened."

Jeremy pointed to one of the reporters who had raised her hand.

"Who on your team encountered the suspect?" she asked, notepad and pen in hand.

"One of the special consultants working with us on this case had a run-in with him while following up on a lead," Jeremy said.

"Who is that?" the woman asked.

"Reese Golden, a local private investigator," Jeremy added. "She's a former police detective as well, and she's worked with us before to successfully solve other cases."

The reporters and other audience members looked around the room, whispering to each other.

Jeremy met Reese's gaze and nodded, so she stood up and introduced herself. She wanted to sit down again, hating the limelight. However, she sensed Jeremy wanted her to remain standing.

"Have you uncovered a motive behind this tragedy?" someone asked.

"Nothing specific yet, but we have theories," Jeremy said.

Another reporter, a man wearing a sweater, a T-shirt and jeans, stood and said, "Isn't it true that after 72 hours, it's highly unlikely that law enforcement will find a missing individual alive?"

Sylvia moaned softly and bit her lower lip, so Reese reached over and squeezed her shoulder.

"Not every case works out that way," Reese pointed out.

"Investigators basically work against the clock," Jeremy explained. "Each passing hour decreases the likelihood a subject will be found. Locating them within that time frame can mean the difference between life and death, which is why it's vital to find the missing person right away."

"Why hasn't the FBI been brought in?" another individual asked. Seated right at the front of the room, the woman stood and looked Jeremy straight in the eye, almost daring him to give a reasonable explanation.

"That's a good question," Jeremy said. "We are sharing information with them, so they are aware of the case. We will reach out to them for help if need be. Right now, they are on standby and they are committed to helping us. We are very grateful for their resources and I'm proud of how hard this department is working."

More questions were shouted from the audience, but Jeremy held up his hand and said, "I'm going to call up Ms. Golden to share her thoughts with you. I want to reassure you the force is doing all it can in this circumstance."

Jeremy stepped away from the lectern and waved her forward.

Reese made her way to the front of the room. It wasn't that she disliked talking to audiences, it just would have been better if she could have prepared beforehand.

"Thank you, detective," she said tersely to Jeremy as she stood behind the lectern.

He only nodded, which she assumed meant that he believed she could handle it. Glancing out at the sea of faces, she cleared her throat.

"Violet Gentry is a daughter, a sister and a valuable member of this community," she said. "We realize her loved ones are anxious to see her brought home safely. Just as Sabrina Byrd's loved ones are anxious to see this monster brought to justice. Rest assured we are working around the clock to achieve those goals. There is nothing more important to us than resolving this case."

"Didn't someone recently contact you with a tip about seeing Violet?" a woman asked.

"That's true," Reese said, gripping the edges of the wooden lectern. "I immediately followed up on that, but unfortunately, it was only someone who looked like her. Believe me, it was a disappointment to us all."

Jeremy leaned toward the microphone and said, "Taggart Gentry would like to say a few words now on behalf of his sister."

Reese moved back and blended in with the police officers. When her cell phone buzzed with a text, she swore silently at herself for not turning off the sound. Pulling it from her pocket, she slid the button to mute. The message came from an unknown number, and the threatening words cut her to the bone.

Stop snooping into things that aren't your business! If you value your life and that of the boy, you'll back off. This is your final warning.

Reese's skin crawled, knowing once again, that their suspect was keeping tabs on her. He was probably even watching this broadcast, feeling triumphant. Where had he gotten her phone number? *Duh, Reese.* It was everywhere, from her website to her business cards. Shaken, she began stuffing the phone back in her pocket, when another text flashed. This one was from Fox.

Called my mom earlier. Told her someone's been prowling around your house and she hurried back to town. Dad's with her, and we're going home. Stay in touch, okay?

How did Fox know what was going on? Maybe Mrs. Mac had mentioned it, or Reese had said something that tipped him off. At this point, it didn't matter. On one hand, she felt relieved that he wasn't in danger from her stalker. On the other, she felt disappointed to think of him leaving.

Okay, she quickly texted back to Fox. **Talk to you soon.** Looking up again, she watched as Tag stepped in front of the lectern.

"On behalf of the Gentry family, I'd like to thank the Meadowlark Valley Police Department, Reese Golden, and the entire law enforcement team who has been searching for my sister, including the police K-9s." Tag's voice trembled, and he stopped speaking for a moment, then resumed. "I'd also like to thank the volunteers who have dedicated themselves to helping distribute missing posters and to search every inch of this town. I'm asking for help from anyone who may have seen Violet or knows anything to call the tip lines provided beneath her picture on the Smartboard screen. Your call can remain anonymous. Whatever you can do to help to bring my sister home, please, I'm asking for that."

"We appreciate all of you coming out this evening," Jeremy said as he once again addressed the audience. "Rest assured that we are continuing to analyze the data pertaining to this case, and we're following up on everything. Just like all cases that cross our desks, we're leaving no stone unturned."

"Why is it taking so long, Detective Savage?" someone at the back of the room called out.

"We share your frustration at the slow progress," Jeremy said. "That's why we're pleading with the public to help provide tips if you can. You might not think it's important, but let us decide whether it is or isn't. It may just be the missing piece of evidence that we need."

THIRTY-TWO

REESE DROVE HOME, HER WINDOW ROLLED DOWN to catch some fresh air. A fiery sunset of orange blaze arched over the snow-tipped mountains, which were accentuated by banks of purple clouds. The plains surrounding Meadowlark Valley stretched into the distance, brown grass, blue-green sagebrush, and autumn wildflowers dotting the expanse.

Pale twilight draped homes, trees, and lawns like a veil, bringing an end to another day. Wind swirled yellow and red leaves across the road. Reese drove through them, watching them scatter as troubled thoughts filled her mind.

"I've got to get some sleep," she muttered, but realized she needed to spend some time in her office rearranging her suspect board. She hadn't found the opportunity to touch it in days, and she wanted to update her progress.

After parking beneath her carport, she got out of the Bronco, then walked inside and glanced around the kitchen. With Fox was no longer staying here, an odd pang of regret reverberated in her chest. She'd grown accustomed to the sounds of people filling her home. However, unusual silence met her as she headed into the living room.

"Mrs. Mac?" she called.

Bo padded into the room, meowing as he wound his way around her legs.

"You love me, don't ya buddy?" She picked up the cat, pressed his silken black fur against her cheek, then placed him back on the floor. He leapt onto a chair and curled up on the cushion.

"Here I am, Reese." Mrs. Mac walked around a corner and handed her a large manilla envelope. Her purple caftan, adorned with stylized peacock feathers, swished around her pink boots. "Fox's mother picked him up."

"Yeah, he texted and told me," Reese said. "I wish I had been here to talk to Tanya, though. I had a few choice words to say about the way she left Fox."

"She said she'll be in contact."

"Hmm, what's your impression of her?" Reese studied the envelope, but wasn't willing to look at the contents just yet.

"She's a pretty little thing with big, brassy hair, floozy makeup, and tight jeans. Thinks a lot of herself, I can tell. She sashayed in here like she owned the place." Mrs. Mac frowned. "I have to admit, she not my cup of tea."

"What about Cash? Did he come along with her?"

Mrs. Mac shook her head. "He stayed in the car, but he had Tanya deliver your envelope."

Curiosity niggled Reese. Because of the photo Tanya had left for her when she dropped off Fox, she knew what Cash looked like. Now she wondered if the two of them shared any similar facial features or physical traits.

Was he a needy type of person, like his wife? Would he expect things from her? Or would he be a delightful addition to her life?

Mrs. Mac tilted her head to the side and gave her a questioning look. "Well?"

"My mother never told me a thing about Cash Nesbitt. At a certain point, I stopped asking who my father was because it always made her cry."

"He might only wish to see you, and maybe talk some."

"I doubt that," Reese said. "After he took off, he put everyone in a bad spot. I think he's probably going to cause trouble."

"You can't be sure until you get to know him."

"That's true," Reese said, still not totally convinced of what she should do.

Why did Cash run from his responsibilities? Was he unable to hold down a job and a family life? Is that why he'd left her mother, Jesse, and her? Was that happening with his new family?

"Some people have trouble keeping their lives on track." Mrs. Mac's brows knitted together. "It doesn't make them bad."

"True," Reese said. "It worries me that he isn't reliable. And that he never even tried to come and visit me or my brother all those years ago. I always felt unloved and unwanted. By him anyway."

"You mother told you he never tried to contact you," Mrs. Mac said. "But what if he did?"

Reese put the envelope on the table. "My mother and my grandparents were always so supportive; why would they keep that that from me?"

"They were doing what they thought was right to protect you and your little brother," Mrs. Mac said. "That doesn't mean it was the right thing to do."

Reese considered that for a moment. She realized her mother would have moved heaven and earth to protect her children if she thought they were in danger. For some reason, she must have believed that Cash would be a bad influence.

Why?

"There's a special bond between fathers and daughters," Mrs. Mac added. "Did your girlfriends ever talk about their dads?"

"Sure, sometimes. They mentioned going fishing with them or attending daddy daughter dances at school. I did all those things with Grandpa."

"Since your grandparents passed, maybe there's an opportunity to develop a connection with your father now. At least discover for yourself what makes him tick."

Reese considered what it would be like to have a father, but it seemed far-fetched. Her grandfather had filled those shoes quite nicely and she definitely did not have daddy issues.

"I think it's too late for that."

"What about Fox? You like him, don't you?"

"I'd like to spend more time with him, sure," Reese admitted. "He's definitely a different unit, but he's grown on me. I want to be a part of his life."

"Then get to know his father," Mrs. Mac said. "You're a grown woman and you can handle the truth. Meanwhile, you'll be in Fox's life in case he needs you."

"What if the whole thing turns toxic?"

"That's a chance you'll have to take," Mrs. Mac said, patting Reese's arm. "If it doesn't work out, you can walk away. Otherwise, you may regret this opportunity the rest of your life."

Reese knew her conscience would eat away at her if she didn't search for the truth. Whether or not getting to know her father was a good thing, she wouldn't be able to drop the issue.

"You've got many important things to decide, so honey, my advice is to take it slowly and don't make any rush judgements," Mrs. Mac said.

"Mrs. Mac, if you were in my situation, would you risk your heart to bring strangers into your life?"

"I'm like that cat of yours. I'm too damn curious and I'd have to try."

"You would?"

"Without a doubt. You see, my girl, you can't hide your head in the sand when life gives you an opportunity like this. It may never come around again." Mrs. Mac yawned and walked toward the door. "I'm going to head home now. I'm bushed."

"You've helped me so much," Reese told her. "Especially with your pep talk."

"I'm always here for you, Reese. By the way, I made macaroni and cheese for dinner and there are leftovers in the fridge."

After a quick wink and a wave, Mrs. Mac left, her caftan swooshing behind her. Reese stood in the doorway, watching to make certain her neighbor returned home safely. Then she locked up and headed back into the kitchen where she propped the manilla envelope on the counter. She studied it briefly, then decided she wasn't ready to look at the contents. It had been a long day and she didn't feel like ripping open any fresh wounds.

Stomach growling, she reached into the refrigerator, or the icebox, as her grandmother used to call it, and pulled out a plastic tub full of gooey orange pasta. After removing the lid and nuking the contents in the microwave, she grabbed a fork and ate.

The rich, cheesy noodles hit the spot—comfort food fit for the gods. Finished, she put her dishes in the sink to soak and headed into her office. She flipped on her computer and turned to face her suspect board. Shock rippled through her when she noted items had been arranged in a completely different order.

"What the heck?" Reese moved closer, her heart thumping. Studying the placement of photos and notes, she finally relaxed, and the tension in her shoulders lessened. Pleasantly surprised, she decided she would have arranged things this way, too.

Then she spotted Fox's note pinned beneath the items.

I finished my homework and got bored, so I came into your office. Don't be upset.

When you told me about your current case, you piqued my interest and I now have my own conclusions. So, I rearranged your murder board to match my theories. One thing for you to keep in in mind while you work on your murder/kidnapping leads, is Occam's razor. It is a theory attributed to 14th-century English Franciscan friar, scholastic philosopher, and theologian William of Occam. A supporter of reason and logic, he believed that when one is confronted with competing theories or explanations, the simpler one is preferable.

Good luck!

Fox, your brother and friend

Reese chuckled and muttered, "Fox couldn't resist the urge to sort out my theories, but he did a great job. There's one final thing I need to add, though."

She plopped in her office chair and brought up her email. Sure enough, Jeremy had sent her a picture of their suspect. After printing out a copy, she tacked it on her board, then stood back to study the man's dark, malicious eyes.

If Jeremy was right, which she believed he was, that monster had traveled all over the county, perhaps even the state, preying on innocent women. He'd abducted them and shaken down their families for money. Then he'd killed his victims.

To what end?

It crossed a powerful borderline to intentionally kill another human being. Most people couldn't behave with such calculating cruelty, but murderers' brains seemed to be wired differently.

Her thoughts turned to her current case and the suspect, who remained at large. Bottom line, what did he want? Money? Revenge? Criminals always had a reason that they believed justified their deeds.

Overwhelmed by all the possibilities, Reese shut down her computer, then rubbed her aching forehead. Passing through the kitchen, she pulled down a bottle of pain reliever from a cupboard, downed a couple of tablets with a drink of water, then headed into her bedroom. Inky clouds etched the sky behind the street lights as darkness enclosed the neighborhood. After drawing the drapes, she put on her nightshirt.

Too tired to even brush her teeth, she switched off the overhead lights and crawled into bed. A second later, Bo jumped onto the covers and settled near her feet in a ball of fur, generating comforting warmth. Reese's mind whirled for a moment as she considered all the loose ends in her life.

She tossed and turned, trying to get comfortable. Resting an arm across her forehead, she murmured the plea insomniacs across the world sent into the universe as they asked for blessed sleep.

"Please, please, let me get some shut-eye."

When slumber finally pulled her into a warm cocoon, her muscles relaxed and she drifted off. At some point, her state went from tranquil rest to troubled dreams.

Stars twinkled like diamonds in a velvet black sky and cool air brushed against her cheeks. At the sight of a feather drifting past, she realized it belonged to her. Amazingly, she'd transformed into a bird with plumes of inky feathers sprouting from her body. Somehow, she'd taken flight.

At first, she panicked and plummeted toward the rocky earth, screaming and crying. The grassy ground, covered in sagebrush, tall grass, and red, rocky outcroppings, threatened to become her grave.

Spread your wings, Reese. It's easy. You can do it.

Gingerly, Reese held up her arms, feeling air ripple beneath them. The updraft lifted her avian form, brushing through her feathers and transporting her to soaring heights. Allowing herself to enjoy the freedom, Reese dipped and spiraled, astonished to journey through the wilds of the backcountry.

Somewhere, an owl hooted. Mice, prairie dogs, snakes, and insects crawled through the underbrush, squeaking and snuffling as they went about their business. Deer, antelope, and sage grouse with their spiked plumage meandered through snaking valleys.

Only a few lonely lodgepole pines thrust up their branches near ravines, daring nature in order to thrive in such barren surroundings. Cactus, yucca, and rabbitbrush covered in yellow blossoms, had adapted to such arid conditions and offered plentiful cover.

With her piercing bird's sight, she saw it all.

A flute's haunting strains drifted through the air, along with drums, the sound guiding her along a ribbon of river gleaming in the moonlight. Sounds of running water caressed Reese's hearing as waves washed over rocks.

Keep flying, Reese. You're almost here.

"Almost where?" Reese whispered.

Only the low, haunting wind answered as it rushed through her hair. Rusty red stone formations loomed ahead, like the back plates of a stegosaurus dinosaur. Shadowy recesses hinted at caves hidden beneath rocky ledges.

Bones. Piles of them lay everywhere. Ringed by jagged red bluffs, they were bleached to an off-white color and covered with a thin layer of dirt. At the chilling sight, she cried out. In her bird's form, it echoed in a sharp caw-caw.

Reese winged downward for a closer look. The sight chilled her, especially when she spotted a mandible bursting with teeth. Human teeth. She flew skyward, hoping to erase the sight from her mind.

"I'm here, Reese," a voice called out. "Don't leave me to die!"

Reese wheeled back down, examining the desert. Violet stood in the shadow of an old, rotted tree truck. Moonlight gave a silver cast to her crumbling dirt dress, and tears streamed down her upturned face.

"How can I find you?" Reese asked.

"Don't forget me," Violet insisted. "I'm far away, but not that distant. Don't let him kill me. Find me!"

"But how?" Reese surfed along a ripple of air. She angled her body to focus on Violet, anxious for the missing woman to provide her with answers.

"You'll know how. I trust you."

Reese tried asking more questions, but her voice froze in her throat. Dread rippled through her. If she didn't find Violet, and something terrible happened, it would be her fault. Thoughts raced in her guilt-laden mind—her mother and Jesse's car accident, the shooting incident while she'd been a DPD detective, and others.

They all added up. She felt responsible.

Lives were entrusted to her every day. The importance of being in tip top shape, both physically and mentally, weighed on her conscience. It would destroy her to let anyone down again.

An annoying noise broke through the cobwebs in her dozing mind. She blinked in the pale glow of morning light. Once again, she was in her bedroom. Furniture, pictures, lamps, and other items appeared to be normal, yet she felt drawn back into the realm of sleep.

That shadowy, ethereal place.

She longed to return. She needed answers.

The jangling cell phone shook her out of a confused, drowsy state. After rubbing her sticky eyes, she collected the phone from her nightstand, noting it was Jeremy.

"Hello?" she asked in a sleep-thickened voice.

"You up?" he asked.

"I am now."

"Get ready. I want you to ride with me over to the Gentry's place."

Hearing the alarm in Jeremy's voice, she sat up. "What's going on?"

"They received a ransom note for Violet."

THIRTY-THREE

BUFF-COLORED PRAIRIE SWELLS, SURROUNDED BY A purple mountain range, filled the large picture window in the
Gentry's living room. Gusts whipped the trees and bushes into a
frenzy, bending tufts of buffalo grass and wildflower stems to the
forces of nature.

Wind always made Reese nervous. She chewed her lower lip,
hoping she wouldn't return home with a flattened fence or ripped
shingles.

As gusts pounded against the walls of the house, Wade Gentry
paced back and forth in front of a large rock fireplace, his bald-
ing head shiny with perspiration. Nearby, a couple of plain-clothed
police officers assembled special equipment to monitor the phone
in case Violet's kidnapper decided to call with more demands.

Reese realized that staring out at the countryside, her nerves in
a turmoil, would not resolve any problems. Specifically, the warning text she'd received from their suspect—it had really rattled her.
What lengths he would go to in order to stop her?

She hadn't decided whether or not to tell Jeremy, otherwise
he'd start threatening to pull her off the case again. And she didn't
want that.

Perched on the arm of a black leather couch with cowhide fabric along the sides, she noted everyone's tense postures, especially
the Gentry's. No one ever wanted to find themselves in a situation

like this. Even though she'd been trained not to become personally involved in cases, she always did.

Wade looked crushed, angry and disbelieving, all at the same time.

Sylvia sat on the couch, her face white and pinched, her arms wrapped protectively around her tummy. Tag stood behind her, dark half circles beneath his eyes.

Next to her, Jeremy propped a booted foot on a carved wooden stool. "Start from the beginning, Wade. Tell us what happened."

"I went out to check the mailbox this morning and found this." Holding up a large white envelope, Wade withdrew the contents and handed them to Jeremy.

Jeremy withdrew a crudely-written note, and began reading. "Pay $700,000 by tomorrow morning, or Violet's dead. Leave the cash in a backpack in the park by the stone fountain. Have it in place by 6 o'clock and don't stick around. Don't be stupid and contact the police, either. If you do, your dear Sylvia will go missing, too."

Sylvia started crying, Tag swore, and Wade's face blossomed a fiery red as he slammed his fist against a paneled wall.

"Bastard!" Wade shouted.

"Don't work yourself up, Dad," Tag told him. "We don't want you back in the hospital."

Wade seemed to calm down, but he looked ready to rip someone in two.

From the envelope, Jeremy pulled out a Polaroid photograph of Violet with her hands bound, her eyes and mouth duct-taped. She looked gaunt, weary, and overwhelmed.

"Proof of life," Reese murmured, disturbed by Violet's condition. Guilt rushed through her like wildfire. If she were doing a better job, she'd have found her client's sister by now.

Tag swore. "We can scrape up the cash, but not by tomorrow morning."

"I'll get on my hands and knees and beg for a bank loan," Wade said.

"But if we pay, how can we trust that this psychopath will even let Violet go?" Sylvia asked.

"You can't," Jeremy said. "We know he's willing to assault, kidnap, and kill. That says it all."

"This guy is cold and calculating, and he doesn't care about hurting others," Reese added.

"Exactly," Jeremy said. "Reese and I recently spoke to the sister of a woman we believe was one of his victims. Her father didn't go to the police and paid the ransom, but the family never saw her again."

"God help us," Sylvia said.

"What am I supposed to do?" Wade rubbed his neck as he continued pacing. His lips were moving, but he didn't speak aloud. In a brittle voice, wracked with emotion, he finally managed to say, "First my . . . my wife disappeared, and now Violet. This family must be cursed."

"Dad, don't think that way," Tag said as he walked over to grip his father's shoulder. Wade took one look at his son, then howled with rage. "How can this be happening? Why us? Why our Violet?"

Tag picked up the newspaper from a tall chest and peered at the front page. "This is what the kidnapper looks like?"

Reese walked over to him and glanced at the police sketch. "Yes. I had a run-in with him."

"He looks familiar," Tag said.

"Are you sure?" Reese asked.

Tag nodded. "He was one of the volunteers who helped search for Violet a while back. The dude even donated to her search and recovery fund."

"He probably got a kick out of playing a concerned community member," Reese said as disgust filled her.

"Yeah, while holding my daughter hostage," Wade said.

"I feel sick," Sylvia said, pressing her face against her palms and sobbing.

"What do we do next?" Tag asked.

"This guy wants a payday, so we're going to give it to him," Jeremy said.

"Does the MVPD have marked bills we can use as bait?" Reese asked Jeremy.

He nodded.

"How does that even work?" Wade asked.

"Reese and I will be nearby when the kidnapper comes for the backpack," Jeremy said.

"And when that happens, we'll close in on him," Reese said. "We'll take him into custody and sweat him until he tells us where he's holding Violet."

"What if he gets away?" Wade asked.

"We'll have a record of the serial numbers on the bills," Jeremy said. "If he buys something with any of them, we can track him."

"Meanwhile, he's got my sister," Tag pointed out.

"It's all we have right now," Reese said.

"Tell us honestly," Sylvia said in a trembling voice, "do you believe we'll get Violet back alive?"

Both Wade and Tag winced.

"I believe the chances are good," Jeremy said. "Especially since the kidnapper sent us that photo."

"We don't know what might have gone on after he snapped it," Wade said.

"Try to stay positive," Reese said.

"It's hard," Tag said.

"Seriously, keep your hopes up," Reese insisted. "In Denver, I worked on case where a teenager was kidnapped by a family friend. Rescuers found her alive in the mountains a week later and her abductor was apprehended. Now he's serving a 25-year prison term."

"When I was with the Sage Police Department, a little boy was taken right from the school grounds," Jeremy added. "We found out a dark van had been cruising the area the day before. When we broadcast the story on the local media, the kidnapper got scared and released the boy outside of a restaurant. Luckily, we found the perp, and now he's got three hots and a cot for the rest of his life in prison."

Over and over, Reese and Jeremy reassured the Gentry's that they had plenty of experience handling situations like this. Bringing Violet home was everyone's priority.

Jeremy's cell rang and he pulled it from a pocket.

"Savage here," he answered. After nodding a few times, he hung up.

"We've got another tip generated by the police artist sketch," he said. "A woman called and said the photo looks like her neighbor's son."

Reese placed her hands on her hips. "What's the neighbor's name?"

"It's Frida Crawford. Her son's name is Wyatt."

"I talked to Frida about the Especial Romeo Cigarros," Reese said, flabbergasted. "She buys them for her son, but claims he hasn't been around in months."

"She's probably covering for him," Jeremy said. "We searched the system to see if Wyatt has a criminal record. He's got a long rap sheet that started when he was 16, when he did time in Juvie. After high school, he got arrested for a couple of DUIs, and a misdemeanor for property destruction. Next, he spent six years in the State Penitentiary for felony aggravated assault and battery."

"Who did he attack?"

"A girlfriend. He punched her in the face, dragged her down some stairs, and choked her."

"Creep," Reese said.

Jeremy headed toward the door, glancing back at Reese. "You know where Frida lives, so let's roll."

THIRTY-FOUR

Jeremy's Trailblazer rumbled down dusty roads that cut through property divided by leaning posts and barbed wire fences. It hadn't been that long since Reese visited Frida's place, so the passing landmarks were familiar.

Did Frida know about her son's checkered past or would she deny it?

"While we were at the press conference, I got a text from our suspect warning me to back off of this case," Reese finally told him. "I forwarded it to your phone."

"Dammit it, Reese. I don't like that he's threatening you," Jeremy said. "Maybe you ought to drop this case. The police can handle it from here."

"I told you before, I'm staying put," she said.

"You are determined," Jeremy said.

"Like a dog with a bone, right? Maybe I should have that stamped on my business cards."

"It's definitely true," he responded. "I'll have our technology department try to trace the text, but I imagine our perp used a burner phone."

With a frown, Jeremy turned down a graveled drive, glancing at the old, two-story home surrounded by blackened and broken tree stumps.

"Looks like that place got torched," he commented.

"My thoughts, too," Reese said.

She studied the decrepit, cantaloupe-colored home that was being reclaimed by tall grass and wandering vines. Sooty streaks made it look like stripes on a prisoner's jumpsuit. The heat of the blaze had broken the windows, giving it the appearance of a gap-toothed mouth.

Next came the ramshackle shed tangled in tall grass and weeds that housed the ancient, rusty car. Around the corner, Frida's new gray house with the blue shutters appeared, along with the nearby, oversize metal garage.

Fresh sod, saplings, a new metal barn, the black GMC Sierra Denali, and a large, fifth-wheel RV dotted the area. Reese got the distinct impression those items were recent adds. Acquiring them would have taken a considerable chunk of change.

After Jeremy parked, he and Reese got out and stepped up on the porch. She rang the doorbell, then hooked her thumbs in her belt. When no one answered, her gaze lowered to the carved wooden bear statue perched next to a flower pot.

"I bet I know where Frida is," she said, patting the bear's head. "She makes these fellows for craft shows."

"She's a chainsaw artist, eh?" Jeremy asked.

"Yep," Reese said, motioning for him to follow her. "She's got a woodshop in that metal barn. I bet she's over there."

Treading across the farm, they passed a flock of hens gathered next to a chicken coop and a pasture that supported several grazing cows. As they approached the outbuilding, Reese pointed toward the chestnut-colored horse nibbling hay in a pen.

"That's the color of horse ridden by the rider who startled Wade Gentry that day out at the reservoir," Reese said.

"It's also the same color of horse ridden by the bank robber," Jeremy said. "That's a common shade."

"If Wyatt Crawford is our suspect, he could have been riding this critter from Frida's barn."

"You've got a point," Jeremy said. "Too bad we can't dust its rump for fingerprints."

"Good one," Reese kidded. "By the way, keep an eye out for Frida. She's got a shotgun and she's not afraid to use it."

"I take it you know from experience?" Jeremy raised his dark brows.

"She shoved one in my face the first time I met her," Reese said.

"What happened?"

"She accused me of trespassing, but eventually backed down."

"Shit," Jeremy said. "I don't need you brought up on charges while you're working for us."

"Bad optics, huh?" Reese lifted her cowboy hat, caught a cooling breeze, then placed it back on her head.

They'd reached a door in the metal building and Jeremy knocked on it. "Frida Crawford? It's Detective Jeremy Savage of the Meadowlark Valley Police Department. You in there?"

No answer.

"It's Reese Golden, Frida," Reese added. "We talked the other day, remember? We only want to ask you a few more questions. It won't take long."

Reese met Jeremy's gaze and shrugged. "Frida's truck is out front. I wonder what the deal is"

"Maybe she left with someone," Jeremy suggested.

"H-help," a trembling voice called, a voice that sounded like its owner was in pain.

Jeremy opened the door and the two of them entered. Chairs, pegboards and shelving full of chisels and screws had been knocked askew. Storage containers were overturned, and blocks of wood spilled across the concrete floor.

It smelled like sawdust, sweat, and blood.

In front of a tool bench, Frida stretched out on her stomach, her head turned to the side. She wore dirty jeans and a ripped T-shirt. Her left arm bent unnaturally and one side of her gray hair was crusted with blood. A large hammer rested nearby; the metal part covered in a rusty red substance intermixed with matted hair.

Reese rushed to Frida's side and knelt down. Behind her, she could hear Jeremy calling 911.

Frida managed to open one swollen, black and blue eye. "I asked . . . too many questions."

"Who did this to you?"

"Wyatt, my boy. He's, he's pissed."

"About what?"

Tears trickled down her dirt-streaked cheek. "He's been so good to me, paid for my cancer treatments, new house, new truck . . ."

Jeremy hunkered down, wincing as he gave Frida an assessing gaze. "Why did he hurt you?"

"He's in trouble, says I'm prying . . ." Frida moaned, then fell quiet.

Fearing she'd passed away, Reese pressed two fingers on her inner wrist, feeling a steady, but weak pulse.

"Hold on," she murmured, hoping Frida would hear her encouragement and take heart.

Jeremy frowned. "I'll bet she discovered Wyatt's behind all the kidnappings and murders."

"Maybe she threatened to report him to the police," Reese added, "so he got desperate."

Frida whimpered.

When ambulance siren blared in front of the building, Jeremy went outside. A second later, he led the crew, rolling their stretcher, toward Frida. Reese stepped out of the way as two EMTS leaned down and began to assess Frida.

"What do you think?" Jeremy asked a short while later.

"Looks like she's got a broken arm and a frontal temporal contusion," one of them said. "There's no telling right now what her internal injuries might be."

After making more determinations, the crew carefully placed Frida on the stretcher and rolled her out of the building. Reese and Jeremy followed, watching as two squad cars drove up, lights flashing.

The officers who exited the vehicles spoke briefly with the EMTs, who then drove the ambulance away with the siren sounding.

"Officer Berry, Officer Ketcham," Reese said, acknowledging the two uniforms walking toward her and Jeremy.

"Do you know what happened?" Officer Ketcham asked.

"Appears to be a family altercation," Jeremy said. "The victim said her son attacked her. Come in the building and let me show you the crime scene."

As Jeremy and the officers scrutinized the woodshop disarray and blood spatter, conjecturing about what had gone down, the CSI team arrived. While everyone was occupied, Reese moseyed through the building, doing her own inspection.

On the other side of two tall wooden bookcases, she found an area large enough to park a vehicle. Both old and new grease stains marked the concrete floor. A rag covered in dry blood sat nearby, along with torn food wrappers, beer cans, and a small, curled paper.

Moving closer, Reese recognized the items—especially the bloody rag. She'd spotted them inside of the suspect's vehicle at Bluff High School. They suspect she now felt certain must be Wyatt Crawford.

After removing her keys from her pocket, she leaned over and used one of them to prod the curled paper until it flipped over. It was a bumper sticker that read, **THE END IS NEAR, SATAN IS AT HAND.**

"Hey Jeremy, have a look over here," she called to him.

A second later he eased up beside her. "What's this?"

"It probably fell off of Wyatt Crawford's vehicle, which I believe he's kept hidden in here." Reese pointed at the garage door along one wall. "He could have driven in and out of here any time he wanted."

"Do you think Frida knew he'd been parking out here?"

"Probably," Reese said. "Wyatt's been helping her financially. She said he even paid for her cancer treatment. A mother's love is fierce. I'm sure she wanted to protect him."

Jeremy shook his head. "I bet Frida finally asked Wyatt what he was up to, and he went off on her."

Jeremy's phone rang and he answered, gave a couple of non-committal grunts, then hung up. "Speak of the devil," he said. "One of our squad cars is in pursuit of an old station wagon like our suspect's."

"Holy smoke," Reese said, her heart racing with excitement.

The two walked over to the officers and the CSI techs. Jeremy spoke briefly with them, then he and Reese headed outside and got in his truck. He placed a temporary siren on the top of his hood and tore down the road.

OFF OF THE OLD BIGHORN HIGHWAY SOUTH OF TOWN, a collection of old stores and gas stations offered amenities to people who lived in older neighborhoods and mobile home parks. Located south of the railroad tracks, this part of town had fallen into disrepair.

City council and community members raised money to pay for the improvement of commons areas, parks, and neighborhoods. Reese found herself impressed with the clean-up efforts and improvements.

Her attention soon turned toward Jeremy, since he was talking on his radio and listening in, blow by blow, to Officer Mick Ventling's vehicle chase. In an unusual turn of events, it wasn't a high-speed affair, but more of a low-speed crawl that had backed up traffic.

"Dispatch, suspect is pulling off of the main road into the Dollar Store parking lot, and I am in pursuit," Officer Ventling reported, his statement ending in static.

"There they are," Jeremy said as he turned off the highway and swerved into the parking area. He eased his vehicle up beside Ventling's squad car with its red and blue flashing lights. A gray, older model station wagon covered in stickers sat nearby with its driver's door wide open.

A short distance away, a crowd of people stood watching. They talked to one another and rolled video on their cells as events unfolded.

"I don't think that's Wyatt's old rattletrap," Reese said as she reached for the car door. She hustled over to check out the license plates, noting they weren't the fakes she'd seen on Wyatt's old station wagon. "It's not him."

She kicked a rock out of frustration.

Jeremy shoved his hands in his pockets, a frown on his face.

From behind a collection of scraggly bushes, a tall police officer with a dark complexion frog-marched a shorter man with a razored haircut toward the squad car.

"Why did you run? Officer Ventling asked the perpetrator.

"Your siren scared the shit out of me," the perpetrator whined. "I thought you'd be hauling me to jail."

"Did you do something I should lock you up for?" The officer asked.

"No," the man said.

The officer tsk-tsked.

"Cops are bad news in my neck of the woods."

"You got a broken tail light is all," the officer said. "I wanted to give you a warning."

"Oh," the man responded. "I been meanin' to get around to that. Got busy, is all."

Officer Ventling uncuffed him. "Next time a police car with flashing lights rides up on your tail, pull over and stop. Don't get out. The police officer will come up and talk to you."

The guy skedaddled to his car, climbed in, and drove off.

"It's not our guy, Detective Savage," Officer Ventling said as he approached Jeremy.

"Thanks for checking it out," Jeremy told him.

"No problem," Ventling he said as he got back in his squad car, and drove off.

Reese and Jeremy climbed into his Trailblazer and he drove away, his face set in lines of frustration.

"I'm headed back to the command post at the Gentry's," Jeremy finally said. "I want to be there in case the kidnapper calls."

Reese reached into her purse and pulled out some lip gloss. She smoothed it onto her dry mouth, thinking about the stack of paperwork on her desk that she needed to tackle.

"Unless you need me out there, can you drop me by my house?"

"Sure thing," Jeremy said. "But I want you with me tomorrow morning at the park."

"Of course, I plan to be out jogging. I'll be hanging around the pick-up point."

"Perfect," Jeremy said, reaching around to rub his heck.

"Tanya picked up Fox," Reese said. "You were worried for no reason."

"I thought sure you'd gotten yourself in hot water."

"It's not over," Reese cautioned. "Fox's dad left me a package of stuff I'm supposed to look through. I'm sure he'll try to explain why he abandoned our family."

"Your dad, you mean?"

"Biological dad, I suppose. While I was growing up, he wasn't in the picture. What good could possibly come from me knowing him now?"

"You'd be closer to Fox."

"True," Reese said, relenting when it came to him. "I have questions for Cash that he probably doesn't want to answer. Mainly, why he never came around. I won't tolerate any lame-ass excuses."

Jeremy glanced over at her with an assessing gaze. "Don't be too brutal on the guy, Reese. He's only human."

"I don't care," Reese said as a lump formed in her throat. "We deserved more."

"I understand why you're hurt," Jeremy said, reaching over to squeeze her hand. "I'm always here to talk with you."

She glanced out of the window, barely seeing the prairie swells covered in sagebrush, scraggly pines, and Yucca bushes covered in soapy white blossoms. A haze of teers obscured her vision.

She'd allowed her career to take the place of family. All of her goals and aspirations were centered on that. Right now, catching a kidnapper and freeing his captor was paramount in her mind.

Getting sidetracked by emotions for a long-lost father and a half-brother might ruin her focus. It could cloud her judgement, make her vulnerable, cause her to make mistakes.

Cash Nesbitt had had written her out of his life long ago.

Why should she care about him now? Why jeopardize what she'd worked so hard to build for herself?

THIRTY-FIVE

After Jeremy dropped off Reese at her house, she meandered into the kitchen. Succumbing to food's siren call, she made a beeline to the refrigerator. Scanning options, she pulled out condiments and luncheon meat. She whipped up a bologna sandwich, grabbed a cold Starbucks drink, then headed into her office.

With a meow, Bo followed her. He jumped onto a small conference table and watched her every movement, his tail switching across the wooden surface.

"You know you aren't supposed to be up there, don't you buddy?" Reese sat at her desk and switched on her computer.

The midnight black feline studied her with unblinking eyes, then began methodically licking his paws. Of course, her spoiled cat could care less about the rules.

After eating her dinner, she got down to business scouring websites and completing paperwork. A couple of hours later, she'd reviewed her emails and finished one of her cases with the Feds.

Background checks often took two or three months to finish, depending on an individual's background and the scope of work that needed to be completed. Reese followed a detailed vetting process to make sure applicants were trustworthy and reliable. Criminal offenses and illegal substance abuse were instant disqualifiers.

The work had become routine and boring; however, no one would ever hear her complain about getting the assignments. The cases Jeremy tossed her way, along with other local clients, provided her contact with the outside world. Otherwise, she'd probably never leave the house. Except for her morning jogs with Kiki.

Knocking sounded on her office door.

Reese typed a final word on her document, hit save, and went to open up.

Kiki breezed into Reese's office wearing stylish camouflage pants, a white sweater, fashion boots, and a black leather bomber jacket. Long, black curly hair swept her shoulders and as she passed by Reese, her signature patchouli perfume lent fragrance to the room.

"You haven't been out jogging for days and I haven't seen you in meditation class," Kiki accused. She plopped into a chair near the conference table and scratched Bo's head. "What gives?"

"Been too busy," Reese said, feeling guilty. She and Kiki each used to jog alone. But after a woman in Yellowstone had been assaulted while out running, the two had decided to team up when they exercised. "I promise I'll get back into a routine soon."

"Newsflash, we are all busy," Kiki said. "At least check in with me when you get buried in work."

"Sorry," Reese said. "You can shoot me at sunrise. I'm a bad friend."

"No kidding, especially when this happened last night." Kiki held out her left hand, showing off a large diamond ring. "What do you think?"

"Brett proposed?" Reese stared, dazed, at the enormous sparkling rock.

"Yes, ma'am," Kiki said with a huge grin.

"Congratulations!"

Reese and Kiki hugged.

"I really like Brett," Reese said. "He's a nice guy and he's good to you."

"But?" Kiki said, raising her brows expectantly.

"Not to be a Debbie Downer, but you two haven't been going out that long, have you?" Reese frowned as concerns filled her thoughts.

"Long enough," Kiki said. "Besides, it'll be a lengthy engagement, I can assure you. If I'm going to spend the rest of my life with a guy, I want to make sure he's definitely the one."

"Are you two going to move in together?"

"Later on, down the road," Kiki said. "Right now, we're taking it nice and slow."

"Good," Reese said. "I mean, I'm happy you're not rushing into anything."

Kiki leaned pinned her with an assessing gaze. "What about you and the lawman?"

"Jeremy and I only work together," Reese said. "And we went fishing the other day. It's not a big deal."

"Uh, huh," Kiki said with a hint of disbelief in her tone. "What's going on with Fox?"

"Fox went back home. His mother came by and picked him up."

"How does that make you feel?"

"I like having my place back, but I kind of miss his motor mouth," Reese admitted. "It's complicated, though. Fox has been texting me, asking when we can visit again. And Cash left me a mystery envelope. I'm afraid he wants a father-daughter relationship."

"I've never known you to be afraid of anything, Reese."

"After all these years of never having a father, it's strange to have him show up."

"It's your decision whether to have him in your life," Kiki said.

"I know," Reese said. "But I keep going back and forth about what I should do. It doesn't help that I'm preoccupied with finding Violet Gentry."

"How's that coming along?"

"Jeremy and I have been scrambling for leads and I'm worried. It's taking too damn long to find her."

"I saw the kidnapping suspect's picture in the newspaper," Kiki said. "And I watched your news conference. You actually ran into this freak?"

"Unfortunately, yes."

"No wonder you have nightmares."

"I never used to get so personally attached to my cases when I worked for the Denver police."

"That's difficult to believe." Kiki leaned back in her chair and stretched out her long legs.

"Maybe it's because I'm a lone wolf these days."

"By going solo, it's possible you feel even more personally responsible for the cases," Kiki said. "I'm not a certified dream interpretation specialist, but I learned a few things in those courses I took."

Reese chuckled. "Is that really a thing? A professional dream interpreter?"

"It is, so don't laugh."

"Seems kind of woo-woo, to me," Reese said. "You know, very unscientific."

"Look at who you're talking to, lady!" Kiki shook her head. "I own a mystical, new age shop. I teach mindfulness and meditation classes. I even give Tarot Card readings, for Pete's sake."

"Sorry, I didn't mean to make light of it. The idea is new to me, kind of far out, you know?"

"So, Miss-Know-It-All, are you continuing to dream about Violet Gentry wearing a dirt dress?"

"I must sound crazy, right?"

"No, I think at some level, you're in touch with things we can't see. Dreams are symbolic. They're not supposed to make sense. What do you think they mean?"

"That's the problem," Reese complained. "I have no clue."

"Describe them and let's try to sort them out."

"Here's my latest version." Reese clenched her hands into fists. "It's dark, and the stars are bright. I'm a . . . seriously, don't laugh. I'm a bird—to be specific, a crow."

"Like in caw, caw?" Kiki's mouth curved with a smile.

Reese frowned. "No mocking allowed."

"Of course not." Kiki made a serious face. "Tell me more."

"I'm flying high above rocky outcroppings, surrounded by a desert covered in cactus and sage," Reese said. "My aviation skills are shaky at first, but I manage to do all these dips and dives. I can even see tiny creatures like mice and sage grouse. And insects—like spiders—are crawling around."

"In your bird form, it seems you are in touch with the heartbeat of nature," Kiki suggested.

"Yeah, okay, that makes sense," Reese said. "During all of this, owls are hooting and soft drumming echoes, flutes play, the wind is blowing, and I hear water splashing. Then a woman's voice tells me I'm almost there."

Kiki's brows arched and her expression filled with curiosity.

"I sail past rocky ledges with caves hollowed out beneath. There are piles of bones stacked everywhere. After flying closer, I see what looks like a human jawbone with teeth. I'm upset and I try to fly away, but someone shouts, 'Don't leave me to die!'"

"That is unusual," Kiki said.

"I see Violet standing by an old tree wearing—you guess it."

"The dirt dress?"

"Bingo," Reese said, rubbing her temples. "I ask her all these questions, like where is she and how can I find her. She claims someone's going to kill her and she's crying. She begs me not to forget her and says I'll know how to find out where she is."

"No pressure, huh?" Kiki said.

"I'm trying so hard—we all are—to find her. That bozo who took her holds the key, and if we catch him, I am sure we'll get some answers."

"You'll get him, Reese. I trust you."

"Funny, Violet said that in my dream. Now you know why I'm so stressed. I can't let her down."

"I don't blame you for feeling that way."

"I hate that I turned into a crow," Reese said. "Aren't crows supposed to mean doom and gloom?"

"No, in fact, in different cultures, they hold many symbolic and spiritual meanings," Kiki explained. "Myths often claim black crows are a good omen. Seeing one, or in this instance, being one, can mean you're getting a glimpse of the future."

"Lordy, you mean I'm psychic?" Reese groaned. "Don't ever let Jeremy hear you say that. He might not want me working with the PD anymore."

"Actually, it would be a good thing," Kiki said. "Your intuitions are most likely on the money. Start journaling your dreams."

"With great reluctance, I did put a notebook on my nightstand so I can jot down what I remember," Reese said.

"Crows often symbolize transformation. Some folk tales say crows are messengers from the gods. The bottom line is they adapt easily to new situations. The universe may be telling you that your life is about to change, Reese. Something could be happening along your personal journey or maybe along your current investigation."

Reese realized she stood on the precipice of meeting her father, regardless of whether the outcome turned out to be good, bad, or ugly.

"I see the dream as you wanting to spread your wings and be free to discover the truth about yourself and also this case," Kiki said. "Although, there could be many interpretations."

"In other words, deep down, you're saying I probably feel the need to meet my father and find out why he rejected me. Also, I'm anxious to solve this case."

"That seems reasonable," Kiki said.

"I'll quit being afraid of these dreams then," Reese said.

"Go with the flow of your intuition and remain curious while you're dreaming," Kiki suggested. "Explore and seek answers. You still might want to talk to a therapist, though. Make sure you're dealing with your underlying emotions in a healthy manner."

"I'm going to take your advice. Meanwhile, I've got an envelope full of stuff Cash asked me to read."

"You haven't opened it yet?"

"I'm dragging my feet," Reese said. "What if it turns into a Pandora's box?"

"You're curious though, right?"

"Of course," Reese said.

"Then let's have a look."

Bo stood up and arched his back, looking back and forth between the two women.

"I think he agrees," Kiki said.

"Or he wants his dinner, which is more likely," Reese said.

They both chuckled.

"I'll go get the envelope," Reese said. "Fox's mom gave me a photo of Cash and my mom, so I know they were in a relationship. With you here for support, I suppose I'll be able to handle whatever else I find out."

THIRTY-SIX

THE DOORBELL AWAKENED REESE. She blinked, and sat up. After Kiki left earlier, she'd cuddled up on her couch with a blanket, and must have fallen asleep while reading one of her mother's letters. Refusing to expose their children to Cash's wild mood swings and drunken rages, Reese's mother had told him to stay away if he couldn't control his drinking.

Reese could tell her mother had been heartbroken. Yet, she'd chosen her children's welfare over her love for Cash Nesbitt. She felt like she knew the woman who had given birth to her much better.

Smoothing hair out of her eyes, Reese got up and hustled to the door. Opening it, she saw Jeremy, a black backpack slung over one shoulder.

"What's in there?"

"Nothing yet, but it's for the bait money I'll get from the police locker in the morning."

Reese beckoned him inside. "I take it there were no new developments at the Gentry's?"

"It was a bust," Jeremy said as he sat on the couch. "The kidnapper didn't call, so unfortunately, we couldn't negotiate anything else."

"We're on for the park tomorrow, then."

"Right." Jeremy unzipped the bag and pulled out a couple of earpieces, handing her one. "I snagged these for us."

Reese fit the piece in her ear to try it out for size. "I haven't participated in a sting operation for a while."

"Here's a chance to brush up on your skills."

"I'll be reporting for duty at zero dark thirty, boss."

"Man, I do love it when you call me boss," Jeremy said. "Makes me tingle all over."

"Show off," Reese said, grinning at him.

"What fresh hell is all of this?" he asked, looking at the photos, cards, and correspondence scattered on the coffee table.

"Kiki stopped by and helped me sort through the items in Cash's envelope," Reese said.

"What did you learn?" Jeremy asked.

"Things aren't as black and white as I'd assumed," Reese said.

"That's usually the way it turns out. What's the story?"

"Cash moved to Nashville to try and get his career started," Reese said. She handed Jeremy one of the letters, then sat down next to him. "It wasn't simply because he wanted to ditch his responsibilities."

"That's good news, right?"

"Right," she said. "I sense Mom really loved him, but she wanted him to get help for his drinking. He refused, so she finally told him to stay away."

"Do you blame her?"

"No, I don't. My brother and I were really young at that time. She was trying to protect us."

Jeremy winced. "Did he ever hurt your mother?"

"According to what Mom wrote, he'd yell and slam things around," Reese said. "She worried he might lose control someday. It's ironic. She was so worried about Cash's drinking, but in the end, she and Jesse were hit and killed by a drunk driver."

Jeremy shook his head. "It's a damn shame."

"Mom refused Cash's marriage proposals. She wouldn't agree to become his wife until he dealt with his addiction. I think she figured that would be enough incentive to make him get clean. But it wasn't."

"That's too bad."

"In one of her letters to him, she even said, 'Damn you Cash, all you care about is booze and country music.'"

"Did he write anything back to her?"

"He insisted he loved her more than life. He told my mom after he got his singing career off the ground, he'd send for her and us kids."

Jeremy lifted one brow. "Have you changed your mind about meeting your father now?"

Tears threatened, but Reese refused to let them fall. "Cash chose booze and mindless ambition over his family."

"That must be disappointing."

"We didn't need anything fancy or expensive, you know?" Reese said. "Having oodles of money doesn't strengthen a family. Love and respect are the glue."

"I agree."

"We'd have all been happy to see Cash at our dinner table every night. It would have been magical if he'd taken us fishing or to the park. Show up at school plays, stuff like that."

"Too bad he missed out," Jeremy commented.

"When Cash heard through a friend that my mom and Jesse had died, he finally made contact."

"You don't say? What happened?"

"He wrote my grandparents a letter telling them he was sorry. He offered to move back to Meadowlark Valley and take care of me. Grandpa wrote him back, warning him to stay the hell away."

"Honestly, I don't blame him."

"Grandpa insisted I'd already been through enough trauma and Cash would only add to it by showing up out of the blue. He said since Cash had left us, he'd lost his father's privileges. He said that's what Norah would have wanted."

"And Norah is, who?"

"Sorry, that's my mom."

Jeremy nodded. "So Cash stayed away?"

"Yep. He told my grandfather he'd honor his wishes and mentioned he'd enclosed some money for my expenses."

"How old were you?"

"I was 12," Reese said.

"Are you upset that your grandfather wanted Cash to keep out of the picture?

"In retrospect, I really wish he'd have told me."

"You were just a kid, Reese," Jeremy said. "I'm sure your grandpa only wanted to protect you."

Reese nodded. "With Cash's drinking problem being such an issue, my grandfather was right to be worried."

"Since Cash is your biological father, he could have insisted on getting to spend time with you."

"I'm sure he probably couldn't pay the legal fees to hire an attorney."

"Maybe Cash realized his unstable lifestyle wouldn't benefit the needs of a preteen girl," Jeremy said.

"He could have at least visited me," Reese said. "Surely, he could have scheduled something with my grandparents."

"People don't always do what we think they should," Jeremy pointed out.

"Yeah, I know." Reese picked up several photographs and handed them to Jeremy. "Since my mom couldn't send him updates about me any longer, Grandma and Grandpa sent pictures."

Jeremy shuffled through the stack and chuckled. "God, Reese, I'm sorry, but you were a goofy looking kid. Look at those horn-rimmed glasses and buck teeth!"

"Thank heavens for laser surgery and braces," Reese said dryly. "Cash left me his phone number, so I've been trying to decide what to do."

"Why don't you meet him? Otherwise, you'll wonder for the rest of your life what could have been. There won't be any dark clouds of uncertainty hanging over your future."

"There's also Fox to consider," Reese said, recalling that Mrs.

Mac had said something along those same lines. "He knows his folks have a drinking problem. I think he avoids reality by burying himself in his education."

"That's a better coping mechanism than turning into a punk to get attention," Jeremy said.

Reese couldn't agree more.

THE NEXT MORNING, REESE DRAGGED HERSELF out of bed and drew her curtains. Inky black shadows encompassed neighborhood homes, vehicles, shrubs, and trees. The mountains just outside of town wore an indigo blanket, with huge dark sky arching overhead that glittered with a smattering of stars.

"Time to go get the bad guy," Reese told herself.

She padded to the kitchen, rubbing sleep out of her eyes. Something was missing, and she realized it was Fox and his ever-present smile. Bo watched her from his window perch, meowing loudly, an indication he wanted breakfast.

"Not until I get some brew started," Reese said. She filled her coffee maker with water, dropped in a filter, then spooned in some dark roast.

Punching the ON button, she yawned. She always had good intentions of preparing the pot the night before so she could wake up to the coffee aroma. Alas, good intentions do not always prod one into action.

Bo meowed again and Reese quit daydreaming. She pulled out a can of kitty delight from the fridge and scooped some into his dish.

"Your highness, your feast awaits."

Bo jumped from his perch and beelined past her, black tail flicking back and forth as he dove into his food.

A hot shower revived Reese. Wrapped in a towel, she headed into the bedroom where she turned switched on the nightstand lamp and fished clothes from her closet. She donned a gray tracksuit with a matching zipper hoodie. Socks and sneakers came next.

In the kitchen she poured coffee into a mug, then savored the hot drink. A carton of strawberry yogurt satisfied her breakfast needs. Before Jeremy had left last night, he'd briefed her about where everyone on the team would be placed and how they expected the operation to go down.

He'd told her that the instant she spotted their suspect, she was to let him know. That seemed clear enough, so Reese wasn't concerned about handling her part. She didn't personally know anyone else on the team, but she knew Jeremy would have assigned competent officers. She glanced down at her wrist watch and noted that it was time to leave.

THIRTY-SEVEN

A S WAS HER USUAL MORNING ROUTINE, Reese walked over to the park, admiring the glowing slice of sunlight tracing the eastern horizon. The rolling lawns were layered with shade and silence filled the morning air.

Jeremy's job was to place the backpack beside the stone fountain, then blend into the surroundings and observe from a distance. Reese spotted his vehicle in the parking lot not far from here, nearly concealed by dense bushes.

Crows flew back and forth among the tall cottonwood branches, making sounds like a scolding mother. A common species in these parts, they seemed more prevalent these days. Or maybe Reese noticed them more. Most likely they were on her mind because they dominated her dreams about Violet.

One week ago today, Violet Gentry had been kidnapped, and her friend Sabrina Byrd had been murdered. Every minute that passed by weighed heavily on Reese's mind. By now, Violet's chances of being alive weren't good. Yet, Reese still hoped to find her alive.

Upon reaching the bubbling stone fountain, Reese realized she wasn't alone. A guy in ragged clothes slept on a bench beneath a large cottonwood, a newspaper covering his face. One of his arms stretched toward the ground, and he clutched the neck of a wine bottle.

Across the sidewalk from him, an elderly lady in a ratty-looking, oversize sweater, a floppy hat, and long skirt pawed through shopping cart items.

A couple of squirrels scampered by, chattering as one chased the other up a tree trunk.

"Coms' check," Reese said, pressing a finger against her earpiece.

"I'm close by," Jeremy responded. "The backpack's in place."

Reese spotted it propped beside the stone base.

"Hey, there's a couple of folks out here. A wino and a bag lady."

"Plain clothes cops," Jeremy said.

"Kind of cliché, don't you think?"

He chuckled. "Whatever works."

Reese did some stretches, noting the sky had taken on a shade of gray-blue. As the atmosphere brightened, bushes, flower beds, and playground equipment became more discernable.

The rising sun set the lake afire, causing it to glitter like a diamond. Aside from the sounds of nature, a hush insulated the land, almost as if it, too, were waiting.

Nerves pinging with anticipation, Reese jogged in place, watching for any signs of movement. It had been a long time since she'd participated in a law enforcement operation. This time, however, she only served as a prop.

A tall man dressed in black suddenly appeared and made his way toward the fountain. "Suspect spotted," Reese said to Jeremy

The man pushed past a couple of bushes, walking along a worn dirt pathway. He wore a long black hooded jacket and kept his head low.Leaning over the backpack, he examined it, then picked it up and resumed walking.

"Freeze," Jeremy said as he approached the man, gun drawn.

The other two officers also approached, drawing their weapons.

"Don't shoot," the guy pleaded. He dropped the backpack and lifted his hands in the air.

"Stop moving," Jeremy warned as the guy backed away. "We only need to talk to you."

"I didn't do nuthin," he complained.

"Good, then don't worry," Jeremy advised.

The suspect pivoted and began running in Reese's direction. When he tried shooting past her, she stuck out her leg and tripped him.

"Bitch," he howled as he jumped back on his feet and tried to land a sucker punch on her jaw.

After ducking, she rammed her shoulder into his chest, grabbed his knees, and dumped him on his back. His hood fell off. He called her every name in the book, things that would cause a sailor to blush. To her disappointment, she realized she didn't recognize him.

It wasn't Wyatt Crawford.

His long brown hair had been pulled tight into a manbun. A snake tattoo slithered down one cheek. Black ink had been used to fill in his lips and his chin bore a what appeared to be a tribal pattern.

"Who are you?" she asked.

Jeremy grabbed the suspect, rolled him over, and clamped handcuffs on his wrists.

The man glared at her, then spit and said, "I ain't nobody, lady."

The plainclothes officers had arrived, and pulled the suspect to his feet. Holding him by his arms, they marched him toward the parking lot.

"You have the right to remain silent," one of the officers said as they headed toward Jeremy's unmarked police vehicle.

"Remember, I've got my fifth amendment rights," the suspect taunted.

"Sure, sure," the other officer said.

Jeremy brushed off his jacket and squared his shoulders.

"Impressive moves," he told Reese.

"Martial arts training," she explained, catching up to him as he followed the officers.

"Came in handy today," he said, then scowled. "But we've got a big problem."

"I know," Reese agreed. "That guy you're hauling off to the pokey isn't Wyatt Crawford."

"Crawford must have sent him to do his dirty work."

"Definitely something he'd do," Reese said.

As they passed by the fountain, Jeremy grabbed the backpack straps and slung it over his shoulder. "We'll question this guy, anyway. See what he can tell us."

"Hopefully you can get him to talk," Reese said.

"I bet he's got a rap sheet a mile long," Jeremy said. "Which means he might have outstanding warrants for his arrest. In that case, we can take him into custody."

"Good luck," she told Jeremy.

"Thanks, we'll need it." He pulled her close and kissed her tenderly.

Reese gasped, delighted to feel warm lips on hers.

Stepping back, he asked, "You're coming down to the station, right?"

Catching her breath, Reese said, "Yep, I'll meet you there."

Jeremy smiled, then turned and jogged to catch up with his team.

Still tingling from Jeremy's kiss, Reese walked home, showered and dressed, then drove downtown to the police department. Blue and white squad cars lined the parking lot in front of the white cinderblock two-story building. She noted that the department had finally hired someone to fix the broken sidewalk bordering the building. Since the roots of a giant cottonwood tree had made a mess of the old walkway, they'd relocated it around the large trunk.

A strong wind whipped past the flag pole, causing Old Glory and the Wyoming flag to flap noisily. The gusts made it difficult to open the entrance door, but she managed.

A familiar black leather couch and mauve chairs met her gaze. Office workers sat at desks, concentrating on computer screens. TV monitors hung on walls. Filing cabinets, printers, and book shelves jam-packed the area. Fluorescent light fixtures gave off the typical harsh glare.

Office coordinator Steve Daniels sat at the front desk. He looked up when she approached.

"Hey, Reese," Steve said. "Detective Savage is waiting for you. Go on back."

"Thanks," she said as she headed down the hall toward his office. She walked into a large room where several uniformed officers seated at desks leaned over stacks of papers, studied their computer screens, or talked on the phone.

"Knock, knock," she said as she entered Jeremy's cubicle.

"Ah, you're here." Jeremy grabbed a notepad and pen. "Let's head down to the interrogation room."

Officer Berry stood outside guarding the door when they reached the place where suspects were questioned.

"Nice to see you, Allison," Reese said.

"Same to you," she responded with a smile.

When they entered the cold blue room, the suspect was seated in a gray metal chair and handcuffed to a matching metal table. Two identical chairs sat near a one-way mirror, which Reese knew police used for observation.

She sat down in one of the seats and Jeremy took the other.

"I'm Detective Savage," Jeremy said. "And my partner here is Reese Golden, a local private investigator."

The guy sniffed and placed his clasped hands together.

Jeremy glanced down at his notepad, then said, "Your name is Chad Wagner?"

"Last I heard," Wagner said.

Jeremy read him his rights again, then said, "I understand you've waived your ability to have a lawyer present?"

"Damn straight," Wagner said. "I ain't done nuthin' wrong."

Jeremy handed Wagner a form and a pen. "This is a waiver I'll need you to sign."

Wagner signed it with a flourish.

"Why did you pick up that backpack at the park this morning?"

Chad shot Jeremy a defiant look.

"What are you afraid of?" Jeremy asked. "You said you haven't done anything wrong."

"Uh, huh," Wagner insisted.

"Did you know what was in the backpack?"

"Nope. He didn't tell me."

"He didn't tell you what?" Reese asked. She crossed her legs, aware he wasn't going to cooperate.

Wagner continued his silent brooding.

"You're not in any trouble, especially if you cooperate." Jeremy paged through some forms, glanced at one, then said. "You've got some significant strikes against you. Let's see, resisting arrest today, for starters. Then there's the violation of a domestic protective order, possession and drunk driving—"

"Cut it out, I know what you're gettin' at," Wagner complained.

"I figured you would," Jeremy said. "Here's how it's going to go. If you cooperate with us, things will be easier for you."

"All right, all right," Wagner finally relented. "Here's the deal. This guy asked me to collect the backpack. He promised to pay me $100 cash."

"What's his name?" Jeremy asked.

"I don't know, I've never met him."

"How do you get the money if you've never met him?" Jeremy asked.

"He always pays up."

"You've done other jobs for him?" Jeremy asked.

"Yep," Wagner said. "I've got an old post office box hanging by my porch, and that's where he drops my cash."

Jeremy withdrew a small journal from his jacket pocket and flipped through the pages. "This belongs to you, right?"

Wagner nodded. "So what? I find out things for the guy and write 'em down. I have to do that or I forget."

Jeremy lifted his brows. "I see addresses and names of women, times, and places of where they go, etc. Looks like you're stalking them."

"Nah, you got it wrong." Wagner frowned. "I'm observing 'em is all."

"Which can be considered stalking," Reese said tersely. "Why does your boss want this information?

Wagner shrugged. "Ain't none of my business."

"We believe the man you're working for is responsible for kidnapping and murderer," Reese said.

Wagner's face paled and his eyes widened with fear. "Hey, I ain't involved in shit like that. I'm just a messenger boy."

"Don't lie," Jeremy warned him. "I talk to a lot of people every day and I know when they aren't telling the truth."

"I ain't lyin'," Wagner fumed, his face turning red.

"How long have you worked for this guy?" Reese asked.

"A few years," Wagner said.

"How do you contact him?" Jeremy asked.

"He gets in touch with me when he's got a job," Wagner said. "He leaves me a note in my old mailbox," Wagner said. "That's how he contacted me in the beginning. After I do what he wants, I put copies of the information in there. The guy comes by and picks it up. And, like I said, he always leaves me money."

"Have you ever seen him?" Reese asked.

"Nope."

"You don't seem like a bad person," Jeremy said, obviously trying to gain Wagner's trust. "You've gotten yourself in some trouble with the law a few times, but that happens. Tell me honestly, have you ever run into this character at any point?"

"No!" Wagner said. "I work at the Coke bottling company during the day, so I figure he probably stops by when I'm at work. Am I still in trouble? Are you going to hold me?"

Reese and Jeremy exchanged glances. She sensed he felt the same as her—this guy was clueless and they were wasting their time questioning him.

"You're free to go." Jeremy uncuffed Wagner and gave him one of his business cards. "If you think of anything else that can help us, call me."

"Sure thing," Wagner said as he opened the door.

"Please escort Mr. Wagner out of the building," Jeremy told Officer Berry.

She nodded, then turned to walk with Wagner down the hall.

Once they were gone, Jeremy pulled his cell phone from his pocket and punched in a number.

"Ketcham?" Jeremy said. "Yeah, put a tail on Wagner. I want to see if meets up with anyone after he leaves here."

Reese smiled. Wagner probably wouldn't realize he was being watched.

"Well, that interview was a bust," Jeremy said. "Hopefully Crawford's mom has improved by now. Maybe she knows where he's hiding out."

"I'm tired of that bastard getting away from us," Reese said as she stood and began to pace. "We've got to outsmart him."

Jeremy sat back in his chair and gave her a discerning glance. "What are you thinking, Reese? You've got that dangerous look in your eyes. The one I know all too well."

"Violet may not have much time left," she explained. "Crawford's going to be pissed that he didn't get his ransom money."

"There's no telling what he'll do now," Jeremy added.

Reese placed her hands on her hips as a small voice in her mind told her what needed to happen. "That's not true, he told us exactly what his next move would be."

Jeremy frowned. "What?"

"He threatened to kidnap Sylvia Gentry, right?"

"We'll put her up in our safehouse," Jeremy said. "He won't be able to touch her."

As Reese considered how to resolve their problem, she remembered Fox's advice about Occam's Razer.

Go with the simplest solution.

"I've got an idea."

Jeremy frowned. "Am I going to like it?"

"Probably not," Reese said.

THIRTY-EIGHT

Later that day, standing in front of a full-length mirror in Sylvia Gentry's bedroom, Reese ran a hand over her fake baby bump. She wore one of Sylvia's flowing maternity tops and stretchy pants. Fortunately, Sylvia and Reese's hair were nearly the same color, so that feature added authenticity to Reese's disguise.

Sylvia, who stood behind her, nodded and said, "Looking good."

Reese had also borrowed Sylvia's blue, cat-eye glasses. She settled them on the bridge of her nose, adjusting her eyes to the slight magnification.

"It's amazing," Sylvia exclaimed. "You could be my twin. Close enough, anyway."

"All I need is for Wyatt Crawford to kidnap me," Reese said.

"I hate the sound of that," Sylvia said. "And I hate that you're putting yourself in such danger."

"That's my job," Reese said.

"It seems above and beyond," Sylvia said.

"My reasons have a selfish edge."

"Selfish?"

"I'm compelled, maybe even driven, to try and make up for my past mistakes," Reese said.

"Like you're making restitution?"

Reese nodded.

"Either way, we all appreciate your dedication."

"I've done plenty of undercover work in my career," Reese said. "If that's what it takes to nail this guy, I'm up for it."

"I can't believe that YouTube video really helped us create a fake pregnancy," Sylvia said, studying Reese's belly. "Who knew you could stuff a baby blanket into a pillow case and then tuck it under a couple of tight tank tops?"

"This blouse style helps," Reese said, running her hand over the flowing, burgundy ruffles. "You can't tell my stomach looks lumpy and bumpy."

Talking strategy, the women walked back out into the living room where Jeremy sat, along with Wade and Taggart. The men lounged on the couch, talking with one another about hunting adventures. When they saw Reese, they all stopped to stare.

Jeremy's mouth even dropped, then he quickly composed himself.

"Do I look like a convincing expectant mother, specifically Sylvia Gentry?" Reese asked.

"Yes," all three men echoed.

"Are you sure you want to go through with his?" Jeremy asked as he stood. "We'll find another way to catch Crawford."

"I've made up my mind," Reese said, hearing the stubbornness in her tone.

"If Crawford takes the bait and tries to kidnap you, I can always have my cops close in and capture him," Jeremy said. "We'll sweat him until he tells us where he's got Violet hidden."

"That could take days," Reese said. "Meanwhile, we don't know what kind of condition Violet's in, whether or not she's got enough food and water, and a million other concerns. We don't have time to let this drag out any longer."

"My police officers are better equipped to—"

Reese held up her hand, and Jeremy fell silent. "The Gentry's hired me to find Violet and that's exactly what I intend to do."

Jeremy's gaze burned into her. She could tell he was concerned, but that he also admired her. That boosted her confidence.

"Frida Crawford is in stable condition, by the way," Jeremy added. "I checked with the hospital and they said she's got a long road ahead to recovery, but she's going to make it."

Reese took a deep breath and exhaled. "Let's do this thing."

All three of the Gentry clan had been watching Reese and Jeremy's exchange, their expressions expectant.

"Don't worry," Reese told them. "Jeremy and I argue like this all the time. It's how we get things done."

Everyone smiled.

"You sure could have fooled me," Tag said as he picked up a suitcase sitting by a wooden hall tree.

"I've got our bag, honey," Tag told Sylvia. "Jeremy's going to drive us to the safehouse."

"I parked my Trailblazer in your garage," Jeremy said. "That way, if Crawford's watching, he won't see you two getting inside. The tint on the windows is dark enough to keep him from spotting you."

Sylvia handed Reese a flowered fob from which dangled a set of keys. "My car key has the red plastic cap. It belongs to the gold Honda Accord in the driveway."

"Got it," Reese said.

Tag and Sylvia donned their coats and headed down the hall toward the garage, with Wade following.

"I want to see that you two get settled in all right," Wade said.

"Thanks, Dad," Tag said.

When everyone had left the room, Jeremy shot Reese a serious look. "It'll take a little bit for me to drive Tag and Sylvia up to the safehouse and get them settled them in."

"I won't go anywhere until it's dark," Reese promised.

"You've got the tracker I gave you, right?"

Reese held up her wrist, displaying the silver friendship bracelet embedded with a tracking device. "Right here."

"Let me know when you get ready to leave," Jeremy said.

"That's the plan," Reese said. "This momma to be is going to have a craving for a Java Chip Frappuccino from the Starbucks downtown. Hopefully, I'll attract Wyatt Crawford's attention and he'll come for me."

"You take crazy risks. You know that, right?"

"It's my job."

To KILL TIME, REESE AND WADE WATCHED a cable news channel on TV and snacked on leftover fried chicken and potato salad. They discussed politics and other current events as if nothing were amiss, even though Reese's tense muscles reminded her otherwise.

Reese's phone dinged with a text message. She lifted it up, noting it was from Fox. *When are you coming to my house to talk to OUR, dad? Don't forget about me, okay? Reese, let me know you're there!*

Reese texted back. *I won't forget you, buddy. I'm just busy finishing up my case. I'll get in touch soon. I promise.*

Being busy with work gave her a good excuse to keep from meeting with Cash. For now. When her case had been resolved, what other excuse could she use?

None.

Her pillow stomach made it difficult to move around. She couldn't help but wonder what a true pregnancy would feel like. She'd heard mothers discuss how their babies, especially during their final months, rested on their bladders and kicked their ribs. Despite the joy of bringing life into the world, she knew it must be miserable.

Reese glanced through the front room's large picture window, studying the gathering evening shadows. They draped the countryside in shades of purple darkness. It would soon be time to head downtown.

She really disliked setting herself up as bait. But time was running out for Violet. What other choice did she have? During a lull in her conversation with Wade, she fished her cell phone from her purse and called Jeremy.

"It's go time," she told him, doing her best to maintain a steady voice.

"It's not too late to back out," he said, as if he sensed her vulnerable state.

"Nope," she said, not trusting herself to say anything else. Now wasn't the time to doubt her abilities.

"We'll be following," Jeremy said.

"We?"

"Rhett Ketcham is riding shotgun."

By the time Reese got off the phone, Wade had retrieved a black puffy jacket and held it toward her.

"This is one of Sylvia's maternity coats," he said. "It should keep you warm."

He helped Reese put on the coat, then wrapped her a huge bear hug. She felt awkward, and definitely didn't know what to say.

"We're beholden to you," he said, sniffling. "The idea that you're willing to risk your life . . . well, I can't thank you enough."

"When I make a promise, I keep it."

Wade wiped his watery eyes as he pulled back.

Reese collected Sylvia's keys, leaving her purse on the table to pick up later . . . if there was a later. Giving Wade a thumbs up, she headed down the entry hall and left through the front door. As the icy wind bit her cheeks, she inhaled sharply.

"Lord," she whispered, "if you're really out there, help me bring Violet home."

THIRTY-NINE

IT GREW INCREASINGLY DARKER AS REESE DROVE DOWNTOWN. She sang one of her favorite old country tunes, her voice trembling. The words always bolstered her.

"Buck up, buttercup," she told herself.

Glancing in the rear-view mirror, she noticed a car following her. With every turn she made, it remained on her bumper. Studying it closer, she realized it was Crawford's old station wagon. Mixed feelings bubbled within her, trepidation, then triumph.

The plan was working.

Fishing her phone from her purse, she called Jeremy. "Crawford's on my tail."

"Roger," he said. "We're watching your every move."

Disconnecting, she dropped her cell back into her purse.

At the coffee shop, she found a parking area beside the building. The area sat empty, and overhanging tree branches provided sheltering cover, the exact type of spot where Crawford liked to attack people.

She got out of the car, but didn't notice Crawford pulling in nearby. Where was he? A chill ran up her spine and she sensed someone watching her. Glancing up into the trees, she noticed a couple of crows. Usually, the birds were squawking their heads off. But they only stared in eerie silence.

Did they sense she was going headlong into danger?

She entered the building where people sat at small round tables sipping their drinks. At the counter, she grabbed a bottle of water and ordered a Frappuccino and a bagel from a young lady. After paying for everything, she stood in the waiting area. Her biggest fear was running into someone she knew who would see through her disguise.

"Java Chip Frappuccino," the barista finally called.

Reese stuffed the bagel and the bottled water into a large front pocket of the coat. The food wasn't for her, it was for Violet in case she was hungry. Picturing the woman alive and in need of sustenance encouraged her. Grabbing the coffee, she headed toward the door.

"Hey, Sylvia, hi!" someone called from one of the tables.

Reese spotted a woman seated beside two young girls, waving her over. They all watched her expectantly.

Shit.

At a loss for what to do, Reese lifted a hand in greeting and called, "In a hurry," then hustled outside toward Sylvia's car. When she reached for the door handle, she sensed a large presence behind her.

Her skin tingled. Panic set in. Even though she'd set herself up to be taken. Even though the plan was working perfectly.

She started to scream, but only let loose a weak cry before someone grabbed her and held a damp cloth over her mouth.

As the toxic fumes drifted up her nostrils—a combination of bleach and nail polish remover—she struggled and kicked. Seconds later, felt herself go limp. The sensation of being carried washed over her, then everything went black.

"WAKE UP, BITCH!"

Feeling hard, painful slaps on her cheek, Reese opened her eyes and shouted, "Stop!"

Moving aside to avoid the blows, she rolled into the trash filling the back of Wyatt Crawford's old station wagon. Wearing his black hooded jacket, he loomed over her like a giant, pinning her with his demonic gaze. He'd jammed a gun into her temples, and he grinned, showing those sharp, pointed teeth.

Reese pushed away a mess of mental cobwebs. Bits and pieces of what had happened flashed in her mind. She heard herself groan.

What the hell did I get myself into?

"Get up, Sylvia," Crawford barked, "or I'll kill you right here and now. I won't even give old Wade Gentry another chance to pay up for both his daughter and daughter-in-law."

Shivers gripped Reese as she attempted to sit up, but failed. Nausea washed over her. Everything in her stomach came up in a rush. Turning aside, she heaved on a pile of rubbish.

"God damn," Crawford shouted, waving his hand back and forth in front of his face. "Couldn't you have upchucked on the grass?"

Crawford grabbed her arm and dragged her out of the car. She stumbled to her feet and scanned the area, recognizing Frida Crawford's barn, along with two saddled horses standing next to the pens. In the cool evening, steam escaped their snorting nostrils, and they pawed the ground impatiently.

Attempting to collect her senses, Reese felt another pang in her stomach. She leaned over and gave a couple of dry retches, coughed, and wiped her mouth on her coat sleeve.

"You better be done with that shit." Crawford set his gun in the station wagon trunk and boosted her into the saddle of the black horse. In a different scenario, Reese would have started fighting him.

This had been her goal, however, to get him to take her. Besides, she felt sick and weak—definitely not strong enough to fight a tree trunk of a man like him.

He grabbed a length of rope from the back of the car and tied her wrists to the saddle horn.

"Who are you? What d-do you want?" Reese asked in a frightened voice, which was not faked. She was honestly terrified, and hoped she could manage to keep her cool. People were counting on her.

"You'd better be able to ride," Crawford growled, ignoring her questions. "Otherwise, you'll wind up with a chapped ass."

He yanked the rope so tight; Reese's hands began to tingle with numbness. Sending out an exploring tongue, she licked her dry lips, but didn't speak. She'd spent plenty of time in the saddle, but it had been a long time since she'd been on a horse. Like riding a bicycle, she didn't believe people ever forgot once they learned.

"P-please don't do this," Reese said, her teeth chattering. "Are you the guy who took Violet? My family just wants to bring her home."

"You'll find out soon enough." With a loud guffaw, he grabbed his gun and closed the station wagon's hatch. Then he swung up into the chestnut horse's saddle and took the reins.

"Cooperate with the police," she pleaded, then realized he'd probably wonder how she knew that. "At my house . . . I heard them talking. They'll go easier on you."

"Sure, sure," he snarled. "I believe that as much as I believe I need a hole in my head."

Crawford grabbed the rope attached to Reese's saddle horn. He kneed his horse and urged it forward, pulling Reese's black horse along with him. They rode away from the farm and onto the vast prairie.

A short distance ahead, soaring purple peaks rose to meet the horizon. Although the sun had set a while ago, lingering light imbued strands of puffy clouds with a pink and amber glow.

Reese's head pounded like a drum and she felt stiff, achy, and sore. Trying to ignore her discomfort, she forced herself to stay awake and alert. The importance of memorizing every detail about the trail swirled in her mind.

Glancing down at her wrists, she noted that the bracelet Jeremy had given her was missing. Holy crap, she'd lost it! Maybe when

Crawford grabbed her it had broken. Now Jeremy couldn't track her location.

I'm royally screwed.

Alarmed, Reese fought to gain control of herself. She'd been in tight spots before. She could handle this. It's no big deal, she told herself, when she knew that it was. She had no weapon to use against Crawford.

Only her wits.

Each cogent thought helped clear her mind and calm her down. Each breath of fresh air cleared her head and cleared her lungs. Peering into the gathering darkness, she did her best to make out distinguishable landmarks.

A patch of yucca covered a nearby slope, a thick line of trees arched over what must be a water source, and three boulders that looked like sleeping grizzly bears rested near a bluff.

"There's no way I can escape," Reese pressed. "You've got me trussed up like a calf at rodeo."

He grunted.

"Tell me where we're going."

He hawked and spit on the ground, then turned to glare at her.

"Only if it'll shut you up," he barked.

"I promise," Reese said.

"I'm taking you to Outlaw Mountain."

FORTY

"NEVER HEARD OF IT," REESE SAID.

"Not surprising," Crawford snarled. "My friend named it."

"Who's your friend?"

"You talk too much."

"But—"

"His name's Jackrabbit!" Crawford rounded on her and held up a fist. "Romeo Jackrabbit. Now shut up, you hear? Or I'm gonna plant this in your jaw. Or shoot you. Your choice."

Reese knew she'd pushed him enough. Resuming steady watch at the countryside, she memorized more landmarks. A grove of aspen appeared as they started up a mountain. Nearby, a pile of branches jutted from patch of grass like an assortment of forks.

Crawford nudged the horses up a rocky trail. With sure feet, they animals began to climb, as if they already knew the way.

He's going to kill you.

A bolt of reality rocketed through her. Crawford never intended to return his victims, just collect his ransom and disappear. The same thing he'd done with Gina Miller and numerous other women.

Fortunately, the drug he'd had used to render Reese unconscious had begun to fade from her system. Her mind took on a sharper edge, she felt her focus sharpening, and strength had returned to her limbs.

CRAWFORD LED THE HORSES DOWN A SLOPE covered in sagebrush and tangled undergrowth. Several feeding deer lifted their heads, noticing their approach. Pointing his gun, he pretended to shoot at them.

"Pew, pew," he said, laughing as the animals bounded off into the woods. "Too bad I'm not out here to hunt. Well, actually, I am."

He looked over at Reese and winked. Disgusted, she looked away. A fallen log surrounded by an orange-yellow blanket of flowers and clusters of red Indian Paintbrush offered yet another marker along the trail.

Burbling water sounds filled the air, then a stream appeared, cutting its way through a bed of stones, logs, and boulders. Crawford guided the horses through the shallow depths. He stopped to let them drink, then urged them up a muddy bank. Connecting with the other side of the dirt trail, Crawford kept the horses moving. Before long, a wide canyon surrounded by rocky red buttes appeared.

As the portrait of a harsh, forbidding landscape unfolded, a sense of Déjà vu nudged Reese. Her jaw dropped when she spotted piles of bones, topped by leering skulls, arranged beside mounds of rust-colored earth. What an inglorious end for Crawford's victims, to rest in shallow graves, exposed to the harsh elements where vultures and other creatures would pick their bones clean.

To her shock, the gruesome sight appeared familiar. Sickening awareness tingled throughout her extremities

Then it hit her. She'd been here before—in her dreams. During her nighttime ramblings, flying across the sky as a crow, she'd explored every nook and cranny.

It made no sense, yet, her nightmares had become reality.

"Caw, caw," crows called, as if scolding the riders. Sitting in the branches of an old, twisted tree growing from a rocky cleft, were several of the blackbirds. Another eerie sensation drifted over Reese, and her skin prickled.

Maybe her unusual dreams came from a good place, signifying her instincts were leading her in the right direction. The idea had merit, and she felt it worth more exploration—if she made it home alive.

It seemed like they'd ridden about a half hour. It was dark now. Crawford had slowed the horses' pace as he guided them through several twists and turns that lead them past towering rock walls.

Eventually the path led them toward a ridge where a weathered cabin perched beside a couple of skinny pines.

"Where are we?" Reese asked.

"Romeo and his gang used to hide out here," Crawford said.

"His gang?"

He grunted. "That's for him to tell you about."

Crawford swung off his horse and pulled her down. Gripping her elbow with one hand, his gun in the other, he led her around to the back of the cabin. An ancient-looking root cellar with a wooden door had been dug into a small hill. Stone and plaster edges surrounded the opening.

"What are you going to do?" Reese asked, apprehension mounting.

"Until Old Man Gentry decides to pay up, you're stayin' here," he said.

"Is this where you're keeping Violet?"

"What's left of her."

Reese remained silent, blood pumping wildly through her veins. Could it be that the dirt dress Violet had worn in those disturbing dreams represented her underground prison? As Crawford dug a key from his pocket and opened a padlock on the cellar door. The clicking sound caused her to tense. She dreaded by what she might find inside.

Crawford shoved her inside, then closed up. The sound of the padlock being secured echoed behind her. She stumbled forward, then steadied herself. A damp stench assaulted her nostrils. The plaster and rock interior reverberated with silence and a camping lantern propped on a shelf provided faint illumination.

When her eyes adjusted to the dimness, Reese noted am oblong lump that looked like a body. Once again, she tensed.

"Violet?" she whispered.

No answer.

Violet, is that you?" Reese walked toward the shape, fearing what she would uncover. Holding her breath, she knelt down and looked.

"Thank God it's you, Violet!"

Reese sighed with relief, even though the woman wasn't moving, and she'd tucked her body into a fetal position. She wore jeans, hiking boots and a long-sleeve sweater. Reese placed two fingers on the pulse at her neck, encouraged to find the throbbing that indicated life, albeit weak.

After unzipping her coat, Reese reached underneath her shirt and yanked out the stuffing that had created her fake baby bulge. She covered the unconscious woman with the small receiving blankets.

Violet stirred and opened her bloodshot eyes, which were ringed with deep hollows. Studying Reese, she cried, "H-help me . . ."

"That's why I'm here." Reese helped the woman sit up, then reached in her pocket for the bottled water. Unscrewing the plastic cap, she handed it to her.

Violet gulped the drink, and rivulets of moisture trickled down her jaw.

"Slow down," Reese cautioned, placing a hand on Violet's shoulder. "It'll make you sick to drink too much."

Violet leaned back against the wall, closed her eyes, and wiped her mouth with the back of her hand. "My friend, Sabrina. Where is she?"

Reese shook her head.

Violet started crying. "It's all my fault."

"You couldn't know that Wyatt Crawford was outside waiting."

Violet's brows shot up. "Is that the guy with pointy teeth who looks like Pennywise the clown?"

Reese nodded.

"I haven't seen him for a while," Violet said. "Romeo's the only one who comes in here."

"Has he hurt you?"

"If you're asking if he's raped me or anything, no. Sometimes he brings a sandwich or two, and a juice box. I suppose I'm lucky he even left me a bucket to pee in."

"What does he look like?"

"He's a big, tall guy with dark hair. Wears western clothes, and a cowboy hat."

"Has he told you anything?"

"He gripes about what my grandfather, many times removed, did over a hundred years ago. I swear he's crazy."

"Sins of the fathers," Reese murmured. She removed the bagel from her coat pocket and handed it to Violet.

"What does that mean?" Violet tore off a chunk of the bread and ate it.

"It's biblical," Reese clarified. "It refers to how sins pass from one generation to the next."

"Who are you?" Violet asked, her face and questioning. "You're wearing my sister-in-law's clothes."

"I'm Reese Golden and I'm working with the local police," Reese said, removing the glasses she'd borrowed from Violet's sister-in-law. "It's a long story about why I dressed like Sylvia. I'll explain it all later. Right now, we've got to get out of here."

"There's no way," Violet said. "Believe me, I've tried. It's locked tight as a drum."

"You said this Romeo guy comes every evening?"

"Uh huh. He always carries a gun and he's big as an ox."

Reese sat on the floor and thought about their predicament. She eyed the old book case, noting that it looked pretty rickety.

"I have an idea," she said.

FORTY-ONE

REESE KEPT A WATCH OVER VIOLET as the woman dozed, her head resting against the stone wall. Deprived of decent food and water for days, she was weak and in early stages of starvation. She'd been traumatized, which had probably worn her down to a point of exhaustion and desperation.

Something tickled Reese's cheek, and she brushed it off, horrified as a spider landed on the dirt-packed floor next to her thigh and scurried away. Shivering with revulsion, she looked toward the ceiling, noting the mass of spider webs directly above.

"Disgusting little beasts," she muttered as she stood and began to pace. Spiders had their place in the world, but it wasn't crawling around on her.

Since being locked in this cellar, she'd managed to break off a leg from the book case, then prop up the bottom of it with the slop bucket. She kept the makeshift weapon tucked nearby. With any luck, she'd be able to catch their captor off guard the next time he visited.

How awful for Violet to have been trapped for so long in this stone prison, wondering if anyone would ever find her. Wondering if she'd die alone.

At last, heavy footfalls outside of the door announced someone's approach. The rattling of the padlock came next. Reese grabbed the chunk of wood off the floor and held it behind her back.

"Wake up Violet," she whispered.

Violet sat up, blinking.

"Remember the plan," Reese urged. "I'll do all the talking."

"Okay," Violet said.

The cellar door opened and a large man entered, pointing a gun in their direction. He wore jeans, a western-cut shirt, a fringed leather vest, and a cowboy hat.

Romeo Jackrabbit.

However, his facial features were identical to those of Wyatt Crawford. Right down to the scar on his forehead. Reese blinked; certain she wasn't seeing clearly. The only thing different was that when he grinned, he had normal pearly whites instead of pointed teeth.

"Wyatt?" Reese asked. "Is that you? Did you remove your fake teeth?"

He only glared at her.

Violet drew up her knees and wrapped her arms around them. Reese could tell she was terrified, and no wonder.

"Wyatt's not here anymore," he finally said. "I'm Romeo."

"Who are you, Romeo, and what do you want with us?"

"You both have to pay."

"Pay for what?"

"You should know," he insisted.

"Well, I don't," Reese said.

He sighed. "The Gentry ancestors did awful things. You married into their clan and now you're going to give birth to one of their whelps."

Relief passed through Reese. She was glad she'd zipped up the coat so he didn't notice her flat stomach. Slowly, she rose to her feet, careful to keep the book case leg behind her back.

"What awful things did they do?" Reese pressed. "It's only right that you tell me. I should know why I'm being punished."

"Wyatt told me you are a big mouth." Romeo moved closer. "The cattlemen took land from me during the Wyoming Range War. They justified it by saying I was a squatter and that I rustled their cattle, which was a lie. I got my land fair and square and I never took a single cow from them. They only wanted to get their hands on my property because of the water rights. Dirty bastards."

"I believe you," Reese said.

He frowned and shot her a puzzled look.

She decided it would be best to make friends with this guy, whoever the hell he was. Could he be Wyatt's a twin brother? Frida never mentioned another son. No matter, he was clearly delusional. The range war he referred to, also called the Johnson County War, began in 1889, more than one hundred years ago. He acted like it had just happened.

"You believe me?" Romeo snorted with disbelief. "You're a lying bitch."

"Seriously, I know what you're talking about," Reese insisted, taking a small step forward. "It wasn't fair that the big cattle barons, with their money, power and influence, were able to run innocent people off of their land."

"They took everything from me," Romeo complained. "Everything I dreamed about, everything I worked for."

"You had a good reason to be angry," Reese said. "I can't blame you, after the way you were treated."

"I had no money, no home," he continued. "I joined up with the other ranchers they'd taken land from, and we decided to get even. We robbed banks, we robbed trains, we rustled cattle. This place was our hideout and we stayed here between jobs. We turned into the outlaws they accused us of being in the first place."

In her research, Reese had read about Wyoming's notorious bandits, one of whom was named Robert "Romeo" Jackson. He and his gang had terrorized the state for years, riding from town to town doing terrible things. The reason for their actions, according to historians, had been to exact revenge against the ruthless cattle companies.

"Is your last name Jackson?" Reese asked.

"Jackrabbit," he growled.

"Did you change it to Jackrabbit?"

"The boys did that," he said. "For an entire month, while we were on the run, the only thing I brought into camp for dinner was jackrabbit meat."

It seemed that Romeo/Wyatt really thought he was a notorious outlaw from the Old West. Did he suffer from dissociative identity disorder? Supposedly it was rare, but people dealing with this condition had two or more personalities.

"Did you and your gang kidnap and kill members of the land baron's families?" Reese asked.

"Only the daughters," Romeo said. "Do you know why?"

Reese shook her head.

"Because the S.O.B.s finally caught me and hanged me, along with my sweet, innocent daughter. Now they know what it feels like to have a child brutally murdered."

"What are you going to do with us?" she asked.

"You two need to be put down. Like the rest of them."

"First, let me talk to Wyatt," Reese said, taking a chance that she'd correctly guessed his mental condition.

"I told you he ain't here," Romeo barked, his eyes flashing.

"I think he is," Reese responded. "I want to talk with him. Now."

Romeo inhaled and exhaled, and his expression changed. When he finally spoke, he said, "It's all Romeo's fault."

"Are you Wyatt?" Reese asked. "I want to be sure who I'm talking to."

"Yeah, I'm Wyatt."

Violet made a surprised sound, but didn't say a word. Reese met her gaze and they exchanged a meaningful glance.

"What is Romeo's fault?" Reese asked Wyatt.

"He made me kidnap those girls," he said with a sob. "I didn't want to."

"I'm sure you didn't." Reese inched forward, now close enough to take the gun if she got the chance. "Hand me the weapon and I'll help you. You don't want to hurt anyone else, do you?"

He continued pointing the gun at her, so she kept him talking, hoping he'd come to his senses or give her a chance to knock the weapon from his grip.

"Why did you go along with Romeo's plan?" she asked.

"He promised when families paid the ransom money, he'd share it with me, and I could help my mother. She doesn't have health insurance and she needed cancer treatments. She needed a better house and car. Romeo convinced me those cattle baron families owed it to us."

"Why?"

"Because Romeo is one of my grandfathers from long ago," Wyatt said.

"How can that be?" Reese asked. "Surely he's dead."

"No, he's been reincarnated. He found me when I was a kid and promised he'd help me. If those cattle barons hadn't stolen his land, he could have passed it on to us. Then the Crawford's would have been wealthy cattle ranchers. Not dirt-poor goat farmers."

Reese recalled Frida's truck, her house and the large outbuilding—all fairly new. Now she understood where the money to purchase all of it had come from.

"Did you kill those women?" Reese asked.

"No, I swear, it was Romeo," he said. "He left some of them where he killed them. And some he brought up here to Outlaw Mountain. That's their bones you see spread all around."

A wave of nausea washed over Reese, but she managed to force it away.

"Romeo had me kidnap your mother," Wyatt said to Violet.

"Is she alive?" Violet asked in an eager tone. "Are you holding her hostage somewhere else?"

"Romeo killed her, too. She's up here with the others."

Violet uttered a strangled cry, then began sobbing.

"Romeo said she had to pay since she'd married a Gentry," Wyatt said. "Gentry kinfolk were part of the posse that hunted him down and strung him up."

"Why did you attack your mother?" Reese asked Wyatt.

"I swear, it wasn't me," he protested. "It was Romeo. I went to see Mom that day, but she accused me of hurting all those missing girls. She was going to turn me into the police. Romeo got pissed. He hit her over and over. I couldn't make him stop."

Tears filled Wyatt's eyes and he made a strangled sound.

"Wyatt, let me have the gun," Reese said, holding out her hand. "You can trust me."

Horses' hooves pounded outside. Distracted, Wyatt twisted toward the cellar door. Reese slammed the chunk of wood down on Wyatt's gun hand. When he dropped the weapon and howled in pain, Violet hustled over and grabbed it. She tripped and rolled into a corner where she sat clutching the gun, breathing heavily, fatigued by the exertion.

"What did you do?" Wyatt howled, lunging toward Reese.

She smacked the chunk of wood against his forehead. Blood gushed from the wound as he sprawled on the floor, unconscious.

When the cellar door flew open, Jeremy burst inside, along with Officer Ketcham. Ketcham produced handcuffs, which he clamped on Wyatt.

Jeremy hugged Reese and asked, "Are you okay?"

"I am now."

Reese trembled in Jeremy's embrace, enjoying his broad, warm chest pressed against her. When he finally released her, he walked over to Violet, helping her stand. He took the gun from her, checked the safety, then tucked it into his utility belt.

"I'm ready to go home," Reese said as she met Violet's gaze. "Unless you want to stay for some reason."

"Hell, no," she said softly. "I can't get out of here fast enough."

"Do you think can ride?" Jeremy asked her.

"Yes," Violet responded. "I might need some help getting in the saddle, though. I'm dizzy."

"Then let's blow this popsicle stand," Reese said.

Officer Ketcham got Wyatt to his feet and walked him out of the cellar, with the rest of them following.

Reese gulped the fresh air. A frosty chill permeated the atmosphere, but it was preferable to being locked in that damp cellar.

"By the way, how did you find us?" she asked Jeremy.

He withdrew a folded paper from his jacket pocket and handed it to her, then shined his flashlight on it. It was a map, crudely drawn, as though a child had made it. A red crayon line marked the trail up to Outlaw Mountain.

"Where'd you find this?" Reese asked him.

"In Wyatt's car, next to the bracelet that fell off your wrist," Jeremy said. "Ketcham and I figured that must be where he took you, so we saddled enough horses for all of us from his barn and rode out."

Reese swung into the saddle on her horse as Jeremy helped Violet onto another mount. Violet grabbed the reins and settled in, no doubt ready to leave this place far behind, and eager to return home.

After he and Officer Ketcham mounted up, everyone guided their horses over to the trail that would take them down the mountain. In the starlight, pent-up anxiety melted away from Reese like ice in the hot sunshine.

Along the trail, Jeremy called for backup with his long-range walkie talkie. By the time they returned to the Crawford's barn, a squad car sat there, lights flashing. Ketcham loaded a complaining Wyatt in the back seat and closed the door. As Ketcham got in the passenger side, Jeremy leaned over and spoke through the open window to the officer seated behind the steering wheel.

A minute later, the officer flipped on his siren, then headed back to town. At the police station, Reese knew Wyatt would immediately be taken into custody on kidnapping charges. Finally, he would be off the streets and justice would be served for all the women he'd hurt and their grieving families. The satisfaction of a job well done warmed her insides.

While Jeremy stabled the horses, Reese helped Violet get into the back seat of his Trailblazer and buckle up, then covered her with a blanket.

"Thanks, Reese," Violet said, tears forming in her eyes. "I thought I'd never get away from that crazy man."

"Sit tight, hon," Reese promised. "You'll be home soon."

After closing the vehicle door, Reese went to stand next to Jeremy, who had returned from the barn and was talking on his cell phone.

"She's all right, Tag, and after we stop by the police station, we'll bring her home." Jeremy disconnected the call and tucked his cell phone in a jacket pocket.

"I'm so glad you're all right, too," he told Reese. He hugged her, gently kissed her forehead, then led her over to the shotgun seat his Trailblazer and helped her inside. After sliding behind the steering wheel, he glanced back at Violet, who rested her head against the side of the vehicle.

"I'm okay," she said in a soft voice. "I only want to go home."

"Soon enough," Jeremy told her.

The drive to the police station didn't take long. Once they entered the building, the department's new victim advocate Charlene Brewster swept Violet into her office. Having had plenty of experience victim advocates, Reese knew Charlene would council Violet about the emotional trauma she'd experienced, in addition to offering information about local support groups.

Reese strolled with Jeremy to the reception area where they sat on a couch, waiting for Violet to finish with her appointment. About a half an hour later, Charlene and Violet, who clutched a blue folder, walked toward them.

"I'm ready to go home," Violet said.

Both Reese and Jeremy stood.

"You don't want to go to the hospital and get checked out?" Jeremy asked.

"Home is where I want to be right now," Violet said, brushing stray hair away from her face.

He looked at Charlene, who nodded and smiled, then said, "Violet has all she needs from me right now."

"Let's go, then," Jeremy said.

Back out into Jeremy's Trailblazer they went, and he drove them to the Gentry Ranch. Once the vehicle stopped in front of the well-lit house, Violet got out and hurried toward the front door. Reese and Jeremy followed close behind as she burst through the entrance.

"I'm home!" she called.

Tag Gentry ran to meet his sister, pulling her into his arms. Tears of joy glistened on both of their cheeks. Grinning, Wade Gentry joined the happy reunion, his arms enfolding his daughter when she turned toward him.

"Thank heavens you found my girl," Wade told Jeremy next, clapping him heartily on the back.

Tag embraced Reese, thanking her profusely for helping him locate his sister, then walked over to Jeremy and shook his hand.

"Come in, come in everybody," Tag said as he waved them all inside. "Sylvia's got a little surprise."

In the front room, Sylvia sat on the couch, holding a wriggling bundle of blue. She stood slowly and met Reese's gaze. "Tag and I never even made it to the safehouse because my water broke on the way over. We drove straight to the hospital and junior here made his appearance a few hours later."

"Congratulations," Reese said. "I'm surprised to see you out of the hospital so soon."

"When Jeremy called to tell Tag that Violet was coming home, I wanted to be here too." She walked over to her sister-in-law, hugged her with one arm, then helped her take the baby.

Violet smiled down at the newborn cradled in her arms, tears rolling down her cheeks. "What a sweet little angel," she said, sniffing. "What name did you and Tag finally decide on?"

"Wade Gentry, Jr.," Sylvia said. She lifted one of his tiny hands and kissed it.

Wade grinned and seemed to stand taller as he puffed out his chest.

"Congratulations are in order all the way around," Jeremy said. "It's been a hell of a day."

"I'll second that," Reese said, thrilled to see the Gentry family reunited, and thrilled that her persistence had paid off.

FORTY-TWO

"HOME IS BEST, ISN'T IT?" REESE told her cat as she sat on the floor with him. Each time she dangled a long piece of red yarn in front of Bo, he'd raise his paw and bat it. Entertaining him as morning sun shone through the front window with its warm, white light seemed such a simple, but pleasurable activity.

At least for now, Reese had no tasks to undertake, no agenda to stick to, and no list from hell to complete. With her police case resolved, and her other work caught up, she'd decided to take it easy for a while.

The cozy surroundings of the small home teased her thoughts, bringing back memories her childhood. The overstuffed couch held a plaid blanket that she and Jesse had put to good use as an indoor tent on rainy days. Images of everyone gathered around the brick fireplace on holidays—talking, laughing, and sipping cocoa—sparked warmth inside of her.

The antique lamps her mother had snagged at an auction gleamed on tabletops. Grandpa's book shelf, still stocked with his favorite novels, helped her envision him sitting in the antique rocker, intently reading. The Hummel figurines arranged the fireplace mantel helped her envision her grandmother dusting their adorable porcelain surfaces.

Even though her family had passed on, Reese felt strongly that they remained with her in spirit. The comforting idea eased the heartache of missing them. As thoughts of Fox and Cash flashed through her mind, she began to brood. Should she call her father and get to know him? As usual, she couldn't make a damn decision.

At least she'd decided how to handle her plague of unusual dreams. Next week, she had an appointment with a therapist to try and sort through her nocturnal experiences, and hopefully gain a better understanding. Then maybe she could get some decent sleep.

When her cell phone rang, she picked it up, noting it was Fox . . . again. He'd been calling and texting ever since his mother picked him up, nagging her about getting together. She'd been using Violet's case as an excuse not to meet him, saying she was too busy. Now that the woman's rescue and the arrest of her kidnapper had been splashed all over the news, she couldn't hide from him any longer.

"How's it going, Fox?" she asked.

"Real good, Reese," he responded in a chipper tone. "Hey, what are you up to?"

She tossed the piece of yarn on the floor and Bo attacked it, scooting it off into a corner. "I've got a mountain of paperwork—"

"You solved your case, right?

"Yes," she said, unable to make any excuses.

"Then you can take off a couple of hours and meet me at the county fair."

"I didn't realize that was happening this weekend."

"It is. I love the fair. Especially the agricultural displays."

Reese smiled. "Not the roller coaster or the Ferris wheel?"

"Nah, those are for babies," he said. "Besides, my grandfather, actually, our *grandfather*, Cash's dad, was a rancher. I like seeing the goats, and cattle, and pigs and imagine what it was like for him to live out in the boonies."

After hearing that piece of history, curiosity niggled Reese. She hadn't considered anything beyond the fact that Cash Nesbitt was her father, and Fox, her half-brother. She realized that Cash's ancestral tree offered more information about who she was and where she'd come from.

"Promise you'll meet me," Fox said. "Puh-leese?"

The walls around Reese's heart began to melt. What would it hurt to go to the fair and hang out with him for a while? She could buy him a corndog and send him home with a funnel cake. Hopefully, that would make him happy.

"Your parents are okay with you going to the fair alone?"

"I'll be with you," he said emphatically. "And I'm no longer a child, as you know."

She did her best not to chuckle at his prickly response. "All right, kid. You win."

"Excellent!"

They agreed to meet at the fairgrounds in an hour, beside the stage. Reese paced for a few minutes, assessing the situation. Knowing Fox as she did, she realized he'd want to spend more and more time with her. It seemed inevitable that she'd eventually run into Cash, and whether she liked it or not, she'd get to know him.

As a sense of vulnerability crept over her, she dialed Jeremy. When he said hello, she began telling him about Fox's request for her to meet him at the fair.

"Sounds reasonable enough to me," he said.

"But I feel like I'm going out on a limb," she said. "I'm not sure that I want to know Cash, but by doing things with Fox, we will interact at some point."

"Yeah, that seems inevitable," Jeremy said. "I don't think you should sweat it, though. It's not like you're donating a kidney to him."

"You're right," she said, surprised her hands were sweating and her heart palpitating. "Will you go with me to the fair?"

"You're not afraid to face a killer, but you're afraid of a kid?" He chuckled.

"No," she said. "I hoped I could count on you for support."

"Reese, you know I'll always be there for you," he said. "I'll be over to pick you up shortly."

She headed to her bedroom and chose an outfit from her closet, since she still wore her ice-blue, baby doll nightie, along with a pair of ratty cutoffs. After dressing, she studied herself in the bedroom mirror. Her jeans, paired with a country print blouse, her boots, and her cowboy hat made her look like a true Wyoming girl. Something she always had been and always would be, no matter where she wandered.

When the doorbell rang, she grabbed her purse and headed into the living room. Opening the door, she smiled at Jeremy, who wore jeans and a western shirt.

"My hero," she said jokingly.

"At your service," he said with a smile.

Jeremy drove them to the fairgrounds, which were surrounded by large fields edged with scrub brush. The sky arched overhead with a clear blue expanse, offering perfect weather for spending time outdoors.

When Jeremy finally found a parking spot, they got out and began walking toward a huge billboard with large red letters announcing they had arrived at The Granite County Fair.

A flurry of activity loomed ahead, the expanse littered with colorful, tall structures and large tents. Music blared, intermingling with loud voices and laughter. The smell of greasy fried food floated through the air. Artery clogging goodies—curly French fries, gooey Nachos, fried Oreos, cotton candy—was offered at booths everywhere.

Like an old movie, flashbacks from yesteryear passed before Reese's eyes. The fair had been one of the places she'd frequented with her family. Yet, she realized she was making new memories that she sensed would be just as good.

She and Jeremy strolled by old-time photo booths, games featuring flamboyant stuffed animals, a whirling carousel, spinning tea cups, and the like. Couples walked arm in arm, with gleefully shouting children bouncing beside them.

Suddenly, Jeremy grabbed Reese's hand and squeezed it. They shared a smile, and she knew she'd made the right call asking him to come. The sensation of his firm, encouraging grip chased away all of her concerns.

"I'm glad you're here," Reese told him.

"Maybe you haven't noticed yet, but I like being with you," Jeremy said.

"You're growing on me too, Detective," Reese said.

They arrived at the large stage where a band played lively music. Reese glanced around, but didn't spot Fox in the crowd. Minutes passed, but he never appeared. Anxiety twisted through her.

"Do you see Fox anywhere?" she asked Jeremy.

"Nope, not yet," he said, his gaze skimming the crowd.

"I knew we should have picked him up at his house," Reese said. "But he wanted to come on his own. If anything happens to him, I'll never forgive myself."

"Give him more time," Jeremy said. "I'm sure he's okay."

The band onstage thanked the audience for listening to their music. Collecting their instruments and equipment, they left. Reese glanced at her watch, realizing Fox was 20 minutes late. It wasn't like him not to be on time.

Another band walked out onto the stage, setting up their music stands, instruments, and speakers. Reese was still searching for Fox when she heard a woman's voice come over the microphone.

"Howdy folks! I'm Tanya Nesbitt and we're the Country Drifters."

"Holy crap," Reese muttered. "That's Cash's group!"

"Are you sure?" Jeremy asked.

"Absolutely," she said as reality hit home. "Fox lured me here. He must have decided that whether I like it or not, I'm going to meet my dad today."

Jeremy chuckled.

"It's not funny," she growled.

"Seriously, Reese," he said. "He only wants his family to know each other. It's not a crime. In fact, I think it's pretty damn clever how he set this up."

Reese relaxed, realizing Jeremy had a good point. Fox didn't want anything different from what she wanted; he'd only bumped up the timetable. She couldn't blame him for that. If she didn't meet Cash today, would there ever be a good time?

Actually, Reese appreciated all of Fox's efforts. Since she'd been waffling about meeting Cash, it was a relief that Fox had taken the initiative to get them together. Wise beyond his years, Fox knew healing the rift between Reese and her father needed to happen sooner, rather than later.

The band started playing a rousing country tune, one of her mother's favorites. Reese's knees went weak. Next, a tall man with light gray hair, wearing jeans and a western shirt, eased up beside Tanya and began to sing along with her.

Reese panicked when she recognized Cash. Blood pumped wildly through her veins, and thoughts rushed through her mind. When a small hand touched her arm, she looked down.

"I'm glad you showed up," Fox told her, resettling his glasses on the bridge of his nose.

"You set me up."

"You need to meet Dad," he said. "It's time."

"It should be my decision," she insisted.

"You'd never get around to it, Reese," he said. "That's why I took matters into my own hands."

She knew he was probably right, but still . . .

"Hey there, Fox," Jeremy said, patting one of Fox's shoulders. "Good to see you again."

"You too," Fox said.

When the music stopped, they all watched as the band members set aside their instruments. Cash sipped from a beer and placed it back on a small table.

"This is a special day, y'all," he said. "My daughter, who I haven't seen or talked to in many years, is here."

The audience clapped and looked around.

"Reese Golden, please come up here darlin' so you can give your daddy a big ol' hug."

Reese's jaw dropped, and Fox nudged her forward.

"Go on, Reese," he encouraged.

Feeling at a loss, she looked at Jeremy, hoping he would advise her about what to do.

"You're beautiful and strong, Reese," he said, releasing her hand. "And you're not afraid of anything."

Reese walked toward the stage and climbed the steps, hearing the roar of applause in her ears. The lights were hot up here, and she began to sweat, especially seeing the grinning man with his arms open wide.

His eyes looked like hers, and the shape of his mouth did too.

"Come here, darlin'," he urged. "We've got a lot to catch up on."

"Dad," she said shakily as she stepped into his embrace.

When the two of them hugged, the audience roared with approval. Whistles and whoops of joy rose into the air. It felt strange to think of having a father, but deep down, Reese knew that another chapter in her life had begun.

Born in Portland, Oregon, Cindy has lived all over the United States and spent five years in Misawa, Japan. She has visited Canada, the Philippines, Samoa, Hawaii, both the western and eastern Caribbean, and New Zealand.

Currently, she lives in Cheyenne, Wyoming, where Cheyenne Frontier Days is held each July. CFD's well-known rodeo is often referred to as the "Daddy of 'em all."

Over the years, she has won or placed in various writing contests. She has also written for and edited numerous newsletters. Her non-fiction magazine articles have been featured in "True West" and "Wild West." She was a book critic for Storyteller Alley and is a freelance writer/editor.

For the last 20 years, she has been a contributing editor and writer for Laramie County School District 1's Public Schools' Chronicle, which has a circulation of approximately 46,000 readers.

From baby alligators to glow worms, Cindy has seen a variety of life's wonders.

www.ingramcontent.com/pod-product-compliance
Lightning Source LLC
Chambersburg PA
CBHW011915130726
47903CB00016B/3041